Lonely Heart Of The Little Prince

Lonely Heart Of The Little Prince

a novel

LeeAnna Neumeyer

Book cover by Yours Truly

Book design by Maureen Cutajar
www.gopublished.com

Print ISBN: 978-0-9911740-0-3
eBook ISBN: 987-0-9911740-1-0

For Norman
Who shared with me his heart and this story.
This is my hug.

Acknowledgements

There were people along the way to which I deeply give my thanks. Morris and Harriet Saxe, who generously opened their door, hearts and memories to me. Norman Orenstein, for his brilliance as a teacher, and all the late night conversations. Bridget Briley, for her invaluable friendship, support and guidance. My mother, Ann, for the encouragement and many visits to the Northport Public Library to gather articles, interviews and anything else she could find in regard to the subject of this book. To the Librarians of the Northport Public Library whom my mother called, "The nicest and most helpful people," and to my dear friend in heaven, Jerry Mannato, for his forever constant and loving support, as well as sharing his own stories about Adele.

Finally, a special thank you to those who said, "yes" to me and/or this project while I was writing it (in no specific order): Paul Neumeyer, Kim Ooi, Erika Coleman, Michael Cristofer, Drew Ruselowski, Fawn Fuso, Melissa Ortiz, Leanne Victorine, Barb Frederick, Gilley, Dr. Barbara Davis,

Sheila Wenzel-Ganny, Rene Ascencio, Johnny & Cindy Neumeyer, Mary Neumeyer, David Crawford, Dylan Crawford, Miranda Crawford, Nathan Crawford, Jonathan Howard, Martha Sanchez, Joe Hipps, Kaitlyn Tafffe, Michael DeWitt, Stevenson Greene, Stephen LaManna, Dorman Nelson, Anne Kim, Andy & Melissa Baumbach, Barbara Balfoort, Rachel Balfoort, Chris and Lindsay Kusiak, Meredith Littas, Jorge Enrique Ponce, Matthew Goethals, Luanne Regis, Giuseppe DeVitis, Natalie Jones, Gayla Nethercott, Adam Orenstein, Jo Orenstein, Ruth Vitale, Nick Gladden, Viresh Hughes and Zack Kaplan. Encouragement goes a very long way. Thank you.

Contents

Chapter 1

The Dream

*A*dele *wandered through the dense fog that blanketed everything around her. Even the pavement beneath her feet was hardly visible, which made it seem as if she were walking on a cloud. She clutched tightly to her thick, black coat since the fog came with a heavy mist that sprayed on her face, dampened her hair and gave her body a chill.*

Gradually, the fog began to lift, and she saw a clearing in the distance. As she walked toward it, she saw what looked like a large hunk of grey metal. When she got closer, she realized it was an airplane, and she was on a tarmac.

The plane was a Lockheed P-38 Lightning, one used by French pilots during World War II. Just as she questioned to herself why it was there, from behind the tail of the plane, out stepped Antoine de Saint-Exupéry, a strong, confident and playful man of forty-four, dressed for flight in an airman's jumper suit and bomber jacket. On his head he wore a brown flying helmet with goggles that had ear-flaps dangling from both sides.

Adele's heart skipped a beat. She'd never seen him in flight gear before, only in casual pants and soft, white shirts with the collar open, and a few times in formal suits with tie and jacket. His round head was perfectly outlined by the leather helmet, his large eyes still had the lazy, seductive allure, and his tall frame gave off a rugged appeal in the jumper. He looked every inch the hero now, which once again fanned the desires in Adele that she had mastered at concealing.

Saint-Exupéry gave a wave and called out, "Mademoiselle Breaux!"

His heavy French accent was like a homecoming as she took steps in his direction and shouted back, "Monsieur! What are you doing here?"

"I've come back to see you," he said, as he moved to the front of the plane.

Adele's eyes widened. "Y-you're speaking perfect English!"

He stopped and gazed warmly at her. "Yes. You taught me."

Adele swooned at these words of acknowledgement, but more from his gaze which caused her to timidly confess, "I...I miss you."

"I know," said Saint-Exupéry as he drew a mischievous smile, one she's seen many times. "I know everything now."

"Everything?" Adele asked putting her hand to her chest, as if to cover her now exposed heart.

Without answering, he looked at her one last time then climbed aboard the plane and into the cockpit. Anxious to get her answer, Adele took several more steps forward and called out, "Everything, Monsieur? Everything?"

The propellers came on blowing the fog and mist in a forceful whirl that pushed Adele back. She held her arm across her forehead, trying not to lose sight of Saint-Exupéry. He had by now closed the glass of the cockpit and sat snug in his pilot seat. A large wisp of fog swept over the glass, then cleared for a few seconds, enough time for Adele to make eye contact with him. He smiled, nodded and gave one more wave before pulling the goggles over his eyes and giving his attention to what was ahead.

Adele clenched the collar of her coat and stared up at her friend, the brave hero, the beautiful artist, the sensitive poet, as the fog quickly fell in front of her and he was gone.

Adele tossed several times in bed before she released a sharp gasp and her eyes opened. Being that it was early morning and still dark, she squinted to focus, then realized it was only a dream. Anxiety set in nonetheless, since the bedroom and everything in it looked unfamiliar; that is, until she remembered she was at her friend Sara's house on vacation. The long flight from New York, where her life and career now existed, made everything disoriented. This always happened on the first night back in Oregon, her home state.

The humidity in the room brought beads of perspiration to her forehead.

It also made her nightgown stick uncomfortably to her body. It was 1944 and August, which meant no reprieve from the muggy nights. There was only a small fan in the corner of the room that circulated warm, stale air that only accentuated the conditions rather than relieved them.

Adele soon forgave these conditions once she began recalling her dream. She enjoyed thinking about Saint-Exupéry, but dreaming about him was better. This was the first time it happened, and it was comforting, since it gave her a sense of connectedness she rarely felt. And with that, despite the humidity and the droning hum of the fan, she turned over on her side, snuggled into her pillow and was able to fall back to sleep.

Hours later, when the sun was up, and as Adele bathed and dressed, she thought more about Saint-Exupéry. She hadn't seen him in over a year, but he was never far from her thoughts. In fact, she thought of him often, daily even, but that was something she never disclosed to anyone.

She wondered why he appeared to her in a dream and what it might mean. Saint-Exupéry had made a plea during one of their last visits that weighed on her mind ever since. It was about a career change that she didn't feel secure enough to make, leaving her job as a teacher to become a translator for the government and help in the war effort.

Being patriotically loyal to his native France, as well as to America, Saint-Exupéry believed it was every citizen's duty to defend and serve when needed. Adele believed the same, but lacked his fearlessness. Reason always won out over risk taking, but this was not something she was proud of. In fact, it was the thing she was most ashamed of about herself and wanted desperately to change.

Perhaps the dream was a "sign" for her to finally take that courageous leap. Saint-Exupéry always detected resistance in her and knew how to playfully bring it to light, so it made sense he would do the same in a vision. The question was, why was she resisting? It had already been a year of weighing the pros and cons of this and confining herself to the classroom while the rest of the world seemed to move forward, including Saint-Exupéry.

The dream was an obvious representation of her life, she concluded. Saint-Exupéry and seemingly everyone else flew high while she was grounded, stuck in a fog. What was she waiting for?

Adele looked at herself in the mirror and finally knew the answer. She zipped her dress with a fixed determination, patted her short, wavy hair until it looked just right, gave her cheeks a gentle tug with her thumbs and forefinger to give her face some color, since she didn't much care for rouge, and left the bedroom with a renewed confidence.

❧

ADELE SHARED BREAKFAST THAT morning with her friends Sara and Beatrice, on Sara's outdoor patio. The three had known each other for decades, having met at Reed College in Portland where they were classmates back in 1915. Adele was the only one of the trio that left Oregon to "see the world," while Sara and Beatrice stayed and did what was expected of women at the time, getting married and raising children.

Because Adele took the unconventional path, she stood out as the more sophisticated one and had a mildly superior attitude toward those she left behind, but never in a cruel or obnoxious manner; it was simply part of her personality. Sara and Beatrice knew her well and never took anything Adele did or said personally when she'd become too "hoity-toity." They also knew how to bring her back down to earth by reminding her of where she came from. It became a playful, unspoken game between the two of them.

Sara and Beatrice wore simple cotton blouses and skirts in contrast to Adele's sharp looking dress that was formal for such a relaxed atmosphere. But that was Adele, and no one made mention of it, just as Adele eyed, with quiet distain, a radio that sat near an open window from which Bing Crosby was crooning a popular tune. Adele preferred Brahms to Bing, but tolerated it for her friends.

"You seem happier than your last visit, Adele. Things are going well back east?" Sara asked as she poured coffee into Adele's cup.

"Yes, very well," Adele said as she motioned with her hand for Sara to stop pouring, then added nonchalantly, "I've decided to quit teaching."

Sara's eyes widened and stared fixedly on Adele. Beatrice's jaw dropped. Their friend had been a teacher for ten years, and it was a position in which she excelled at, even boasted about.

"You're quitting? What on earth for?" Sara asked.

Adele took a sip from her coffee then set the cup carefully back on the saucer. "I've met someone," she said with a sly smile.

Both Sara and Beatrice's brows lifted in astonishment. What was going on here? They knew Adele well, or so they thought. Adele was set in her ways, being in her forties, and as long as they've known her she had never spoken about, let alone hinted at, any affairs of the heart.

There was also the fact that, although she wasn't unattractive, she had a severity in her manner and dress that hid the necessary femininity to attract a man's eye. And there was also her work. Adele taught French at a high school in New York, Long Island, to be exact, and boasted incessantly about her beloved students, the school's high standards, as well as her commitment to being one of "the best" educators in the district. In short, she treasured her career. Now here she was talking about – love?

"He's an aviator," Adele began with that hint of pretense, "and a writer. He's written several wonderful books, all on the New York Times bestseller's list."

"Gosh, how'd you meet him?" asked Sara, flabbergasted, as if no one who matched that description could possibly penetrate her simple existence, let alone Adele's.

"Well, he's French…" Adele began.

"Oooh, French!" Beatrice squealed as a sly grin spread across her face.

Adele shot her a disapproving glance, then continued, "And he needed someone to help him with his English. I was hired to give him instruction."

"And now the two of you are…?" Beatrice asked as she sat forward in her seat eager to hear every salacious detail.

"Friends," insisted Adele, "Just friends. He was on Long Island to write a book, but was also helping coordinate the war effort in Washington between the US and the French Resistance. He's a fascinating man. Talented. And charming." She then smiled warmly, adding, "Very charming."

"Sounds like more than 'just friends' to me," Beatrice chuckled with raised eyebrows. "Come on, Adele, tell us what's going on between you two."

"There is nothing 'going on,' Adele snapped. "I have nothing to spin for your entertainment, Beatrice."

"Are you kidding? A French aviator and a small town school teacher?" cracked Beatrice as she looked over at Sara with a knowing smile. "Sounds like a hell of a story to me.

Adele's lips tightened. "Unlike you, I have complete control over my thoughts and emotions."

Beatrice took no offense to this, even though she knew it was a jab at her character, since she was already on her second marriage. What Adele clearly forgot was Beatrice never cared much about what others thought. So, she let out a wisecrack sounding, "Right" in response to Adele's comment and leaned back in her chair, unconvinced.

"I do have control!" Adele insisted, her voice high-pitched, designed to accentuate her truth, but this only caused Beatrice to shake her head and laugh.

"Then don't ever fall in love, Adele, because you'll never be able to control your heart."

Adele shifted in her seat and directed her attention to Sara, ignoring Beatrice completely.

"Anyway," Adele continued, "he suggested I use my skills of English and French for the war effort. He even wrote me a strong recommendation."

Sara had always encouraged Adele, but this was something she found difficult to get behind and asked bluntly, "You're throwing your entire career away for him?"

"It's not for him," Adele corrected her, "it's for our country. I'm needed."

"But, Adele, your life is…"

"Stuck behind a desk…in a classroom," Adele interjected.

"There's so much more out there. It's time I experience the world."

What was she talking about? Sara and Beatrice thought at the same time. As far as they were concerned, Adele had already experienced the world. She traveled to Europe several times before the Depression and was for-tunate to settle in a good, steady career, and in New York of all places!

Sara knew that reminding her of this would only cause Adele to feel she was not getting the support she obviously was expecting, so she took a gentler approach and asked the name of this mysterious aviator.

"Antoine de Saint-Exupéry," Adele answered with pride.

Sara tilted her head slightly. "I know that name. I think there was mention of him in the paper today."

"I wouldn't be surprised," said Adele, "He is quite famous."

"Let me see if I can find it," Sara said as she got up and stepped into the house, leaving Adele and Beatrice to sit in silence.

But Beatrice couldn't help herself and, just to be playful, asked suggestively, "Antoine?"

Adele's eyes narrowed, causing Beatrice to let out a hearty laugh.

"Incorrigible," muttered Adele under her breath.

"Oh, come on, Adele, I'm just trying to save you from ending up a lonely old lady."

Adele angrily slapped her hand on the table. She had enough. But just as she was about to give Beatrice a piece of her mind, Sara came back out with the newspaper. She folded it open, found the article and studied it carefully.

"What does it say? Read it aloud," Adele requested, wanting to soon forget Beatrice's nonsense.

Sara glanced at Beatrice, eyes troubled, hesitant. Beatrice noticed and squinted back, confused. With lips trembling,

Sara read aloud, "Count Antoine de Saint-Exupéry, 44, best-selling French aviator-novelist is…missing in action."

Adele's eyes stayed on Sara as her face went rigid. Sara swallowed hard as she continued, "While on a reconnaissance flight over Europe, Saint-Exupéry, a veteran of over 13,000 flying hours, was…"

As if this was a sick joke the two were playing on her, Adele quickly stood and snatched the newspaper from Sara's hands. The blood drained from her face as she read the article.

Beatrice rose from her seat slowly, filled with remorse. "Adele, I'm so sorry," she sputtered, then switched to optimism, "I'm sure they'll find him. Soldiers turn up weeks, even months later. He'll come back."

But it was no use. Adele wasn't listening; her face sagged in pain. Still holding the newspaper, she wandered off the patio and onto the lawn. The meaning of her dream was all too clear. Saint-Exupéry had only "come back" to say goodbye. Even though the reports listed him as "missing" she knew instinctively that he was gone. The loss hit hard, like a punch to the stomach, because she now understood the meaning of his saying he knew "everything" in the dream. She gasped and nearly retched at its consequence.

Sara and Beatrice watched helplessly as Adele limped to a nearby tree, holding her waist with one hand, and the paper in the other. As if about to collapse, she let go of the newspaper, allowing it to scatter to the ground, and then put her hand on the tree for support and hung her head in broken-hearted defeat.

Chapter 2

Northport

*T*he single-engine Caudron Simoun airplane flew through rough turbulence, jerking spastically and bouncing as if it were pounding a sidewalk. Adele sat inside its cramped cockpit, face ashen and gripping the rim of the console in front of her. She turned her terrified eyes to the pilot, Antoine de Saint-Exupéry, who sat calmly steering the plane, unfazed by the chaos outside.

"Y-you've crashed planes before?" Adele asked, knowing the answer but desperate for reassurance.

"A few," Saint-Exupéry answered in French and with a grin, almost proud of the fact. He then casually changed the subject, "So, tell me – how do you say in English, "I love you?"

Adele shot an incredulous stare in his direction. How could he ask such a question – especially now? Suddenly, the winds hit the plane hard causing it to pitch to the left and right at sharp angles. It then made a decent downward with the engine sputtering.

Adele watched swirling fog slam onto the plane's windshield as she white-knuckled the console shouting, "Monsieur! Monsieur!"

She looked over at Saint-Exupéry, but he was gone. No pilot! Setting her eyes forward, she watched in horror as the plane spiraled *toward earth. The muscles in her face tightened and her eyes shut tight ready for the inevitable crash.*

When her eyes opened, Adele jolted up in bed, barely able to breathe. She fumbled for her glasses on the nightstand and put them on. They helped to place distance between her and the nightmare. The year was 1964. Gone was her youth. She resembled now what best could be described a spinster. Her hair was grey with wisps of white. Her skin was withered and lined. Her frightened eyes, filled with tears, darted around her bedroom, while she held her hand over her racing heart.

It has been twenty years that the pilot she held so dear began visiting her dreams. They came sporadically, usually when it got closer to summer. Sometimes there was only one dream, sometimes several in a row, but all were friendly and welcoming. Time never diminished her wanting to keep him at the forefront of her thoughts, so the dreams helped with that. However, this was a nightmare and one she wanted to erase completely.

As recognition of the present set in, Adele layed back on her bed and let out an exhausted sigh. Wearily she removed her glasses, placing them back on the nightstand and concentrated on the breeze that blew in from a screened window. It reminded her that summer was fast approaching and another year was coming to an end. She based her years on the school's calendar. September was the start, late June the end. But thinking this didn't make her feel any better, just older.

Adele couldn't shake the nightmare. She tried setting her mind at ease by recalling how she was younger, as she was back in 1944. She was young in all of these dreams. She appreciated that and, of course, seeing Saint-Exupéry again, but chose not to place any meaning to them since she failed miserably in her interpretation of that first dream two decades earlier.

As much as she tried, she couldn't fall back to sleep, and

had a few hours left before she had to get up and get ready for school. School! That took her mind off the nightmare fast. She had an important meeting later in the day with the principal and administration regarding her possible promotion to Language Department Chairperson. Being the school's French teacher for thirty years, a promotion like this was long overdue and she was sure to be a shoe-in. Construction for the new high school began a year earlier, and that kind of expansion came with more hiring's and advancements. They needed to promote her, she reasoned.

The thought of this excited her, but Adele knew she wouldn't get back to sleep if she continued to think about it, so she changed her thoughts to something more mundane. The final class assignment took her mind off it, as well as grading each student. Then there was the summer ahead, the garden in her backyard that needed tending and her car, a French imported Renault that she had since early 1940, would need a tune up.

Suddenly, Morris Saxe sprang to mind, the close friend whom she knew since 1950, the year he was hired as one of the new English teachers. Morris was the patient sort, and understood her better than her other colleagues. He was also younger than she was. At forty-four he had an intellect much higher than most, and a friendly, wry sense of humor that could disarm anyone. In the course of his fourteen years at Northport High School, he had advanced to the position of English Department Chairman.

She had lunch with Morris in the teacher's cafeteria at least three times a week where they would discuss such topics as great books and their favorite European cities. Sometimes they would talk about the business of teaching, but preferred keeping this time to subjects outside of school. Adele would talk mostly about her gardening and French cuisine, Morris about his passion for flying. He was a recreational pilot and owned his own airplane, which he loved to take up on weekends.

Adele smiled when thinking about Morris and his plane. She loved to hear his descriptions of the clouds, the feeling of being one with the sky, the care and discipline it took to avoid all the risks of being thousands of feet above earth. She had never been in Morris' plane, but wondered what it would be like to sit in the tiny cockpit.

Oh, no – the cockpit! Why did she think about that? Once again, the image of her alone in Saint-Exupéry's plane as it plummeted at a deadly speed flashed before her. Fear set in again, so she quickly sat up and turned on the light.

෴

ADELE REMAINED AWAKE UNTIL the sun came up, then went through her morning routine, the same one she's had since 1934, the year she began teaching. Though fatigued from lack of sleep, she managed to make her usual simple breakfast of coffee, a croissant lightly buttered, and a small glass of orange juice. After she bathed and selected one of her conservative floral print dresses, she applied her lipstick, and rouge, now a necessity to give her face color.

She gathered her lesson books and papers, and placed them evenly in the leather satchel that she's been using for the past twenty-five years. No one would ever suspect the bag was vintage, as she kept all her belongings in nearly mint condition. It was something she took pride in. There was evidence of this all throughout her home, a small, two-bedroom bungalow filled with the finest antiques and furniture that appeared timeless. The only thing that seemed to age in Adele's home was Adele. Time was never kind to anyone.

Leaving the house, Adele made the short walk from her

front door to the Renault in the driveway. The small, light blue car was another of her possessions that she kept in pristine condition. Because she rarely took the car any farther than to the high school, a ten-minute drive away, maintenance was minimal. The mileage was considerably low, even after twenty-four years.

Once inside the car, its cramped quarters and dashboard controls triggered flashcard images from her nightmare of being in that cockpit with Saint-Exupéry. Moments passed before Adele realized she was staring off, lost in those images, mostly the one of Saint-Exupéry having disappeared when she screamed for him. It brought on a profound sense of sadness and loss that was beginning to overwhelm her.

Needing to shake the mounting feeling of despair, she checked her watch and started the car. There was a special place on Main Street in the village that she often went to that would remedy her gloom and pull her back from going over the cliff of desolation. She knew she needed to get there soon, and thankfully there was enough time to do it before school.

The drive was short, being that the village of Northport was a small one, located on the northern shore of Long Island, about an hour train ride from Manhattan. Adele always enjoyed driving into the tranquil waterfront village. She was pleased and stimulated by the current growth in its population, as well as the stores and businesses that had sprouted since her arrival during the Great Depression. Back then it was more rural and country, barren almost, which, to someone like Adele, was stifling.

By 1964, Northport's Main Street had open sidewalks filled with friendly locals, and was lined with quaint shops and diners that led to a picturesque park and harbor where boats bobbed gently on the water. There seemed no end to this town's charm.

Driving into the village with her windows rolled down helped clear her groggy head, and gave boost to her troubled spirit. Parking was plentiful, due to the early morning hour, but there was only one parking spot Adele wished to have, one she considered her sanctuary and would easily restore her equilibrium. It was at the corner of Bayview Avenue and Main Street, just steps from the park and a short walk to the harbor.

To her dismay, a black Mustang, the new and popular Ford car, was parked there. A row of empty parking spaces sat beside it, but Adele wanted that spot. She *needed* that spot, and stubbornly put her blinker on waiting for the owner of the Mustang to return and leave.

According to her watch, Adele had thirty minutes before her first class. With no one in sight, she began to worry. Driving away was not an option. Although she tried to talk herself out of this silly idea, her heart wouldn't allow it. She needed to be in that spot. It was the only thing that would set her body, mind and soul at ease.

Five minutes passed. She now had only twenty-five minutes before her first class. The anxiety began to build. She cursed under her breath at the Mustang and its owner, hating whoever it was that created this small distance from her and her peace of mind. She watched as cars pulled into nearby spots and parked, the drivers giving her odd glances as they got out. Adele looked away, pretending not to notice the perplexed stares. She looked at her watch yet again. Nineteen minutes now until her first class.

Suddenly, a young man stepped out from a doorway across the street, carrying a bagged lunch and darted toward the Mustang. He removed the keys from his pocket, about to unlock the car when he saw Adele sitting in the Renault and noticed the blinker. Catching her eye, he pointed to the parking space to see if that's what she was waiting for. Adele gave him a relieved smile and nodded yes.

The young man saw the row of empty parking spaces next to his car. Shaking his head, he got into the Mustang and, just to be cool, revved the engine before pulling out. Adele eagerly edged into the spot and turned off the car engine.

Taking in the details of where Bayview and Main Street met, Adele sighed. Her eyes smiled at the cracks in the concrete sidewalk, the few cobblestones that protruded from beneath decades of pavement and the weather worn street sign. A common corner to anyone else, but to Adele her secret nirvana.

She closed her eyes as a gentle breeze blew in from the harbor, carrying the fresh scent of salty air. It was just what she needed. Although physically fatigued, she was now mentally prepared to go to work. She looked at her watch. With only fifteen minutes to get to her first class, she started her car and pulled out. She gave the space one last loving glance, as if bidding a friend adieu, and drove off.

ço∞ç

NORTHPORT HIGH SCHOOL SAT on a sloping hill, surrounded by thick woods. In front was a large parking lot for the staff and students. Adele's Renault sputtered up the hill and parked. Grabbing her satchel and purse, she got out of her car and made it into the building just as the first bell rang.

The day was long for Adele. As she was finishing her fourth class of the day, the lack of sleep was beginning to take its toll. In her thirty years of teaching French, she had never once slacked in her duties, bringing the same passion and commitment as when she started, but on this day she was uncharacteristically drained. The nightmare by now just a memory, but the effects wore brutally on.

On the blackboard, Adele wrote French sentences in chalk. She pointed to one. *"Quel can be used after the preposition. Example, 'A quelle heure veux-tu partir'?"*

A female giggle came from the back of the room. Adele immediately turned and saw Rebecca, a pretty female student smiling coyly at a male student on the other side of the room. As Adele was about to reprimand her, the school bell rang. The students quickly grabbed their books and headed out the door.

Adele came around her desk and called on Rebecca as she walked past with the other students, still smiling from the flirtation. She stopped for Adele as her friends left the room. Adele looked at Rebecca and spoke kindly yet with a fixed purpose.

"You are one of my brightest students," Adele began, "Please don't give in to distractions."

"Distractions?" asked Rebecca, eyes squinting.

"Boys," Adele said pointblank. "You have a very promising future."

"I'd like to get married one day," Rebecca countered, with a slight hint of authority toward this older, unmarried teacher.

"Yes. Love is grand, but a mind such as yours shouldn't be limited to just a domestic life. Devotion to profession is where true reward is. Keep that in mind."

"Yes, Miss – er, Mademoiselle Breaux," Rebecca answered with teenage assurance, and then left the classroom.

Just then, Morris Saxe sauntered in announcing, "Lunchtime," in his friendly, casual manner.

He was a good-looking "guy's guy," slender rather than tall, his hair greying at the temples, a twinkle of humor in his eyes and a welcoming sight for the wearied Adele.

"It's about time," Adele exhaled ready for a break. She went back around her desk to organize, but clumsily knocked a stack of papers to the floor. Bending over to collect them, Morris quickly did the same to help.

"I'm a little off today."

"Everything all right?" Morris asked.

Adele stood, placing the papers on the desk. "I had a nightmare last night. It kept me up."

"You've had those before," Morris said with concern. Being that she was seventy, he took it upon himself to be conscientious in detecting anything out of the ordinary with her, as one would be toward an aging parent.

"They often occur this time of year. The anniversary of his –" Adele stopped, changing the sentence, "When he disappeared."

Morris knew who "he" was and asked in disbelief, "He's still on your mind?"

Adele didn't like how Morris stressed the word "still", as if it was wrong or shameful. She angrily grabbed the papers from his hands.

"What's on my mind is being chairperson of the language department when we move to the new high school. I have an appointment this afternoon with Principal Allardice."

She slammed the papers on the desk and brushed past him to the door. Morris, taken aback, stood watching. When Adele reached the doorway, she turned to him and decreed with impatience, "Lunchtime," then made her exit.

Morris' shoulders slumped. "Oh, it's going be one of those days," he muttered as he followed out the door.

The two made their way to the teacher's cafeteria through the crowded school hallway. Adele walked in stoic stride as students rushed to classes, zigzagging past her. She hardly noticed. Morris kept up in relaxed step with his hands in his pockets. His informal strut perturbed Adele, but she chose not to make comment.

"I've worked long and hard for this promotion, Morris," Adele initiated, speaking with her usual air of superiority,

"Being department chairperson will finally bring reverence. Status. Appreciation!"

"Along with lots of red tape and headaches. Believe me, I know," Morris groaned.

"Yes, but with the title comes respect," Adele retorted.

Morris chuckled. "You already have respect, Adele."

Adele looked at him, eye narrowed, resolute and declared, "I *want* the title."

⚜

IN THE LUNCHROOM, ADELE and Morris sat at a table with several other teachers. Among them was Carmen, a dark-haired, haughty Spanish teacher who was dominating the conversation.

"If the Language Department is assigned a Chairperson, I think an administrative background, which I have, should be the deciding factor."

"It should be based on seniority," Adele cut in.

Carmen shot Adele a competitive look. Adele shot one right back. This tension brought silence from the other teachers.

Morris, breaking the ice, remarked, "And I think it should go to whoever can get the kitchen to make a better meatloaf."

Relieved laughter spread across the table as Adele and Carmen continued to give each other hateful glances. Morris kicked Adele's ankle under the table to get her to stop. Adele gave a startled jolt and shot him an irate stare. He ignored it by jabbing a piece of meatloaf with his fork, mixed it with some mashed potatoes and brought it to his smiling lips.

A short time later, Morris walked out of the teacher's lunchroom, patting his satisfied stomach. Adele was next to him, gritting her teeth.

"I expected you to back me up," she growled.

"The point of lunch is to eat and relax, not battle for position, Adele," Morris responded, not in the mood for a fight.

"Well, I couldn't just sit there and allow that shrew to think she would be chosen over me."

"*Shrew?*" Morris chuckled, "Don't you think that's a bit harsh?"

"No," answered Adele, "I was being kind."

"Well, I know better than to get between two angry women. I'd be better off putting my hand between two fighting cats."

Adele stared at him, insulted. Morris noticed.

"OK, I promise the next time you two get into it, I'll flick a spoonful of mashed potatoes right in her eye."

Adele was not amused. Her stare turned icy. In return, Morris gave her a wink and a smile. This was how their friendship lasted so long. She was uptight, he wasn't. And although he respected and cared greatly for this lonely yet proud woman, he knew how to remind her not to take everything so seriously even if it brought on the more than occasional look of disapproval.

As he headed in the direction opposite hers, Adele asked where he was going.

"I'm in charge of hiring for the new building. I have to check out an applicant, a teacher coming in from New Jersey."

"Now?" Adele asked, knowing he already has a busy day.

"Come on, Adele, you know..." Morris began then, annunciating his words in perfect imitation of her, "It's all part of the *reverence, status* and *appreciation* you talked about earlier."

He didn't wait for a response, because he didn't want one, but more because he didn't want her to see him grinning, as he turned and walked away.

Adele, tight lipped, grumbled, "Incorrigible."

Chapter 3

The Visitor

Adele walked down the empty school hallway long after the last bell rang and all the students were gone. The clicking of her heels echoed on the polished concrete floor as she made her way toward the principal's office. Her aspiration to become part of the high school's administrative team was just moments away.

She was more than ready to accept the honor and, in her mind, was trying to decide how best to receive it. Should she do it with stoic pride, warm and graciously, or maybe a mixture of both? Her choice was to leave it up to the moment. One thing she definitely needed to do was hide her excitement. She didn't want to come off too eager, like some giddy schoolgirl, nor did she want to appear desperate. This was a promotion she deserved; it was long overdue. Still, it was hard for her to contain the thrill of it finally coming to fruition.

When she approached the door to Principal Allardice's office, she stopped to press out a few wrinkles on her dress with the palms of her hands, and primped her hair with the tips of her fingers. Ready, she pushed her shoulders back and opened the door with confidence, entering with chin out and head held high.

Adele sat upright in a chair across from Principal David Allardice who sat across from her behind a desk. He was a handsome, serious man, in his early-fifties, with a fair and compassionate manner. He became principal just two years earlier, having first arrived to Northport High School in 1943 and being hired as Dean of Boys. He and Adele have been colleagues for over twenty years now, which was another reason why she was confident of this promotion.

Standing next to Principal Allardice was a school superintendent, a man of middle age, unfamiliar to Adele. He was there more as a witness than any other purpose, she surmised.

Principal Allardice pulled his chair forward. "You've given a lot to Northport High School, Adele," he said with sincere appreciation.

"Thirty years," she said with no humility.

"And we are grateful for each one of them, which is why it is with deep regret that we...have to let you go."

"Let me..." Adele's voice trailed off as she tried to take in what he just said. She stared in disbelief at both men. "I – I don't understand," she stammered, "I am an excellent teacher."

"Your skill has nothing to do with this decision," Principal Allardice said fast and sincerely, hoping it would soften the blow.

"Then – why?" Adele asked, a faint thread of anxiety in her voice.

"In preparation for the move to the new high school –," he began.

"A move I expected to be a part of," Adele interrupted. "I helped with the planning of that building. We all did." She sat forward, in need of understanding. "Have there been complaints? Have I failed at giving nothing but total dedication and commitment to the students and staff?"

The men looked at each other in search for delicacy. Principal Allardice shifted uneasily in his seat.

"Adele, it is the Board's policy that teachers retire at age seventy."

Age? What stood between her and her goal was her age? Adele gave a chuckle to this minor technicality that could and would easily be rectified.

"Well, the board obviously knows who I am. I'm sure they'll make an exception," she said dismissively.

With no hint of even trying, Principal Allardice said, "No, it's district policy."

A look of pained defeat passed over Adele's face. The superintendent next to Principal Allardice remained silent as he lowered his eyes to the floor in pity. Adele looked at Principal Allardice as her voice broke miserably.

"Please, David...make an exception? For me. Teaching is all I –,"

Principal Allardice shook his head. "It's mandatory, Adele, and state law as well. I'm sorry."

He looked at the superintendent and slightly shook his head signifying how difficult this was, but the superintendent never looked up.

The finality of Principal Allardice's words was crushing. Adele tried to breathe without gasping, opening her mouth just a little to suck in as much air as her lungs would allow. She sat still, numb, forcing this to sink in, and it did. This was a final decision made by a faceless team of men and women whom she had never met, who didn't know, or even cared about all the years she'd sacrificed for the school that had become her very life. But that didn't matter any longer. She had become obsolete in a matter of seconds.

It wasn't like her to beg, cajole, plead or raise any sort of hell. She had too much dignity for that. Her fate was sealed and there was nothing she could do about it. Instead, she slowly rose from her chair and silently walked to the door with what little pride she had left.

As she opened it, Principal Allardice called out, "You will be missed," in a sincere tone that, to Adele, sounded like a stale afterthought.

Adele stopped with her hand on the door handle, insulted by this weak attempt at consolation. She turned and glared at him with burning, reproachful eyes.

"By *whom?*" she asked then walked out, slamming the door behind her.

She barely got a few paces from the office before she side-stepped to the wall, bracing herself against it with an out-stretched arm; the other covered her waist, as she let out a mournful gasp. She quickly swallowed the sob that was rising in her throat and fought back her tears. She refused to succumb to her emotions, but tears filled her eyes nonetheless.

After a moment, she composed herself, though her head stayed bowed, her body slumped in defeat, and walked alone through the late afternoon shadows that now darkened the empty hallway.

THE SCHOOL CAFETERIA WAS filled with a cheerful gathering of teachers sharing wine, cheese and chitchat. It was the end of the year faculty party. The job of grading tests and papers was over, and the arrival of the long summer break was welcomed by most in the room. The only one not in harmony with the rest was Adele. She stood off in a corner, holding a small glass of white wine with Morris, who looked like he would prefer to mingle than stand next to her understandably sour mood.

"Did they have to *broadcast* my retirement?" she said in a frustrated whisper.

"Retirement isn't that bad, you know," Morris responded, good-naturedly.

"Involuntary retirement *is*," she answered in bitter resentment.

Morris gave a supportive nod. She had a point, one he couldn't, and didn't want to, argue with. A moment passed when suddenly, a small cluster of teachers nearby broke into raucous laughter. At the center of the group, basking in the attention was Carmen. Adele eyed her with contempt, clenching her teeth.

"I can't take another minute of this. Let's get out of here," she said placing her wine glass on a nearby table. Morris did the same, after he downed his first.

As they started to unobtrusively pass the group, Carmen saw them. She took a step forward, blocking Adele.

"Adele! I do wish you the best with your retirement," she demurred with mock sincerity.

The other teachers murmured the same sentiments, although theirs were genuine. Adele managed a smile, then took a step to pass Carmen without looking at her.

"Rest assure the department will run smoothly with me as the *most qualified* chairperson," Carmen boasted, enjoying the obvious sting it caused Adele.

Adele stopped and gave her a hostile glare. "Most qualified? You only have the position by *default*."

Carmen took offense. "I'll have you know, I visit Spain every year to polish up on the language – thus *proving* my immense dedication."

Adele snickered. "Polish up? That was never necessary for me – French being my *native* language."

Carmen gave her a competitive, hard stare, then pulled out the heavy artillery. "Several of my former students received scholarships to Yale, Princeton, Duke *and* Northwestern."

The teachers looked at Carmen impressed. Adele, not to be beaten, smiled, confidently.

"And one of *my* former students was Antoine de Saint-Exupéry – author of *The Little Prince!*"

The group turned their attention to Adele, in awe, murmuring "wow," "really?" and "no, kidding!?"

Not able to top that, Carmen bristled with indignation and walked away leaving Adele now to bask in the glow and attention. Morris watched her, amused, but was also relieved, since this was the better way for her to finish her career – with admiration and respect.

Though the party was still in progress, Adele and Morris were in the school parking lot, walking to their cars. Adele exhaled a long sigh of contentment as she swung her purse happily.

"Did you see them, Morris? Did you see how impressed they were?" she asked with exhilaration.

"Yup, I saw," Morris answered, mildly amused.

"Serves Carmen right for being so blatantly obnoxious."

"Yeah," Morris replied wryly, "you showed her."

"And those administrators. I bet now they regret forcing me to retire."

"Yeah. They're just kicking themselves," Morris jokingly agreed.

Adele halted. Annoyance hovered in her eyes. Before Morris spoke to diffuse Adele, Betty Bradley, a sweet natured, grey-haired woman who was Chairperson of the guidance department, and had worked at the high school as long as Adele had, approached them.

"Adele, good luck with retirement," she said with fond sincerity.

"Oh, you, too, Betty," Adele said taking Betty's hand in both of hers and squeezing them tenderly.

"Well, not yet," Betty responded with a hint of weariness. "I was asked to continue for another year."

Adele's body stiffened in shock. "But we're the same age, Betty, and the district has rules about teachers over seventy," Adele said, her mind reeling with confusion.

"I know, but you know how persuasive Dave Allardice can be. He got them to grant me an extension, so I'll be back in September."

They gave *her* an extension? Adele's blood pounded, causing her face to grow hot with humiliation. Morris hung back, looking surprised and embarrassed for Adele, saying nothing.

Not noticing she had just dropped an insulting bomb on her now former colleague, Betty said affectionately, "Best of luck to you again, Adele. And you have a good summer, too, Morris," then turned and walked away.

Adele waited for Betty to get beyond earshot then looked at Morris, her eyes conveying the fury within her.

"How could you not tell me!?" she hissed.

"Me? I didn't know!" Morris shot back, flabbergasted.

Adele clutched her purse tight and stormed toward her car, furious. Morris swiftly followed.

"Adele, wait –"

She didn't wait and kept moving at a vehement pace. When she reached her car, she jabbed the key into the lock, opened it and tossed her purse onto the passenger seat. Morris reached her before she got in.

"Adele –," he began in a calm tone.

Adele would have none of it. "Teaching was my *life*, Morris," she boomed in anger. "It's all I had! People retire to their children and families, but I have neither because I gave *everything* to my profession, to that school. What I've sacrificed!"

With that, she climbed inside, slammed the door shut and fumbled with her keys. Morris gingerly approached the car window and tapped on it lightly for her to roll it down so they could talk. She ignored him as she found the key, shoved it into the ignition and started the engine.

"Adele...come on, let's talk about this," shouted Morris over the engine she revved for effect.

She didn't even look at him as she backed out of the parking spot, put the car in drive and sped angrily away. Fortunately, Adele traveled this course for thirty years, since she drove half blinded by her fury. Any other destination and it's doubtful she would have made it there alive. Images of thirty years of service as a teacher flashed before her. She crazily tried categorizing which ones to put under satisfaction and which under regret. She had none yet for satisfaction.

When she turned onto Chestnut Circle, her quaint provincial street, her foot was still on the accelerator, causing her to careen into her driveway. Realizing where she was, she slammed her foot on the brake, causing the car to come to a screeching halt. Her body nearly slammed forward, but she braced it by holding onto the steering wheel. She released one panicky breath and turned off the car.

The sudden silence made the screams of defeat in her head more deafening. She became immobile, slouched in her seat. A moment passed before she glanced out the side window where something caught her eye.

At her front door stood a mature woman, close to her age, balancing a large box and purse in her arms as she tried to knock with a free hand. Adele stared quizzically at this woman as she got out of her car and made her way up the small brick path to her home.

"Can I help you?" Adele asked.

The elderly woman turned around. It was her old friend, Sara, from Oregon. She, too, was now in her seventies, greyer and slower, yet her warm and gentle personality had not aged a day. A look of surprise and delight came across both their faces.

"Sara?" asked Adele, just to be sure. It had been years since they've seen each other.

Sara smiled affectionately. "Hello, Adele. So good to see you."

ℕℒ

SARA FOUND ADELE'S HOME warm and welcoming. She was impressed how impeccably decorated it was with fine art and antiques. Because it was Adele who always made the trip west to Oregon, she had never been to Adele's house before, or to Long Island for that matter. But this was close to how she'd envisioned Adele to live. It fit her friend's personality and temperament to the tee.

They sat at the dining room table having tea and cookies, and spent the first hour talking about how they have been, Sara's impressions of Northport, and giving each other false yet flattering remarks about their appearances. Both knew the other was being way over kind, but that's what friends did.

When Adele asked Sara if she were living in the same house back in Oregon, Sara delicately placed her teacup on the saucer and told her she had recently moved to New York.

"I'm living upstate now, near Buffalo, to be with my son and the grandchildren. His job transferred him a year ago. I do miss Oregon, but at my age it's important to be near family."

Adele nodded her head, agreeing, yet envious upon hearing the word "family." Her parents were long gone and she never married. It was times like this when she was forced to face the fact that she was very much alone in that sense, but learned how to hide the disappointment.

"You and I will be closer now, Adele. No more shuttling back and forth across the country for sporadic visits," Sara said with a smile.

Adele managed a smile of her own, knowing they wouldn't see much of each other, if at all. It had already been so many years since her last visit to Oregon. In her mind she tried to recall when exactly she was last there. Was it some time back in the late 1940's, perhaps the early 50's?

Sara was thinking the same, but didn't let on then changed the subject.

"So – how is teaching?"

This instantly brought Adele back to the dreadful present. Not wanting to admit the truth and go into insufferable detail, she took the coward's way out and lied.

"Oh. Good. It's good," she replied, distracting any sign that it wasn't by smiling while breaking off a piece of a cookie and nibbling on it.

"I've always envied you, Adele. So dedicated to your work. It must be nice to still be part of something."

Adele's smile weakened. She was no longer a part of anything, and now it was her turn to change the subject.

"How is Beatrice?"

Sara's face became somber. "Actually, that's why I'm here. She passed away before I left Oregon."

Adele slowly put down the cookie, and listened with rising dismay.

"It was cancer...but she was in great spirits right till the end," Sara explained. "Her children were there. And her third husband."

Though Adele was heartbroken, she let out an affectionate chuckle. She had lost count of exactly how many husbands, let alone children, Beatrice had.

"Her daughter went through her things and found this box," Sara said, lifting the large box she was holding at the front door and placed it on the table. Adele looked at it with both intrigue and trepidation.

"Inside are items that belong to you. You left them behind on your last visit. Beatrice kept them."

Adele stared at the box wondering what relics from the past would Beatrice possibly hold on to, let alone thought even important to.

"I thought of mailing it, but this gave me a reason to see you again," Sara said with a grin though she knew it was really more a way to say one last and final goodbye to both her friends.

Adele knew this, but didn't let on and simply returned the grin. She gave a quick glance to the large box not daring to open it in Sara's or anyone's presence. And Sara knew already not to ask her to. The thought, however, did cross Adele's mind why Sara wasn't asking and wondered if it was because Sara knew its contents. Either way, the subject was soon dropped.

It was late in the afternoon by the time Sara was ready to get into the taxi that was waiting in front of Adele's house. Before she did, she turned to Adele and gave her a strong embrace. Adele held tight to Sara, knowing this would be the last she'd see of her friend. Sara then pulled away and climbed into the backseat of the taxi. After the door was closed, Adele reached into the open window and shook her friend's hand.

"Take care of yourself, Sara," she said holding on to Sara's hand as long as she could, knowing once she let go, she'd never feel its touch again.

"You, too, Adele," whispered Sara, having the same thought. They looked into each other's eyes with an impossible hope that maybe they were wrong. Maybe they would see each other again one day.

That hope was dashed once they released each other's grasp and Adele stepped away. Neither woman could bear another sad moment, especially with the reality that they were old and time was cruel, so Sara stared down at her lap as Adele turned and headed back to her house. There was no final wave as the taxi drove off.

Chapter 4

The Journal

Not soon after Sara left, Adele stood in her dining room staring at the large box on the table. She hesitated opening it, wondering if she should continue this trip down memory lane and play seesaw with her emotions, or simply toss it. She already had an emotional day; why add to it? Surely what was inside that box must be useless after so many years, and knowing Beatrice, it was probably filled with outdated, sentimental rubbish.

But curiosity got the better of Adele, so she took a deep, yet blasé breath, carefully removed the lid, adjusted her glasses and peered inside. A quizzical look came across her face as she reached in and started removing the strange items one at a time.

The first one she took out was a very primp and proper, 1940's style blouse. Given the color, a light shade of solid grey, and its conservative, delicate collar, it was most certainly something Adele once owned. She held it up to her chest, hoping it might still fit. Not quite, she thought, but appreciated the fact that the shape of her body hadn't changed too much in the past twenty years.

She carefully set the blouse next to the box then reached in and took out several old black and white photographs. She held them closer to her face as she studied the past like a probing archeologist. They were of Sara, Beatrice and herself in the 1940's. A few were of them sitting casually on Sara's patio, but the others were typical staged poses of each one in front of Sara's house.

The sight of Beatrice's wide smile is what made Adele chuckle recalling her rebellious, uninhibited spirit and intrusive comments. They annoyed Adele then, but were now missed and fondly remembered. Though Adele would never admit it aloud, she appreciated Beatrice's bold honesty and knew this was why they were friends in the first place.

Adele placed the photos carefully on the blouse then reached in and pulled out sheet music of a popular song from that decade. The corners were yellow and chipped, so Adele handled it with special care as she looked at it, with interest.

On the cover was a picture Bing Crosby and The Andrew Sisters. The song title was splashed across the top, "I Can Dream Can't I?" On the top corner was an inscription. Adele brought it closer to see and read it silently to herself: *Adele, Don't let your heart be a 'sad affair' – Love, Beatrice.*

Adele was once again struck by Beatrice's bold honesty. Even as if from the grave she had insight into what Adele needed to be most careful of. Beatrice was right. She always was, Adele admitted to herself, and it made her sad. She wished Beatrice were alive so she could tell her that. Adele let out a sigh of regret, understanding that it's always when something is lost that one begins to truly appreciate it.

Adele placed the sheet music with the photos and then took out an old bottle of French perfume. It was a small, delicate bottle and half full. The idea of smelling the past as well as looking at it appealed to Adele. After a few tug and turns, she managed to unscrew the cap and held the bottle to her nose, taking a cautious whiff. The smell was old, sour and hideous. Adele whipped her head back, away from the bottle. She winced and quickly put the cap back on.

She carried it into her kitchen, opened her trash and dropped it in with a good riddance. Holding her nose, Adele returned to the box. She reached in and took out an old French lesson book. A small, blue booklet filled with lines of French sentences made in faded pencil. Adele smiled as she flipped through the pages. She held the book to her nose, taking in the familiar musky scholastic smell, an attempt to erase the old perfume still lingering in her nostrils. As she did this something in the box caught her eye. She placed the booklet on the table, reached in the box and pulled out an old, leather journal.

A slight pain of recognition showed on her face as she placed the journal on the table and stared at it as if it was a telegram bearing bad news. Hesitant, she opened it. It was filled with loose, yellowing pages of handwritten notes. Adele picked up the first page and slowly took a seat. The words were hers, written so long ago, and she began to read…

May 5, 1942. There was nothing to give hint that the pattern of this day would be any different from what the days, months and years had been since I arrived in Northport – redundancy, solitude, loneliness.

The entry brought a sad recollection that caused her to look up at the ceiling momentarily. Was she up to remembering moments long faded in time, as if viewing a series of short films in her mind? Yes was her answer, based on the fact that she had just lost her job as well as the possibility of ever seeing one of her dearest friends again, even her beloved state of Oregon for that matter, so there wasn't much in the present to hold on to. The past felt strangely more secure.

So, with that, she looked back at the page and braced for whatever memories were about to come forward.

That first entry made her recall that day in 1942, standing in front of a small class of twelve students. She read the French sentences slowly and with emphasis, knowing that hearing the words pronounced properly was just as important as seeing them. The students recited the sentences along with her. When the school bell rang the students gathered their books and made their exit, causing the room to grow eerily quiet. Adele hated an empty classroom, the ending of a busy day. It meant only the beginning of an evening of forced solitude.

"At the end of the day I wondered if all the years ahead would be the same dismal routine. My only contacts were colleagues who faced the same fate."

Teachers with unsmiling, stoic expressions passed the open door of Adele's classroom. She watched knowing not one would step inside for small talk. She then wearily gathered her books and papers and stuffed them into her leather satchel.

"I was a teacher and an outsider. Neither valued by such a small town both in size and mentality. The majority of my personal hours were spent by myself."

It was later that evening when Adele walked by herself down Main Street. It was a dark, quiet town after 6pm in 1942. Most of the locals were home with their families having dinner, although there were people mingling about and some of the shops still open. The five and ten cent store, the diners and, of course, the movie theater.

But taking this stroll was not to shop or take in a movie for Adele, it was more a way to stretch her legs, breathe a bit of the salty air and, more importantly, to feel a part of something. Being in the "flow" of this small town's energy, even if it was small, gave her a sense of connection, and temporarily eased her feelings of isolation.

"It was the farthest thing from my mind that this evening would be the start of something grander than I could have ever imagined."

As Adele passed a bookstore, she stopped and looked in the window. Reading was vital to her, an inexpensive travel to "anywhere but here" when the loneliness became overwhelming. The bookstore was still open, much to Adele's relief, so she decided to go inside.

The wooden floor creaked under her feet when she entered. It was a familiar sound coinciding with the small bell that rang when the door opened. Adele liked the sounds. It was a small acknowledgment that she was there when otherwise no one would have noticed or cared.

Adele made her way to the large wooden table in the center of the store that had stacks of the new arrivals, as well as the most popular on the New York Times Best Seller's list. She would start there. Touching these new books, she smiled with delight. Most on the table held no interest to her, such as the romance novels, the westerns or the latest from Hemingway. She perused right past those. She was ready to move on when suddenly one book stood out, catching her eye.

On the cover was a sketch of a small plane flying over a desert. The title, *Wind, Sand and Stars* was in bold letters above it. But it was the author's French name that grabbed her attention: *Antoine de Saint-Exupéry.*

Adele balanced her satchel and purse on her arm as she opened the book and started to read the first page.

"As soon as I began reading the author's exciting adventures, all time and space ceased to exist."

Hours had passed. Adele was sitting on a stool in the back of the store engrossed in the book when the front lights in the store dimmed. Since she had no one at home waiting for her, no one to even know where she was, it was easy for her to not pay attention to time. Realizing the store was closing, she quickly collected her purse and satchel and made her way to the front to purchase the book.

Later that night, Adele was tucked in her bed with Saint-Exupéry's book opened and balanced on her chest. She read each line carefully, completely mesmerized.

"The aviator's words spoke to me. There was a beauty in his language of being alone in a cockpit above an unforgiving, lonely planet. My spirits were restored knowing the sky and stars were much friendlier."

The next morning, Adele was sound asleep in bed with the book lying open across her chest. It was the pounding on her bedroom door that startled her awake, along with the voice of her roommate, Ann, another single teacher and colleague who moved with her from a boarding house to Adele's two bedroom flat not far from Main Street.

"Adele! You'll be late for work!" shouted Ann through the door.

As Adele became more alert, she saw the book on her chest. Recalling her new discovery, which seemingly connected her to everything now, Adele grinned, grabbed it and hopped out of bed.

At school, later that afternoon, Adele sat at a table in the teacher's lounge talking with animated excitement to several of her colleagues. Her enthusiasm was more like that of a girl describing her first crush than a woman giving a thoughtful book review.

"His words are so wonderfully descriptive," she gushed. "The sky is no longer just blue with clouds or black with stars. There is a whole world above us, and he lifts you right up into it!"

The other teachers nodded their heads with interest. Including one male teacher who stood at the tea station. He glanced over his shoulder more than once engrossed in what Adele was saying. When all the other teachers rose to return to their classes after the bell rang, he took a seat across from Adele.

"What's the book?" he asked, intrigued.

Adele held it up to show him. The male teacher saw the title and author's name then grinned.

"Ah, Saint-Exupéry. Excellent writer. Are you going to his lecture?"

"Lecture?"

"He's addressing the members of the American Association of French Teachers at NYU in a few weeks. You should go," he said as he slowly took a sip from his tea.

Adele's eyes lit up with excitement. Going to the event was all she could think about after that moment.

෧ං･ැ

THE DAY OF THE lecture couldn't have arrived soon enough for Adele, but when it did, she took a train on the Long Island Railroad out of East Northport and got into Penn Station hours before it was to start. Although it was exceptionally early, the station was crowded with people, mostly military troops arriving and departing.

America had entered World War II just six months earlier, so it was now a common sight to see young GI's kissing and consoling loved ones before boarding a train that, more than likely, would take them to a dangerous, far away place without promise of return. Adele maneuvered her way through these crowds to the stairs that led her up to the city streets.

Once at street level, she debated between taking a taxi or

the subway to NYU. Being that the weather was close to perfect, and wanting to save the fare, she decided to walk. She headed west on 32nd Avenue to Broadway then turned south to 16th Street. The forty-minute walk was invigorating, in huge contrast to the limited size of Northport. It also helped her to burn off some of the overwhelming excitement she was feeling for the day ahead.

New York University was a sleepy campus that Saturday morning when Adele finally arrived. A spattering of only the most ambitious students were found strolling toward the library to study, or head off for sports practice. Even though Adele had already traveled nearly fifteen blocks by foot, she walked at a clipped pace toward the lecture hall to ensure herself a good seat. She could not wait to see and hear the brilliant author of this book that had captured her imagination.

When she entered the building where the lecture was being held, Adele walked eagerly down an empty hall. At the end of it, a yawning, student usher, whose uniform jacket was still open with his clip-on bow tie dangling from his shirt's collar, stood lazily by the auditorium doors. Adele didn't even notice or care about his shabby appearance as she approached him with impatient zeal.

"Hello! I'm here for the Saint-Exupéry lecture," she announced, out of breath.

The usher shot her a peculiar look then checked his watch.

"Lady, you're a couple of hours early," he said a bit annoyed.

"I wanted to be sure to get a good seat. I've read almost all of Monsieur de Saint-Exupéry's books. They're quite inspiring. I'd have to say my favorite is *Flight to Arras* although *Night Flight* was just as wonderful," said Adele, oblivious that this young man was not in the least bit interested.

Although against policy, the student usher opened the

door and let her enter. It was something he could be reprimanded for it, but he would rather take the punishment then
be alone in the hallway with Adele listening to her chatter.

Once inside the empty auditorium, Adele gave it a quick
look over before moving down the front aisle, taking a seat
near the center. Sitting alone in the sea of empty chairs, she
glanced over her shoulder and, changing her mind, got up
and took a seat a few rows back. Just as she got herself comfortable in that seat, she noticed a better one at the end of the
row. She got up and tried that one.

Not liking it, she then moved to a seat closer to the aisle –
then to another one nearer the center. She did this several
more times until she finally found the perfect seat, closer to
the front. As she settled in, she looked up at the podium content and smiled. Yes, this was the best seat in the house, she
said to herself with certainty.

It would be a couple of hours before the lecture began, but
be it hours or all day, it didn't matter. She would have waited
an eternity if

The time passed fast for Adele, even more so once others
began coming in and filling the seats. It thrilled her to hear
people nearby speaking to each other in French. It wasn't
eavesdropping; she just loved the lyrical sound of her native
language.

Within a short amount of time, the auditorium was
packed. Adele sat anxiously in her seat when finally a distinguished looking man in a suit walked across the small stage to
the podium and made a brief announcement.

"Good afternoon, Ladies and Gentlemen. On behalf of *The
French Review*, it is my great honor to introduce to
you...Captain Antoine de Saint-Exupéry."

Applause exploded in the auditorium. Adele clapped with
boundless enthusiasm and was instantly mesmerized when

the tall, stoic looking Saint-Exupéry approached the podium wearing a dark suit and tie. Instead of speaking directly to the audience, he pulled up a chair and faced it sideways. He then sat and began discussing military aviation in French, much of the information going way over Adele's head since she knew little about the subject. And yet, it didn't stop her from staring, completely infatuated, at Saint-Exupéry throughout the entire lecture.

"He appeared nervous and spoke in a soft tone, quite the opposite from his commanding appearance. I was taken by his stature. His dignity. His...virility. Seeing him had the most appealing effect on me. It was something I would never forget."

Adele's hands trembled after reading this last entry. It was true, she never did forget the first time she saw Saint-Exupéry, or the last time. Nor any time in-between. Reading this made him seem alive again, and made her feel as if it were only yesterday that she attended that event at NYU. But the feeling was fleeting. She knew it was only a memory, and although wistful and nostalgic, she was also pained and distressed by what she'd lost so long ago.

Her hands continued to shake and she felt an upsurge of sorrow begin to swell in her heart. With the loss of her job, and Sara's visit overwhelming her, she knew she shouldn't be adding to it with bygone memories, especially ones that only magnified her sense of loss. She needed to put distance, more accurately, time, between herself and these recent events, more importantly, the past.

Moving fast, Adele shoved the papers back into the journal and put it back into the box. She was now angry that its contents found their way back, invading life. She quickly grabbed the blouse, photographs and sheet music, shoved them all inside the box and snapped the lid shut. Yes, time and distance was what she most needed.

Chapter 5

In Control

*A*dele was sitting in the cockpit of a small plane, once again the reluctant co-pilot to Antoine de Saint-Exupéry. As he steered the plane through calmer skies, he happily sang and hummed a silly tune in French, much to Adele's irritation. Her annoyed glances indicated a deeper, more nagging issue than just his singing. She did her best to hold her tongue, but his insistent good mood was grating way too much on her bad one.

"You left me," she finally blurted out, angry and hurt.

"Pardon?" Saint-Exupéry asked, startled.

"You disappeared. Vanished," Adele said sharply, waving her hands to dramatically stress the point.

"No, no, Mademoiselle, you have it wrong. It is you who has left me," he exclaimed.

"I did nothing of the sort," she said dismissively, shifting in her seat.

Saint-Exupéry looked at her, shaking his head in disappointment, then let out a heavy sigh.

"Ah, it is a shame. You've missed so much."

"What have I missed?"

"The ability to lose control," he said with sincerity.

"I don't like to lose control," she grumbled.

Her words made him grin. He looked at her with playful eyes.

"Ah, but when we love we lose control," he said giving her a knowing smile, then added, "All control." He followed that with a suggestive chuckle.

"That is not my experience of love," Adele responded, not amused.

Saint-Exupéry let out another heavy sigh with a wounded look in his dark eyes. "No. Your experience is loss."

"Absurd," Adele muttered.

"Is it?" he asked.

She didn't answer. Wanting to make his point more clear, he decided to turn this into a game.

"Here then," he began, "I will teach you about love, and in exchange...you teach me control."

He leaned forward, flipped a switch on the flight panel, took his hands off the wheel and sat back.

"There! Now you are in control," he said pointing to the wheel. "Show me."

"Monsieur, no!" Adele shouted, terrified.

"But are you not the teacher?" he asked. Before Adele had a chance to reply he said, "Oh, of course – not anymore. You lost control of that."

Adele shot him a surprised and embarrassed look.

"Now what will you do?" he asked with cool casualness.

Just then the plane jerked. Adele gripped the control wheel petrified.

"Ah, good! Now you will show me," Saint-Exupéry said eagerly.

"I-I don't know how," she shouted, her hands shaking on the wheel.

"But you must! You are the one in control," he shouted, his voice turning from playful to stern, as if an order.

Adele pushed the control wheel forward. The plane started to descend immediately, making a searing sound, cutting fast through wind. Saint-Exupéry laughed.

"H-help me," Adele begged as her eyes stared transfixed on the swirling clouds outside the window. "Please...Monsieur."

She turned and looked at Saint-Exupéry in desperation. He was gone. A whisper of terror ran through her as the plane started to make a steep descent. Adele pulled back on the control wheel, but it was too late. The plane wouldn't climb and began to nosedive. Adele's eyes grew wide with terror as she saw the clouds thinning out with earth not too far away. The sound of the plane's metal cracking and wind hissing was ear piercing. She covered her ears in pain then, seeing the plane about to crash, shielded her eyes with her arms and screamed.

Adele jolted up in bed, this time screaming with her arms folded over her eyes. The scream seemed endless until she quickly stopped, shocked by her own outburst, and did her best to catch her breath.

"I am not losing control. I am not losing control..." she repeated between sharp gasps as she frantically put her eyeglasses on and got out of bed. She stepped into her slippers, but didn't think to turn on the light. Instead, she made her way out of the dark room, touching the walls and furniture with her hands, as if she were blind.

She quickly moved down the hallway as though she were being tormented and chased by some unseen force. When she reached the hall closet, she opened it, grabbed her coat and put it on over her nightgown. She then fumbled around looking for her keys, which she found on a table, raced to the front door, flung it open and ran out as if fleeing for her life.

Outside was pitch black, but Adele was too hyper to notice or care, until she stumbled, nearly falling, but even that didn't stop her. She made it to her car, her hands trembling as she found the right key, opened the door and got in.

"This can't happen. This can't happen," she repeated hysterically, as she started the engine and turned on the headlights. Their shine cut through the darkness as she put the car in reverse and peeled out of the driveway.

Adele drove, slowing down for nothing, but fortunately, there were no other cars on the road at that hour. She swerved down empty streets, bounced violently over pot holes, never letting up until the Renault took a sharp turn down one last darkened street and pulled into Morris' driveway, where it came to a screeching halt. She jumped out of the car and slammed the door shut.

Clutching her coat, she raced up the porch to the front door and began pounding on it with her open palm. Moments passed before the porch light came on and Morris opened the door, half-asleep, wearing his pajamas under his robe.

"Adele? What in the world...? It's almost three in the morning. Here, come inside," he said as he held the door open.

Adele stammered, with an edge of desperation in her voice, "No, I – I need to talk with you...out here. I had another..."

She stopped when she saw Harriet, Morris' attractive and good-natured wife, also in her robe step up behind him, sleepy-eyed.

"Morris? What's wrong?" she asked before seeing Adele looking uncharacteristically disheveled on the porch.

"Oh, my...Adele! Are you all right?"

Harriet had been Adele's friend for as long as Morris, though Adele had more of a kinship with Morris since he was a colleague and they saw each other nearly every day at school. Even though Harriet and Adele were close, Adele still clutched her coat and stepped away, embarrassed at having Harriet see her so distraught.

Morris looked at his wife as if to say he'll take care of it and stepped out on the porch. Trusting her husband, Harriet went back inside and closed the door just slightly to give them privacy.

Adele peered uneasily over his shoulder to make sure no one else was listening then, voice shaking, confessed, "I had another nightmare, Morris. It was…*horrible*."

"They're only dreams, Adele," Morris said, stifling a yawn as he tightened his robe.

"They're *more* than that, Morris. Why else would I drive all the way out here?"

"Because you're under a lot of stress."

"No. This is *not* stress!"

"It is, Adele. Retirement can be confusing, even when…"

"This has nothing to do with retirement. It's something else. I don't know how to explain it. It's as if he…he's *haunting* me."

"Who is? Saint-Exupéry?" He wanted to laugh, though he wouldn't dare. "Adele, they're just dreams. It's been over twenty years, and you said yourself it's close to the anniversary of his…"

"No," Adele shouted adamantly, then quickly lowered her voice. "Tonight was different. He sees me, Morris. He's talking to me."

"He's *talking* to you?" asked Morris, now worried.

"Yes," Adele answered in just above a whisper as her eyes darted suspiciously at the darkness.

"Then maybe you need to talk to someone," said Morris. "Like, a doctor."

This sent Adele over the edge. "A psychiatrist, you mean. Absolutely not! I am *not* crazy, Morris."

Morris glanced down at her bedroom slippers. Being on his porch dressed like that at 2a.m. isn't crazy? Morris scratched his head, knowing he would have to take a more practical approach.

"OK...in these dreams you're in a plane and it's about to crash, right?"

"Yes," answered Adele, blinking her eyes, eager to hear whatever theory Morris may have.

"I have an idea. Why don't I take you up in my plane this weekend," he said with a slight yawn. "You'll be safe, and then you can see there's nothing to fear..."

"No! I don't want to get on any plane. That's what killed...*no*! How could you even suggest such a thing?"

Morris let out a frustrated sigh. He rubbed the back of his neck, clearly out of ideas. Adele began to wring her hands, her anxiety increasing.

"I can't figure out why, Morris...why now? Why does he keep returning as if he wants something from me?" The question stabbed at her heart.

Morris looked at her, sympathetically.

"Maybe *"he"* doesn't want anything. What do *you* want?"

"What do I want?" as if thrown by the question, then spoke in a heartfelt plea, "I want the world to go back to the way it was...when there was hope and youth, and...the chance again to tell him..."

She caught herself and quickly changed to a flat, inflectionless voice.

"I gave little thought to it ending. Who knew it would be so hard? After all these years of dedication and *this* is what it all comes down to?"

Morris looked at her, confused. "Wait, are you talking about teaching or Saint-Exupéry?"

Adele looked at him, confused herself and unsure how to answer. Morris, tired, again scratched his head and asked simply, "OK, how about a book?"

"A book?" she asked, perplexed.

"Yeah. Write a book about the guy. Maybe that will help." Morris gave a casual shrug.

Adele dismissed it immediately. "Oh, you and your silly ideas. There are things I could never put in a book."

"Then write around them."

"Impossible!"

"What are we talking about anyway?" he asked.

"What do you mean?"

"What can't you put in a book? You were there with him, Adele. You knew the guy. Maybe if you wrote about how he obviously affected you –"

"How he *affected* me?" Now she was insulted. "I was hired to be his instructor."

"Yeah. And...?"

"And, what?"

"Well, there's gotta be something that happened between the two of you to make you so...to cause all this." Morris was becoming irritated.

"There was nothing else, I assure you," said Adele averting her eyes from his.

"Nothing else?" asked Morris.

"No!" said Adele sternly.

"Then why are we outside discussing this at two in the morning?" Morris asked, exasperated.

Adele shot Morris a guilty look, then quickly snapped, "I am not a writer. I am a teacher!"

"Hey, it was only a suggestion. You don't have to bite my head off," said Morris defensively with raised voice.

Alarmed by this, Adele's eyes widened. Seeing this, Morris lowered his voice and said with resignation and compassion, "Look, Adele, I understand..."

"No, you *don't!*" She turned to leave, frustrated and angry.

Morris reached out and grabbed her arm. "I *do*!" he insisted. "You said it yourself – you didn't think about it ending, but it *did*. It's hard to let go of something you still love, but you have no choice. You can't *control* every thing life throws at you."

A shudder ran through Adele's body upon hearing the word "control." That was the word Saint-Exupéry's used in the nightmare. Her heart squeezed in anguish as she silently wondered what all of this meant.

Tired, weak and confused, she pulled away from Morris' hold, clutched her coat tight and said despairingly, "I – I'm sorry to have disturbed you, Morris. Please tell Harriet I'm sorry," then turned to leave.

"Adele – are you going to be all right?" Morris asked, worried.

She nodded, not because she was all right, but to ease his concern, then stepped off the porch and walked into the darkness. Morris watched until she made it to her car, got in and drove away. He then rubbed his eyes and went back inside.

◌

IT WAS STILL DARK when Adele arrived home. She tossed her keys on the table and, without removing her coat, entered her living room and sat on the couch. The room was lit only by the moonlight that streamed in from the windows. Drained and exhausted, Adele removed her eyeglasses, and covered her eyes.

Her thoughts played over her conversation with Morris. The more she thought about it, the more embarrassed she felt having bothered him and Harriet like that, and in the middle of the night no less. She let out a soft groan then decided she would find a way to make it up to them, as well as explain...explain what, she wondered. Even she didn't have an answer as to what possessed her to react so irrationally. Was it stress as Morris said? Was she losing her mind? She had no answers, but knew that she couldn't let that happen again, behaving like a madwoman to her friends, but more importantly, she had to stop the nightmares.

She shook her head, at a loss for a solution and slowly put her eyeglasses back on. She glanced across the room and saw the box from Beatrice sitting on the dining room table. It had a disturbing presence and yet she looked at it with curiosity, recalling the items inside, especially the journal. As the image of it focused in her memory, it brought her back to…

෴

A HOT AUGUST EVENING in 1944. It was earlier that day when Adele first learned about Saint-Exupéry's disappearance at Sara's house. They had since moved to Beatrice's home where a weary Adele sat in the living room, as Sara turned the dial on the radio searching for a news report of Saint-Exupéry's missing plane.

Beatrice entered cheerfully with a tray of tea. "Any news yet?"

Sara looked up and shook her head no. Beatrice set the tea tray down in front of Adele and spoke with a hint of sarcasm, "If they can go on and on about Hitler, they can surely squeeze in something about your friend."

"They probably don't know anything yet," Sara said.

Adele, looking numb and troubled, spoke softly, "There is something I never told him…"

"*Don't*, Adele," Sara said refusing to let defeat fill the room, "Everyone regrets not saying goodbye. But it's not time for that. He's only missing."

Goodbye? That wasn't what Adele was talking about, but

she didn't dare share that. She was now past defeat and had moved onto sadness as terrible regret assailed her.

"He was so strong – so intelligent," she whispered in anguish.

Beatrice was on Sara's side and offered with assurance, "And that's why he's probably still alive. Don't put him in the past tense. You'll drive yourself crazy."

She took Adele's hand and squeezed it. Then, getting an idea, she left the room. Sara kept searching for a news report as Adele sat there, growing more despondent. Beatrice came back with a handsome leather journal and held it out to Adele.

"Here," she began, "You need to write everything down. Every moment…every memory. It will keep him alive – for you."

Adele slowly took it, appreciating the gesture.

"Then, when he comes back – and one day he *will* – everything you wanted to say – will be right here," Beatrice added with a warm smile.

"When he comes back," thought Adele as she slid her hand wearily across the soft leather…

ৎৡৼ৵

ADELE LET THE MEMORY fade. She put her glasses back on and stared hard at the box sitting on the dining room table. It seemed unfeasible to her how the past that was so vast and filled with thousands of memories could fit so easily into such a small compartment.

The past. It was a better time, she thought. Better than the callous and unsympathetic present. And what future did she have with her career gone? She had no plans. They gave her no time to make any. She felt cast adrift and now needed to find her bearings. Perhaps what was in that box was her answer.

She slowly rose, walked over to it and placed her hand on the lid. It gave her a new sense of comfort. She had only to remove it and what once was would return. She could be young again, filled with hope for an exciting future, but more importantly, she could be with him. Her heart leapt at the thought as she slowly removed the lid…

Chapter 6

The Teacher From
New Jersey

Adele drove fast down the winding road that led to Eaton's Neck, a long, narrow peninsula that extends out to Long Island Sound. It also connects the Village of Northport on the "mainland" to Asharoken, a small community that was first developed as a summer resort for upper class families. By September of 1942, it was an affluent area of year round homeowners.

Although the scenery, while driving through the constricted main road on Eaton's Neck, was limited to small brush and sand dunes, it felt expansive due to the majestic blue skies and the frequent glimpses of stunning beaches and ocean.

Adele had the car windows rolled down to take in the crisp, autumn sea air, much to the annoyance of her friend and roommate, Ann, who was in the passenger's seat. She was a short, rotund woman, ten years Adele's junior, who taught Home Economics at the high school. She covered her head with her hands to protect her hair from the salty wind.

"The Bevin House should be at the end of this road. Look for a sign marked *Private*," Adele shouted with enthusiasm, oblivious to her friend's discomfort.

"Why are you in such a hurry?" Ann was perplexed by the speed Adele was driving at even though there were no other cars on the long stretch of road.

"It's Antoine de Saint-Exupéry!" exclaimed Adele as if that were an obvious reason. "I saw him speak a year ago," she swooned, "He was so...so..."

"So...?" Ann eyed Adele, wondering why her middle-aged friend was acting suddenly like a star-struck teenager.

Adele realized she was gushing and answered, "Dignified," in a more matronly tone.

"Don't forget, we're going there to meet his *wife*," Ann said hoping that would keep Adele's feet, and heart, firmly grounded.

Of course Adele knew they were on their way to meet with Saint-Exupéry's wife, Consuelo, who was residing temporarily at the Bevin House, a large, white Victorian mansion in Asharoken that sat on the edge of Duck Island Harbor, a small inlet of Northport Bay. Adele had been referred to Consuelo who was seeking English lessons, and since Adele was a language teacher, she was the ideal candidate. However, Adele wasn't as interested in Consuelo as she was in meeting her husband.

Adele ignored Ann's emphasis on the word "wife" and kept her eyes on the road when suddenly she shouted with excitement, "There it is!"

The Renault turned slowly into the drive, passing tall trees and thick underbrush until the grand white mansion revealed itself. Both Adele and Ann looked up at its intimidating stature as Adele slowed down and rolled to a stop. She turned off the car and the two continued to stare at the opulent house with its beautiful landscape.

Adele got out first, ready to get to the porch and see more. Ann sat there, still in awe until Adele turned and anxiously waved for her to follow. Ann got out of the car and limped cautiously behind because of an injury sustained as a child.

Nervously, they climbed the stairs to the porch and slowly approached the huge front door. Adele gave Ann an excited "here we go" look and knocked. A moment passed before the door opened and a heavy-set man with a big moustache appeared. Adele turned on her natural reserve and spoke respectively in French.

"Good day, Sir, I'm here to speak with Madame de Saint-Exupéry."

The heavy-set man gave both Adele and Ann a suspicious look then seeing they both appeared harmless, frowned and said, "I am sorry. She's not here now."

"Oh," said Adele, crestfallen.

She did her best to hide her disappointment as she thought what message to leave when, from behind the heavy-set man appeared a tall, lone figure dressed causally in brown slacks and a soft, white shirt. He was in his mid-40's, but looked boyishly quizzical and shy.

Adele recognized him immediately and was able to catch the slight gasp in her throat before it came out, although inside her heart felt as if it was about to leap out of her chest. Antoine de Saint-Exupéry stepped forward to get a better look at Adele. This gave Adele a better look at him. Unable to hold her excitement any longer, she lost all composure, and went star struck, gushing in French.

"Monsieur de Saint-Exupéry! I love your book, *Wind, Sand and Stars*. The translation is beautiful."

Saint-Exupéry looked down at his feet for a moment, embarrassed by the unrestrained compliment then looked back at Adele. He spoke back in French, the only language he knew.

"Thank you," he said softly, then his tone changed to suspicion and asked sternly, "Now why are you at my house?"

Adele, not the least taken aback by his manner, responded, "I was told your wife was in need of English lessons. I am a teacher."

"My wife speaks fluent English," he answered, maintaining his authority. "I am the one who needs lessons. Consult with her. Phone next week."

Before Adele could say anything, Saint-Exupéry turned and went back into the house. The heavy-set man gave a slight smile, bowed politely and closed the door. Just like that, it was over. Adele stood there in astonishment, unable to move, except to swap a side-glance with Ann, who was just as surprised. They both broke into grins, stifled giggles and hurried back down the stairs of the porch, with Ann limping fast, and then to the car like two eager school girls...

THE CLACKING SOUND OF typewriter keys broke the usual silence in Adele's home as she sat at her dining room table engrossed in the memories she was committing to page. The notepapers from her journal were strewn about. Yellowing from age, they were all over the table and chairs, including a small stack next to her that she was typing from.

Adele stopped and brought one of the pages closer to her face, trying to make out at a word she had written so long ago in her messy handwriting. She lifted her glasses, nearly holding the page to her nose and squinted. It came to her. Smiling, she placed the paper back down and continued typing.

Suddenly, loud sounds of objects collapsing and folding were heard from outside, as well as mumbled voices. At first Adele ignored it, not wanting to disrupt her creative flow, but its continuation became overwhelmingly distracting. Exasperated, she let out an irritated huff, stopped typing and went to the window to investigate. She drew the curtain back slightly with her fingers and peered out.

A large moving van was parked across the street in front of a charming Cape Cod style house. Norman Orenstein, a tall, slender, slightly balding 30-year-old was out front helping direct movers carrying boxes. His younger, dark-haired wife, Josephine, was helping direct them through the front door.

Adele curiously observed her new neighbors, liking how Norman's black, horn-rimmed glasses gave him a mature, studious look.

"He looks like a reader," she whispered to herself, "And his wife looks like one, too."

She enjoyed the little game of sleuth she was playing with herself when suddenly there was a knock at her door. Adele's body jolted, as if she were found out, and let go of the curtain. When she composed herself, there was another knock. Adele nervously looked over at the papered mess in the dining room, embarrassed there was no time for her to straighten it out.

She was proud of the fact that her home was always in order and welcoming to any visitor. Today's disorder was a rare exception and an embarrassment as she walked to her front door, hoping she wouldn't have to let whomever the unannounced intruder was inside. She opened her door slowly, with trepidation. Standing there was Morris.

"Oh, it's only you," she said with blasé relief as she walked back inside.

"And a warm hello to you, *too*," replied Morris, sarcastically, letting himself in and closing the door behind him. "I haven't heard from you in weeks...not since you showed up on my porch in the middle of the night. I've been worried, you know. Harriet, too," he said as he followed Adele into the dining room.

"I do apologize for that night, Morris. Forgive me," she answered, though her tone was dismissive since her mind was more on her work.

She approached the table and began to organize. Morris, knowing how fastidiously clean Adele was, took one look at the chaos and took a surprised step back.

"Jeez – what happened here?"

Adele smiled, excitedly, "He's returned, Morris!"

"Who?"

"You know who," grumbled Adele, not in the mood to play games.

Knowing whom she was talking about, but thinking she couldn't be serious, he quipped, "Are we seeing ghosts now?"

"Don't be smart, Morris. No," she answered. "Saint-Exupéry has returned so I can write a book."

"No kidding? Writing a book? Now that's a brilliant idea. Come up with it all by yourself?" Morris asked, mockingly.

Adele ignored him.

Morris let out a sigh of relief. "Well, I'm glad. At least now you'll finally get closure on that relationship."

"Relationship?" Adele asked sharply, insulted. "What relationship? I'm writing only the facts about his time here. Anything else would be just sentimental nonsense."

"But people love sentimental nonsense," Morris encouraged.

Adele shook her head with disapproval. "Leave that to the dime store paperbacks. My book will express only my sincere veneration."

"What about what he meant to you?"

The question sounded intrusive to Adele. She shot him an offended look. Morris noticed and held up his hands.

"Just the facts. Gotcha," said Morris, backing off.

Adele went back to organizing and continued her train of thought. "I'll need someone who will help me stick to those facts. Someone obedient, yet smart, who won't steer me off course," she said as she carefully stacked several papers.

"You mean someone who will tolerate you."

Adele stopped and gave Morris an icy stare. Morris smiled. How he loved to jibe her. It was all in good fun.

"I'll be happy to help you with it," he offered sincerely.

"Thank you, but I'd rather have help from someone who doesn't have an agenda," she said with contempt.

"What agenda do I have?" Morris asked, feeling the subtle sting of insult and rejection.

"*Sentimentality,*" she countered. "Now, if you don't mind, I need to get back to my work."

"Spying on your neighbors?"

Adele went speechless, embarrassed and caught, as Morris walked over to the window and peered from the same curtain Adele was looking out of earlier.

"I saw you peeking when I got out of my car. His name is Norman Orenstein."

"You've met him?" Adele asked.

"Met him? I hired him. He's our new English teacher," he said letting go of the curtain.

Adele's eyes widened, intrigued, as she wondered aloud, "So, he's the new English teacher..."

"Yeah. He taught for several years in New Jersey. Some place called Cranford, and needed to get out. Stu Goldblatt in the Social Studies Department recommended him."

"Why did he need to "get out?" she asked.

"Problems with the administration."

"A trouble maker?"

"Not in a bad way. Kind of like yourself," Morris grinned.

Adele was getting tired of his wisecracks. Morris saw this
and spoke more deliberately.

"He's one of us...a dedicated teacher. In Jersey they asked
him to teach a class of slower learning students, so he gave
them Dante's *Inferno*."

"And that was too advanced for the students?" asked Adele.

"No, for the administration. They wanted him to stick to
their curriculum, *Readers Digest* of all things, but Norman
knew the kids were much brighter than that. But because he
bucked the system, they started to make his life uneasy.
Threatened his tenure, that sort of crap. That's why he had to
get out," Morris said then chuckled. "You know what he said
when I asked him why he became a teacher?"

Adele looked at him, interested to hear the response.

"To fight the war on ignorance."

Adele smiled. "Good answer."

"The best I've ever heard," said Morris as he drew back the
curtain and peered out the window again. Adele came up behind him and peeked out as well.

Chapter 7

Welcome

Norman and his wife, exhausted after spending the entire day moving and unpacking, were finishing a Chinese take-out dinner in the kitchen of their new home when they heard a knock at the front door. They looked at each other wondering who it could be since they just moved in and weren't expecting anyone. Norman got up and left the room to answer it. When he opened the front door, standing there was Adele, holding a freshly baked chocolate cake with beautifully whipped vanilla icing.

"Hello," she announced in a high-pitched, friendly voice. "I live across the street. My name is Adele Breaux. Welcome to the neighborhood!"

Norman pushed the door, his style easy and collegial. "Hi. I'm Norman Orenstein. Please come in."

When Adele stepped into the house she saw that some of the rooms were still bare, filled only with boxes waiting to be unpacked. Norman apologized for the appearance as he led Adele into the kitchen where his wife, Josephine, was washing the few dishes they had just used.

"This is my wife, Josephine," Norman said, smiling. "Jo, this is Adele. One of our new neighbors."

As Josephine quickly dried her hands on a dishtowel, Adele handed Norman the cake then warmly approached Josephine and shook her hand.

"It's a pleasure to meet you," Adele said sincerely.

"Hello," Josephine said with a shy smile.

"I just thought I'd come over and welcome you to the neighborhood," said Adele as she turned and caught Norman eyeing the cake's mouthwatering frosting. "And I wanted to make you something special for the occasion. It's chocolate," she beamed then quickly changed the subject. "So, you're one of the new teachers at Northport High School?"

"Yes. English," replied Norman.

"I was in the language department. I taught French there for thirty years," Adele semi-boasted.

"No kidding," said Norman, instantly feeling comfortable in the presence of another teacher.

"That was until I was forced to retire this past June," Adele said, trying to hide her bitterness but failing, adding snidely, "My reward for getting old."

There was an awkward moment of silence between the three, with Norman looking at Adele, not knowing what to say. Just then, a baby's cry was heard from a back room.

"Oh, please excuse me," said Josephine in relieved urgency, and walked out of the room.

"That's my son, Adam," Norman grinned proudly, as he placed the cake on the kitchen table. His thumb purposely grazed the side of it getting a lump of frosting on it. He licked it off, enjoying its sugary sweetness.

"Have you seen much of Northport yet?" Adele asked, happy to have Norman to herself for a few moments.

"We drove around after I got the position and were looking

for a house. I love it," said Norman. "It's very scenic compared to where we lived in New Jersey."

"It is very charming, yes, but it can be a lonesome place when you're by yourself as I am," she said wistfully. "But it can also surprise you – out of the blue – and be quite magical," she added with a smile.

"Magical?" asked Norman, intrigued.

Adele's eyes twinkled. "Yes. When you least expect it, you may find yourself enchanted by what Northport can bring."

The moment was quickly disrupted when Josephine returned with an adorable cooing baby in her arms. Adele clasped her hands together happily and stepped forward for a better look.

"He's beautiful," she said tenderly, though with a hint of regret, for a child was something that she had never herself produced. She would never know a husband and family.

"Would you like something to drink?" asked Norman, warming up to his new and curious neighbor.

Feeling an intruder on this happy domestic scene, Adele withdrew and said, "Oh, no. I don't want to keep you. I just wanted to introduce myself." She then smiled warmly at Norman's wife. "It was a pleasure to meet you, Josephine."

" A pleasure meeting you, Adele, but please call me Jo, and thanks for the cake," said Josephine as she rocked her son in her arms.

Adele nodded then turned and left the room. Norman followed her to the front door. He stepped ahead and opened it for her. Adele appreciated his manners and disarming friendliness as she stepped outside.

She turned to him one last time and said, "And it was a pleasure meeting *you*, Norman."

As Norman was about to say the same, she asked, "Before I go, tell me, when does school start?"

"In two weeks," Norman said with a sigh. Adele noticed his tone of resignation.

"Oh, don't get me wrong," Norman quickly said seeing her concern. "I'm looking forward to it, but it's been a real whirlwind for us the last two months – selling our house in Jersey, buying this one here. We could have used more time, but I'm ready. I love the classroom."

"Good for you," said Adele, appreciating his enthusiastic attitude. "Should you need anything, especially in regard to the school, let me help. I know all too well what it's like to be the new person, so don't hesitate."

"Thanks," said Norman as he watched her take several steps away from the house.

Then suddenly, as if an after thought, Adele turned and called out, "Oh...and good luck with the fight against ignorance!"

This caught Norman by surprise as Adele winked and walked happily back toward her home.

Chapter 8

Lesson One

Norman was a bit anxious his first day teaching at Northport High School. Although he had been in front of classes for several years, a new state, new town and a new school was a bit daunting. Still, he was excited and at his professional best when he stood in front of the classroom, even as he took attendance.

"Janet Clarke," he called out.

"Here," shouted a female voice from the third row.

Norman glanced over at the pretty student and smiled. He looked back at the roster and called out, "Jack Doleman."

There was no response. Norman looked up. "Jack Doleman?" he asked as he looked around the room.

Again, there was no response. He waited a few more seconds then noticed an empty chair in the back of the room. Regretfully, he put a check mark next to the boy's name and continued his roll call. Although all of the other names on the list were in attendance, and this first class went exceptionally smooth, he liked the students and they liked him, but seeing that empty chair and the absence of that one student troubled his unwavering sense of responsibility as an educator.

Later that day, after several more successful classes that helped erase his anxiety, Norman entered the administrative office carrying his briefcase and wearing a confident smile. He approached one of the secretaries, a pleasant older woman, and asked if he could use the ditto machine that was located in a small room near her desk. He needed to make copies of a lesson assignment for one of his afternoon classes.

The friendly secretary told him he was welcome to use it, and that in the future there was no need to ask her permission. Norman appreciated her kindliness and went into the small room. Inside there were shelves stocked with paper and supplies, as well as a long table with a bulky 1964-style hand cranked ditto machine on it. Norman checked it out, impressed that the school knew the importance of keeping up to date with the latest equipment.

He opened his briefcase, removed a class lesson that was typed on a sheet of paper and placed it carefully in the machine. He loaded the attached tray with printing paper and started to manually crank the handle. Soon, the unique smell of fresh ink began to fill the room. The print came out a blue-purple color and slightly blurry.

Norman stopped for a moment, taking one of the copies in his hands to see how it looked when, unfortunately, some of the ink smeared on his fingers. Norman didn't mind, however, since there was hardly a teacher that got through a day without that ink staining their hands. He placed the paper back in the tray, continued to crank the handle, and tilted his head to make sure the copies were coming out straight.

Suddenly, and without warning, Carmen, the recently promoted language department chairperson, stormed into the room with a stern and angry look on her face.

"What do you think you're doing?" she shouted as if scolding a child.

Norman turned around, startled and wide-eyed.

"I-I'm making copies of..." he began, but Carmen cut him off.

"Who said you could use the machine?" she demanded.

"The...secretary," answered Norman, hesitant, hoping this wouldn't get the kind woman in trouble.

"That's *my* ditto machine," Carmen barked as she stepped up to it, yanked out Norman's lesson assignment and handed it back to him.

"I need to make copies. You can't use it until *I'm* done!" she said with overbearing authority then she spun around and walked out.

The room became eerily quiet, much like after a tornado passed through a town. Norman stood there, confused. He looked at the machine then at the clock on the wall. He still had time before his next class, so, not wanting to overstep any boundaries, especially on his first day, he collected the printed copies already made and leaned against the table waiting for Carmen to return. He had waited at least ten minutes before Morris casually passed by. Seeing Norman, he entered the room.

"Making copies?" Morris asked curiously seeing that Norman was hanging idly around.

Norman, wanting to make a good impression, quickly stood, cleared his throat and lied.

"Uh, I just finished," he said as he gathered his copies, shoved them into his briefcase and snapped it shut.

"Great, I'll walk you to your next class," said Morris, as he headed out the door with Norman fretfully behind him.

As they walked down the hall, Norman hoped his new supervisor didn't think him lazy, as well as kept a nervous eye out for that horrible, aggressive woman who claimed to own the copy machine.

Morris walked in his usual casual stride, smiling. "So, how's the new house? Settled in?" he asked.

"Almost," Norman answered, happy to be talking on a more personal level with his superior.

"You picked a good street, Chestnut Circle. Good neighborhood."

"Oh, speaking of," Norman began, "I met one of my neighbors, Adele Breaux. She said she taught here?"

Morris grinned. "Yeah, Adele. She's a good friend...and an interesting woman. She taught French here for years."

Just then, two students passed. They smiled at Morris and gave him friendly "hellos." Morris nodded to them.

"Was she really forced to retire?" asked Norman returning to the subject of Adele.

"She told you that already?" asked Morris with a laugh. "Yeah, she hit seventy, had to let her go. But there's still a lot of life in her. Retirement's tough, but she'll be all right."

At that moment, several school jocks passed. They all gave Morris hearty salutations, as Morris gave them a friendly salute in return. Norman couldn't help but notice nearly every student that passed said or shouted, "Hey, Mr. Saxe" to Morris, with Morris giving each one a smile or wave back. Was he that popular? Norman wondered.

"Adele's an interesting woman," Morris continued, "A little on the daffy side, but intelligent and kind once you get to know her."

As they approached Norman's classroom, a group of girls strolled by carrying books close to their chests and called out, "Hey, Mr. Saxe."

"Ladies," he said in response as they passed.

Norman watched, envious. "Maybe one day I'll be that

popular with the students."

"Something to strive for," Morris said wryly as the school bell rang and he walked away.

With his first day of school over, Norman pulled into his driveway, happy to be back to his new home and family. As he parked he saw Adele at her mailbox from his rearview mirror. She waved. Norman got out of his car holding his briefcase and waved back. Feeling neighborly, he tossed the briefcase back in the car, and strolled across the street to her, ready for a friendly chat. Adele smiled as he approached.

"How was the first day, Norman?" she asked with interest and envy.

"Not too bad," he answered with a slight sigh.

"Your colleagues are wonderful people."

"They are," he said, then winced slightly, "Well, except maybe one. I think her name is…Carmen?"

Adele's face tightened upon hearing the name and said tersely, "Carmen. Yes, she teaches Spanish. Let me guess – she wouldn't let you use the ditto machine?"

"Yes!" Norman exclaimed, relieved it wasn't anything he did wrong in that small copy room.

"Ignore her," Adele said dismissively. "She's a *rustre vache.*"

Norman looked at her, uncertain. Adele noticed and smiled.

"Saint-Exupéry would have laughed at such behavior," Adele said shaking her head.

"Who?" Norman asked.

Adele looked at him with eager surprise. "Come with me," she said with a smile and headed for her front door. Norman followed.

Adele stepped inside her house, with a happy bounce, almost forgetting she had someone behind her. Norman entered with discretion. She hadn't asked him to come in, so he was hesitant to go past the entrance then heard Adele call out from another room, "Come, come…let me show you something."

Taking that as his cue, Norman followed her voice to the living room. Like Sara, he was instantly impressed with the beautiful antiques and exquisite artwork that filled her tiny bungalow. This woman had class, was worldly, though a tad eccentric, but that was part of her charm, he thought as he stepped inside the room.

Adele went to a shelf and reached for a small book. She held it with care as she turned to Norman and handed it to him.

"Ah, *The Little Prince*," said Norman as he looked at the cover. "My wife is a children's librarian and recommended it to me, but I never got around to reading it."

"It was written here," Adele smiled with pride.

"In Northport?" asked Norman, surprised, since he knew the book was by a French author.

"Yes. Saint-Exupéry was looking for a quiet place to write it. He found a mansion by the beach in Asharoken down in Eaton's Neck, The Bevin House. He would stay up very late to work on it, sometimes falling asleep at his desk. The next morning he would be in the same clothes from the day before," Adele said, her smile now warm from the memory.

Norman looked at her, fascinated. "You seem to know a lot about him."

"I should. I was there when he wrote it."

Norman's eye widened, surprised and impressed. "You were? That's incredible. I've read a few of his other books, *Wind, Sand and Stars* and *Night Flight*, years ago."

It was Adele's turn to be impressed by Norman's knowledge of Saint-Exupéry's work. "Oh, wonderful! You're familiar with his writing!"

Norman nodded as he flipped the pages of *The Little Prince,* checking out the drawings.

"Then you'll be interested to know that I have started writing a book about my time with him," she said with gentle authority.

Norman looked up. "Wow, that'll be a great read," he said then tried to give the book to Adele.

"No, keep it," she said with a wave of her hand. "For your son."

"I'll be a while before he can read it, but thanks so much," Norman said, appreciating her generosity.

"You read it first, then read it to him," she affectionately suggested as she led Norman to the front door. Norman thanked her again after he stepped outside. He took only several steps away before Adele called after him, "Oh, Norman...!"

Norman turned around.

"*Rustre vache.* It's French. It means...boorish cow." A sly grin came across her face as she slowly closed the door.

৽৽৵

SAINT-EXUPÉRY SAT COMFORTABLY *in his cockpit, staring straight ahead and concentrating on the clouds as the plane glided effortlessly through the sky. Adele was in the co-pilot seat, smiling and looking pleased.*

"I'm writing a book," she announced proudly, then waited for a positive response from Saint-Exupéry.

He continued to stare straight ahead, not paying attention, lost in thought. Adele looked at him, perturbed.

"I said, I'm writing a book," she repeated, this time with annoyance in her tone.

Saint-Exupéry looked over at her, expressionless then went back to staring straight ahead. Adele shifted in her seat, disappointed.

"I thought you'd be pleased," she said with a disappointed huff.

"What is the subject?" Saint-Exupéry asked never taking his eyes off the clouds.

"You!" Adele nearly shouted to emphasize the ridiculousness of his question then added, *"So you'll be remembered."*

"What matters is only that you remember me," he said, glancing at her.

"Of course," said Adele, *"but the world should, too."*

"Why? They've never met me. They'll never know me."

"Hence, the purpose of the book," Adele answered.

"Is it not for you?" Saint-Exupéry asked innocently.

"Most definitely not!" Adele said, insulted.

Saint-Exupéry chuckled. Adele heard it and turned to him.

"Don't tell me you wrote your books just for your own pleasure."

"Of course! Why else write?" Saint-Exupéry asked then broke into a naughty grin. *"I love to pleasure myself."* He let out a jovial laugh at the double meaning.

Adele sat back in her seat, not amused. He watched her then softened.

"Mademoiselle, to write is the greatest adventure for yourself. You will go much farther and higher with it – more than this plane could ever take us," he said smiling then winked. *"You will see."*

Adele looked at him, puzzled, when outside the sky suddenly turned dark and ominous. Loud claps of thunder cracked down unexpectedly as if hitting the plane. Lightening followed. It ripped and dazzled the sky. The plane jerked violently. Adele bounced in her seat, terrified as she fought to keep her hands tightly on the control panel.

"Monsieur!" she shouted and looked fearfully over at Saint-Exupéry.

He was gone.

The plane once more began a spiraling descent. Adele's screams were caught in her throat. She shut her eyes when she saw the plane was seconds away from hitting the earth.

Adele quickly jolted up in bed, gasping. Once again, she glanced around the dark room, trying to focus and gather her bearings. She let out a deep sigh then wearily leaned back on her pillow, resting on one elbow, and hung her exhausted head.

Chapter 9

The Dropout

Several days later, Norman stood again at the front of his first period classroom taking attendance. When he called out the name, "Jack Doleman," to his dismay there was no response, only chuckles and snickers from several of the students. When he looked up, they stopped. Seeing the empty chair in the back of the room, he regretfully put yet another a check mark next to the boy's name.

After class, Norman was walking down one of the halls packed with students. In the near distance he spotted Principal Allardice and quickly weaved between and around the students to get to him.

"Principal Allardice!" he called out.

Principal Allardice turned and stopped as Norman caught up to him.

"I need to talk with you about a student," Norman said, in a worried tone. "Jack Doleman. He hasn't been coming to class."

Principal Allardice glanced at the passing students who, fortunately, were too preoccupied to hear him.

"I know," he said, quietly with regret, "He dropped out today."

"I'll call his parents," Norman eagerly offered.

"No. We've tried."

"But shouldn't I..."

"Norman, there are some kids you just can't reach. Focus on the ones you can," he said flatly, then turned and walked away.

Norman stood there, disheartened. Suddenly, the memory of why he left New Jersey flashed vividly through his mind, of him, just several months earlier, standing in front of irate school administrators in a small, sterile room with one of the head officials speaking to him as if he was a student being chewed out for deviating from their curriculum. The memory both disturbed and disgusted Norman as he watched Principal Allardice turn a corner and disappear. Had all administrators forgotten what it was to be a teacher?

Later that evening, Norman walked over to Adele's house in much need of advice. Adele was at her dining room table, typing furiously when she heard the knock at her door. She ignored it a first, then after the second and third time, she made a careful note of where she was on the page, got up and answered the door. Sagged against it, looking defeated was Norman.

"One of my students dropped out," he said without even saying hello.

Sympathizing, Adele held open the door and Norman entered. Neither said a word as they walked into the living room. Finally, Norman spoke.

"I never even met the kid, but just the thought of a student giving up, you know?"

"I do know," said Adele as she turned and wandered into the dining room.

Norman followed. "I keep thinking of the promising future these kids have, but only if they have the proper education. Without that, the world will be overwhelming and their choices limited. I don't know, I guess I care too much. That's what everyone tells me."

"I don't think we can ever care too much, Norman. It's what we're supposed to do," Adele said as she approached her table.

On it, near the typewriter, was a beautiful watercolor on antique onion skinned paper of a king sitting on a throne. It was about the size of a record album with faded colors of yellow, blue and orange. It immediately caught Norman's eye.

"Hey, what's that?"

"An original by Saint-Exupéry. He did all his own illustrations for *The Little Prince*. This was a discard," she answered, her eyes studying it with loving tenderness.

"Oh, that's right. He did. You saw him do these as well?"

"Yes," said Adele, softly, never taking her eyes off it. "I saw them all."

"It's beautiful," Norman said, stepping forward to get a closer look. "I take it this king is a character in the book?"

"He is," answered Adele.

They both stood in silence admiring the artwork. Then Adele snapped out of her wistful stare and said, "I'm sorry about your student, Norman."

Norman sighed, "Thanks. Did you ever have a student drop out or so resistant to learning?"

Adele smiled fondly. "Yes. One. And he fought me nearly every step of the way. Our first lesson was like a game of alpha versus alpha, although played by him," is how she began sharing her story…

❧

THE DOOR TO THE Bevin House's parlor room was held opened for Adele by a reserved butler with a blank facial expression. Once she entered, he closed it behind her without making a sound. Adele stood quietly, wearing a black coat with her leather satchel slung over her shoulder.

Standing across the room at a table, with his back to her, dressed casually in wrinkled pants and a white shirt was Saint-Exupéry. He was staring down at something on his table, preoccupied, when suddenly he spun around, faced Adele and spoke impatiently in French at a fast, demanding clip.

"I am a very busy man. When I am not called to Washington I spend my time writing. You're only here because that was my agreement with your government. So, don't expect me to study. All I want to know, and need to know, is how to hail a taxi."

He then took several steps toward her, finishing, "At what time will we have these lessons?"

Adele was taken aback. His tall stature gave him an overpowering sense of authority to her petite frame, but she wasn't intimidated and answered him politely.

"I have classes until 2:30. It would have to be after three," she responded back in French.

"Good," Saint-Exupéry snapped, "Then three thirty will be our time." He then eyed her suspiciously. "So, you are French?"

"I am American, but my heritage is Canadian. French-Canadian," she responded hoping this would win some favor with him.

Saint-Exupéry stared as if studying her then asked, "You've been to France?"

"Yes. I studied in Paris."

"You studied French in France?" he asked.

"No, Monsieur. Music. French is my native language," Adele replied.

Saint-Exupéry smiled at this. He looked her over again. "So, you will teach me this mystery of English and…of you?" his tone turning soft and seductive.

Adele looked at him, shocked. "Of me? No, there is no mystery of me," she said, suddenly feeling self-conscious.

"Every woman is a mystery," he said with a sly grin.

"To men, I suppose," Adele shrugged hoping this strange turn in conversation would end.

"Perhaps to themselves?" Saint-Exupéry asked, testing her.

Now he was crossing a personal line, Adele thought and responded sternly, "I will teach you English. That is my job."

Saint-Exupéry paused. He was impressed. She had pluck. "Of course," he said, "Then show me your *job*."

He motioned for her to remove her coat. As she did, he watched, interested to see what lay underneath such a heavy garment. He hid his smile when he saw her simple, grey conservative dress with no jewelry or accessories. She looked very much like a teacher, at least the teachers he had as a child, and yet he sensed a vulnerability that he understood she was programmed never to reveal. This charmed him.

With his hand he motioned for her to sit. As she did, he took the seat next to her.

"Do you know any English?" Adele asked as she removed a piece of paper and a pencil from her satchel.

"I know numbers," he replied. "And I can make out words on signs, but I do not understand people when they talk."

As he said this, Adele began to write something on a piece of paper. Saint-Exupéry leaned forward, watching. His overpowering manner slowly transformed into curious schoolboy. Adele finished what she wrote and handed it to him.

"Here...I've listed some sentences. You said you could make out words. Can you pronounce these?"

Saint-Exupéry took the paper, looked at it and announced confidently, "Yes."

Adele waited for him to start. He studied the page for about a minute, trying to hide his anxiety. He gripped the paper tight in his hands and spoke in slow, broken English.

"Ple-ase. Call me tax," he read.

"Please call me a taxi," Adele corrected him.

Saint-Exupéry looked at her, not liking to be corrected. He imitated her English. "Please call me a taxi," he repeated back then looked at the paper and continued again, slowly, in broken English, "How-ze mooch iz it?"

"How much is it," Adele corrected him again.

Saint-Exupéry didn't smile as he, again, imitated what she said, "How much is it." He then looked back at the paper and read aloud, "The boyz...titty."

Adele looked at him, unsure. He glanced up to see her reaction then read it again.

"The boyz...titty."

Adele held the same unsure expression. Saint-Exupéry looked at her waiting for a response. Becoming angry and agitated, he nearly shouted, "The boyz *titty*!"

"The word is *tidy*," Adele calmly corrected him.

He looked at her, insulted. "Tidy! I just said it."

"You said –," she hesitated, not wanting to say the word. He looked at her, waiting. Finally, she gave in. "*Titty*."

"I said tidy. Just now. Tidy!" he said defensively.

"Tell me what it means," asked Adele, standing her ground.

"No, you tell me what it means," he said defiantly.

Adele stared at him. She didn't like playing this game of wills, but was determined to win it.

"Orderly," she said stiffly, in a lofty tone. "The word 'tidy' is closer to Old English. The word "orderly" is French."

"Correct!" Saint-Exupéry shouted as he clapped his hands together. "Very good, Mademoiselle!"

Adele looked at him, icy and insulted. "Monsieur, you are forgetting that *I* am the teacher."

Saint-Exupéry's eyes narrowed as if angry then squinted with amusement as he broke into a mischievous grin. "Yes, that is correct. *You* are the mean and severe one."

Adele's eyes flashed outrage. Saint-Exupéry laughed. Angry, she snatched the paper from his hand. This only made him laugh harder.

"Incorrigible," Adele whispered under her breath as she quickly stood and put the paper back in her satchel. All the while Saint-Exupéry's eyes wandered inconspicuously over her womanly form as he continued to laugh...

ॐॐ

ADELE SMILED AFTER SHARING the memory with Norman.

"Was he that difficult?" Norman asked.

"He could be, but he was very kind once you had his trust."

Sensing this was the perfect moment, Adele leaned her hip against the table and said, "Speaking of trust...I would like very much if you would help me with my book."

Norman looked at her with surprise. "Really?"

"It will be for grammar and spelling mainly, but also for content...if it's not too much to ask."

"Not at all," Norman said, flattered. "I'd be honored to."

"Thank you, Norman. I knew you were the kind sort. It's in your eyes," she said sincerely as she led him to the front door. She opened it, but blocked him before he could leave.

"Now, Norman, about this student…it's important to never give up on a pupil. As teachers that's our duty, but they have to be our pupil. If, or when, he returns, that's when you fight the good fight." She raised her thumb in solidarity.

Norman nodded. "Thanks, Adele."

"Thank *you*," she replied. "And I look forward to working with you."

As Norman walked away, she closed the door and returned to her dining room, smiling that she was able to secure the help she needed. She went to her table and set aside the watercolor. She then found five pieces of paper she had next to the typewriter and began to carefully lay them out on the table. On each page was written a month and a year:

"September 1942"

"October 1942"

"November 1942"

"December 1942"

The last one had the date "July 1944." She placed the pages she'd already written under each page to keep track of her time line. Some had more pages than others.

The paper with the date "July 1944" on it was the only one without pages underneath it.

Chapter 10

Please, in French

It was a chilly afternoon, late September 1942, when Adele entered the parlor of the Bevin House prepared to teach her reluctant student English. Saint-Exupéry stood across the room and watched in quiet amusement as Adele removed her coat and hung it carefully over a chair in an efficient manner.

"Are you ready for your first lesson?" she asked.

"This is our second," he said correcting her.

"That was not a lesson; it was our initial meeting," she said as she placed her satchel on the table and pulled out a note-book and a piece of paper. "I needed to see how much you knew and for me to best plan how to instruct you."

"I see," said Saint-Exupéry scratching his chin. "Then what have you found to instruct me?"

"We will start with verbs. I have a list. But first you need to know and understand the verb *"to be"* – which is an irregular verb.

"Irregular?" he asked, intrigued.

"Yes. Can you say *"to be"* for me?"

Saint-Exupéry repeated the words to her in English.

"Very good," she said then explained in French, "*To be* is irregular because its conjugation follows a different pattern. For instance, a regular verb such as 'live" conjugates to "lives" and "lived." To be conjugates as 'am I'…'is your'…and 'were you.' Hence, irregular."

Saint-Exupéry nodded, though Adele wasn't sure if he understood.

"Here," she said as she sat down and placed the paper on the table, "I've written some questions to show how '*to be*' works."

She motioned for him to come closer. He did, standing near the table.

"First question – *Is your* house for sale?"

"No," Saint-Exupery answered.

Adele looked at him. Was he trying to be funny? He wasn't smiling, so she ignored it and continued with, "*Am I*…bothering you?"

"Yes," he answered.

She looked at him again, unsure. He still wasn't smiling. She looked back at the paper. "*Were you*…ever in love?"

"Many times," he answered.

Adele stopped and gave him a bothered look. "Do you understand me, or are you playing a game?" she asked him in English.

Saint-Exupéry stared at her, confused. "Please, in French," he requested.

She was about to repeat it then waved her hand as if to say, "forget it" and decided to move on. "All right, let's try something else…"

She took out another piece of paper, and a pencil and made another quick list. Adele pointed to the words with her pencil.

"Let's go down this list together. I am…you are…he is…she is…it is…we are…they are…" she said aloud.

He looked at the paper then at her and shrugged, clueless.

"I will ask a question and you will answer with one of these on the list, all right?"

Saint-Exupéry nodded, although from the expression on his face, boredom was starting to set in.

"*Who is* going to sleep in your bed tonight?" she asked in French.

Saint-Exupéry raised an eyebrow and grinned.

Adele quickly realized that was a bad example. "Oh dear...let's start again. *Who is* standing next to me?"

Saint-Exupéry looked at the list carefully. Adele pointed out the answer with her pencil.

He answered slowly, "I am," in English.

"Very good!" exclaimed Adele. "Let's try another one. *Is your* wife out of the house today?"

Again Saint-Exupéry looked at the list. Adele pointed to the answer.

He looked at it and said again, slowly, "She is."

"Very good!" Adele said proudly, but Saint-Exupéry gave no expression of being pleased with himself. He was becoming irritated.

"Let's keep going," she said then asked, "*Who is* in this room right now?"

"Intolerance!" Saint-Exupéry snapped in French.

This startled Adele. Saint-Exupéry angrily grabbed the paper and read from it rapidly in broken English, "I am, you are, he is, she is, it is, we are, they are!"

He slapped the paper back down and shouted in French, "I am a *Frenchman*! I want only to speak my language! You are wasting my time!"

He marched to the door, swung it open and stormed out, slamming it behind him. Adele sat there, stunned. She stared at the door wondering if he were coming back. Moments passed. He wasn't.

"Well, then…" she said calmly to herself as she rose from her chair and began collecting her notebook, paper and pencil, putting them back in her satchel. As she did this, slowly the door creaked open. Adele heard it, but didn't turn around. Saint-Exupéry sheepishly peered in. Seeing she was packing her things, he entered and walked over to her.

"Am I scaring you away?" he asked.

"No," replied Adele easily.

"Good!" he said loud and happy.

Adele took her coat off the back of the chair and began to put it on.

"Where are you going?" Saint-Exupéry asked, looking confused.

"Home," she answered flatly.

"Our time is not up, Mademoiselle," he said, as he glanced at his watch.

"You don't want to learn. It's obvious," she said pushing her arms into the sleeves of her coat.

"I don't," he said.

"Well, then…" she said as she straightened her coat on her shoulders and reached for her satchel.

He looked at her, waiting for her to finish whatever she was going to say. She pulled the satchel over her shoulder.

"Well, then…what?" he asked.

"It was you who made a promise to those people in Washington. Just remember that," she said firmly, then added, "Good day."

As she headed for the door, Saint-Exupéry shouted in English, "*I am*…"

Adele turned and looked at him. He thought for a moment then, in French said, "Sorry.

Adele was impressed. He softened and took a step toward her.

"*You are…*" he said in English then, in French, "Right."

Adele smiled. "Very good, Monsieur."

Saint-Exupéry pulled out her chair and said, "*You are…*sit."

Adele approached the chair and pulled the satchel off her shoulder, placing it on the table.

"Sitting," she said correcting him.

"Sitting?" he repeated in English, unsure what it meant.

She removed her coat and, as she began to sit in the chair, stopped mid-way and pointed to her bottom then at the seat of the chair.

"Sitting…*sitting*…" she said.

"Sitting?" he repeated, looking at her more confused.

"Yes…sitting…" she said pointing again to her bottom and then to the seat of the chair.

"Ah, yes!" Saint-Exupéry exclaimed, craning his neck to check out her bottom, "Derriére! *It is…*" he said in English, then finished the sentence in French, "a very nice one, too, Mademoiselle!"

Adele's face blushed a bright red as she quickly sat down. She shot him an irate look then diverted her eyes, still blushing. Saint-Exupéry burst out laughing. Adele let out a huff, grabbed her satchel and began fumbling for things inside it. His laugh softened into a chuckle, as he reached for a cigarette, put it between his grinning lips and lit it.

"Incorrigible," she grunted as she once again pulled out her notebook and slammed it hard on the table…

ADELE QUICKLY RIPPED THE page from her typewriter and glanced over the memory of her trying to teach Saint-Exupery verbs before she crumbled it with both hands and muttered;

"I can't put that in my book."

She tossed the crumbled ball of paper into a nearby trashcan, scrolled a fresh piece of paper into the typewriter, then sat and stared at the blank page. She would have to think more carefully of what to put in her book and what to leave out.

Chapter 11

Misfit

It was many weeks before Adele decided it was time to show some of her pages to Norman. She arrived at Northport High School in the late morning. It never occurred to her to plan the visit or let him know she was arriving. She was on her own schedule and assumed others would simply stop all they were doing to take time for her. And she had no hesitation returning to her former place of work, though if she didn't have the few chapters tucked in a file folder under her arm, perhaps it might have been different. She was accomplishing something of great value that gave her purpose now, and that made it easier for her to return.

She walked stoically down the school hallway, carrying her purse and the file folder with pride. As she passed the familiar classrooms, she smiled at the memory of being a part of this institution. When she came upon her old room, she stopped and peered into the door's window.

Inside, a young female teacher was writing French sentences on the blackboard. Adele squinted her eyes to carefully read the words, making sure they were proper and right. She then noticed two giggling male students tossing a paper airplane at each other. Adele, at first, frowned at the disrespectful sight then a distant yet pleasant memory came to mind. She smiled as she recalled…

உு∞஧

BEING BACK IN 1942, and pulling into the driveway of the Bevin House for another of her scheduled late afternoon appointments with Saint-Exupery. They had a few lessons by this time and were past formalities, although it was still difficult to get him to take her instruction seriously.

After she parked and turned off her car, a small paper airplane fell unexpectedly from the sky and slammed into the windshield of her car. Adele jumped back in her seat, startled. Seeing what it was she quickly got out, grabbed the paper airplane and looked up, wondering where it came from.

From a top floor window was Saint-Exupéry, peering down like a naughty schoolboy. Seeing her looking up at him, he swiftly ducked away. Adele hid her amusement as she fiercely clutched the paper plane in her hand and started for the house.

A maid opened the front door, letting Adele inside then led her down the hall to the parlor. She held open the door as Adele entered. Saint-Exupéry was sitting in a chair, pretending to be reading his lesson. When he heard the door close he looked over, saw Adele and stood up.

"Ah, Mademoiselle! I am prepared for my lesson!" he said with guilty enthusiasm.

"Are you?" Adele asked suspiciously.

"Of course," he said with a smile. "I've been practicing."

"Yes. I've seen how you practice," she said as she put the paper airplane on the table.

Saint-Exupéry looked at it and innocently protested, "That

is for my work in Washington."

Adele, not buying it, said sarcastically, "Let me guess, your secret plan to defeat the Germans?"

"Yes! I study air currents for our planes," he said without hesitation.

She looked at him, again, not buying it. Saint-Exupéry smiled.

"Ah, what is invisible to the eye…you see only a game, whereas I see a successful fleet above Berlin!" He held out his arms as if they were wings of a plane.

"I'm glad to see our government is putting you to good use," Adele replied, bothered that he would think she was that stupid to believe his story.

Saint-Exupéry frowned, lowered his arms and spoke with bored sadness.

"No. They have me in a small room looking at maps of deserts. I used to be a mail carrier flying back and forth across the Sahara. They are only interested in my former routes."

Adele was moved by his honesty, but confused by what he said.

"Mail carrier? But you are royalty. A count," she argued.

Saint-Exupéry winced upon hearing his title then stated, "By birth."

"You are also a hero," she added, feeling strange to have to remind him of this.

"Only in the skies," he sighed. "On earth, I am a misfit."

Adele was surprised by the way he downplayed his importance, but could relate to being what he just called himself. But how strange to have this magnificent man standing before her and make such an admission about himself. Such things, though felt, or worse, true, one never divulged. Quickly, her teacher instincts kicked in, as well as her natural ease at encouragement.

"Why not go back and fly – fight this war?"

Saint-Exupéry let out another sad sigh. "I am too old. According to them. Forced retirement."

He reached for the paper airplane and began fixing one of its folded wings as he added, "So now…I only test for air currents."

As he was about to toss the plane in the air, he stopped himself, folded it open and placed it on the table next to a sketch of a little boy with a scarf around his neck. It caught Adele's eye.

"Who is that?" she asked moving the sketch slightly with her finger to see it more directly.

Saint-Exupéry's mood quickly brightened. "Ah. A little fellow I carry around in my heart. He is a prince. A little prince," he said.

"A misfit on earth?" Adele asked, looking at Saint-Exupéry.

Saint-Exupéry gave her a shy, vulnerable look then broke into a warm smile…

✽✽✽

ADELE STEPPED AWAY FROM the window on the classroom door, smiling from the tender memory, and made her way down the hall. As she turned a corner, Morris appeared.

"Adele!" he said surprised to see her. "What are you doing here?"

"Hello, Morris. Do you know where I can find Norman?"

"Norman? He has a class now," Morris answered, perplexed. "Do you want me to take you to him?"

"No, I don't want to disturb him while he's teaching."

"Well, I'm heading over to the cafeteria for lunch. Care to join me?"

Adele hesitated for a moment. The cafeteria meant eating with other teachers. Former colleagues. Was she ready to sit among them and hear them muse about students, assignments and grades? All the things she sorely missed. Clutching the file folder, she smiled at Morris, feeling armed and ready, and allowed him to lead the way.

As they walked down the hall, Morris asked casually, "So, whatcha here to see Norman about?"

Adele hesitated telling him then said with confidence, "He's agreed to help me with my book."

Morris shot Adele a surprised look and chuckled, "So, you picked Norman. The poor, unsuspecting victim."

Adele glared at him, not amused. "He's someone with a clear objective."

"He's also a very bright guy. Be careful, he might read between the lines."

"What lines?" asked Adele, annoyed. "I've nothing but history to share. And I expect you to help as well."

"Do what? Divert attention?" Morris kidded.

As they approach the cafeteria, Adele stopped before entering and turned to Morris. "Why is it you think I have something to hide? As if I'm guilty of God knows what, with your imagination."

"Come on, Adele, I've been hearing about this guy, Saint-Exupery, for almost fifteen years now. It's all you talk about – and what's with you with those nightmares? How can I *not* think there was something more," Morris confessed.

Adele's face went flush. She tried to mask it by going on the defense.

"This 'guy' as you keep referring to him, was an important man, Morris. He and his work will remain long after you and I are both gone."

"Which is why you should tell everything in your book."

"My God, Morris, you act as if there was something scandalous between us."

"I know it wasn't scandalous. Not with you," he said assuredly.

"Should I be insulted by that remark?" she asked, losing her patience.

"Adele, you think gardening is living on the edge."

Adele lowered her chin to her chest, offended and stared at him from the rim of her glasses. Morris lowered his chin, imitating her and stared back.

"Anything you want to say?" he asked.

"The offer no longer stands. I don't need your help. I'll do just fine with Norman," she said raising her head in a lofty manner.

"Have it your way, Adele. But let me give you a piece of advice, if you have nothing to hide...stop acting so damn guilty."

Adele let out an embarrassed huff.

"Let's go, I'm hungry," said Morris as he passed her and walked into the faculty lunchroom.

The room was crowded mostly with old, familiar faces eating from cafeteria trays as Adele sat at a round table of several teachers with whom she still had a good professional standing with. At her right sat Morris, who was carefully cutting his meatloaf into small chunks.

Sitting directly from Adele was the young female French teacher Adele saw earlier teaching in her former classroom – a natural beauty with an open, friendly air about her. She watched Adele with eager reverence and a bit of intimidation. Adele would give her only a passing, cordial glance that held a hint of resentment.

"How's retirement, Adele?" one of her former colleagues asked, breaking the ice.

Adele slowly wiped the tips of her lips with her napkin

and replied with a regal casualness, "I'm writing a book about my time with Antoine de Saint-Exupéry."

Just as the other teachers were nodding with interest and approval, the young female teacher exclaimed in excitement, "You *knew* Saint-Exupéry?"

Adele quickly corrected her, "*Monsieur* de Saint-Exupéry. Yes."

The young female teacher was too impressed to notice that Adele had no interest in speaking with this underling whom she had been replaced with, and gushed, "The Little Prince is one of my favorite books. I saw his wife, Consuelo, a few years ago in a museum in Paris. I wanted to introduce myself, but lost my nerve. Did you know her as well?"

Just the very mention of the name Consuelo caused Adele's features to tighten. Morris glanced at Adele, knowing this was not a subject she cared to discuss, but curious how she would handle it. Always one for manners, Adele responded, but the words were forced and to the point.

"Yes, I knew her. Although she was often in the city studying art and painting."

"May I ask what is she like?" the female teacher asked with intense curiosity.

Adele strained to be polite. "There were a few occasions when Monsieur went to Washington on last minute business. He'd ask if I would stay and have dinner with Consuelo to keep her company," Adele replied, repulsed by the memory then added, "I did so rather reluctantly…

ADELE SAT ALONE IN the dining room of the Bevin House early one evening. With Saint-Exupéry away on business, the house felt empty, even though the help was around and his wife,

Consuelo was somewhere. Adele had heard from whispered gossip that Consuelo was self-centered and loved the attention that being married to a famous and influential man brought. She was proving it that evening by keeping Adele waiting.

Adele had just allowed herself to slouch in her chair, having sat straight up for a good twenty minutes, wanting to show good posture to the lady of the house once she arrived, when suddenly the massive doors to the dining room swung open and in swept Consuelo de Saint-Exupéry, a woman with dark hair and attractive features. Adele quickly sat up.

Although petite, she entered like a *grande dame* more to intimidate than impress. She was dressed in dark slacks and a white cotton blouse with embroidered ruffles. She spoke loudly in English accented with some Spanish and French as she approached the table.

"Tonio told me you were staying for dinner. Too bad he had to leave," she said grandly as she took a seat across from Adele.

There was an awkward silence at first between the two as Consuelo eyed Adele carefully though acted with disinterest. She then began to speak in a quick and patronizingly manner.

"I was surprised that he would ask someone of your station to dine here. I don't believe you know French as well as I do," she said brazenly, as if testing Adele.

Adele looked at Consuelo with startled offense. Just then, one of the servants entered and placed dinner salads in front of them.

"I said this to my husband – about your French. Do you know what he said?" she asked.

Adele's eyes lit up, eager to know. Consuelo noticed and purposely took a bite of her salad, taking her time. Adele waited patiently for the answer.

"He said you speak French slowly, but that I will *never* speak it so correctly or beautifully even on my dying day."

Adele was flattered by the compliment, but didn't want to show it, so she brought her napkin to her mouth to hide her smile.

Consuelo then added in a condescending tone, "I am from El Salvador, but you are an American. No American can fully grasp another language."

As Adele opened her mouth to speak, about to defend this, Consuelo kept talking.

"Tonio doesn't like American women. He finds them forward and too aggressive."

Adele stared at her, unsure how to take these remarks.

"When my husband told his publishers that he was taking English lessons, they were shocked that they were with a country school teacher. They offered to get him someone good – someone with a reputation, but Tonio told them that he would work only with you and no one else."

Adele was pleased to be in such favor with Saint-Exupéry, but made sure not to show any outward emotion about it for fear it might cause Consuelo to become belligerent or worse, jealous.

Jealous? The thought of that seemed absurd to Adele, although it did give her a bit of an ego stroke that this attractive, worldly woman would be threatened by the likes of a small town schoolteacher. Nonetheless, Adele was careful to acknowledge this simply with, "Madame, I am flattered that your husband is pleased with my abilities."

Consuelo quickly changed the subject. "I wish to write a book!" she blurted out.

Adele was startled by this sudden announcement, especially since it came out of the blue.

"Tonio is against it. He said if I ever did I was not allowed to use his name. The name Saint-Exupéry will only be used for his work alone."

Adele did her best to maintain a neutral expression as she listened carefully to Consuelo's complaint.

"He's trying to stop me from writing. He would never encourage me, or anyone else to write, but no matter what his opinion, I *will* write a book!"

"If you don't mind my asking," Adele cautiously asked, "What will be your subject?"

Consuelo looked at Adele stumped. She had no answer. Just then, a cook entered with two plates – a thick steak on each. He placed them on the table. Consuelo got hers first, of course, then Adele. Consuelo took one look at it, stood up and flew into a rage.

"You stupid fool! You overcooked it!"

The cook, dumbfounded and embarrassed, attempted to speak, but before he could utter a single word, Consuelo grabbed the plates and shoved them at the cook, shouting, "Throw these out! I'll cook them myself!"

She then charged into the kitchen with the cook following shamefully behind. Adele watched with obvious unease and sat once again alone in the large, and silent room...

৩৩৩৩

BACK IN THE FACULTY lunchroom, all the teachers sat enthralled by Adele's telling of this story and watched as she slowly, almost calculated, took a small bite from her plate.

Morris carefully eyed the small audience then asked Adele in his usual, casual manner, "So...how were her steaks?"

"Cafeteria style," Adele responded, deadpan.

The teachers laughed. Adele looked across at the young female teacher, testing her reaction. She glanced at Adele and feigned an unsure, nervous smile.

Chapter 12

The Prince, The King

After lunch, Adele was walking down a hallway, on her way out, when the school bell rang. This caused the students to scatter like rats on a sinking ship to their classrooms. Adele giggled. Watching this suddenly brought back a memory for her. One that she had stored away in her heart so long ago...

A MALE STUDENT WAS standing by his desk butchering sentences in French. As he struggled to pronounce the words perfectly, the rest of the class winced with each mistake he made. Adele was at the front of the class, listening, but was too preoccupied with eyeing the clock on the wall.

Suddenly, the last bell of the day rang and Adele shouted, "Excellent," causing the rest of the class to glance at each other, confused. He was far from excellent. As they rose and collected their books, they watched even more perplexed as Adele excitedly shoved her materials into her satchel and was the first one out of the room.

She skillfully weaved and bobbed through the sea of students in the hallway to the front doors of the school, stopping for no one. The sight of this middle-aged teacher making a mad dash to get out made the students who saw her laugh.

Once outside, Adele ran to the parking lot and to her Renault. She threw her satchel on the front seat, got in and started the engine. She hurriedly put the car in reverse, screeched out of the spot and sped off.

Adele drove fast through the familiar village streets with great precision, finally arriving at the boarding house where she shared living quarters with her friend, Ann. After she parked her car, she grabbed her satchel, got out and rushed through the front door.

Adele sprinted up the staircase to the small flat. Once inside, she dropped the satchel on a chair and headed for her bedroom. She stopped abruptly when she saw a note next to the telephone. It was written in her roommate's handwriting.

Adele,

ST. EX. phoned. He's back from Washington and is expecting you. At least that's what I think he said. I don't understand French!!

– Ann

The message fueled Adele with anticipatory adrenaline. She folded the note and went into her bedroom. It was a small, sparse room with a bed, a desk and dresser. A tiny closet held her limited wardrobe. She stood in front of a mirror that hung over her bureau and primped herself as if preparing for a date then quickly dashed out of the bedroom and was once again out the front door.

Back in her car, she drove fast again on the roads that led

out to Asharoken toward the Bevin House. The rush of excitement along with the cold air blowing through her open windows made her feel young again. She was no longer just a middle-aged teacher in a small town, nor did she feel bored and alone. She now had purpose.

Adele had fast become a part of the Bevin House routine of being welcomed at the front door by a maid then led down the hall to the parlor. On this day, by the time they reached the parlor's doors they were sprung open by Saint-Exupéry with a welcoming smile on his face.

"Mademoiselle!" he shouted happily, then stepped back, allowing Adele to enter. "My wife is in the city today. We won't be interrupted," he told her as he closed the door and followed her inside.

Adele was unbuttoning her coat when she saw there were watercolors and illustrations strewn everywhere. She was pleased to see such vibrant, creative disarray, but kept her professional composure as she slipped off her coat and carefully put it over the back of a chair.

"Are you ready for your lesson?" she asked placing her satchel on the floor and taking a seat next to the mass of artwork.

Saint-Exupéry pulled a small book of English verbs from his pocket and boasted, "Yes! I have been practicing."

He opened the book and started to read sentences aloud in his best, though broken, English.

"Jill fow...found the keys in her coat. He show...should not go to the bank. The car is blue."

He looked up, ready and excited for Adele's pleased reaction, however her attention was on something else. She was eyeing a beautiful watercolor of a king sitting on a throne.

Realizing he was done, she looked back at Saint-Exupéry and said, "Very good. And you understand what you just said?"

Saint-Exupéry was offended that she would think he only sounded out words instead of also knowing what they meant. He irately went to the table, found a key and spoke again in broken English.

"Jill found the key," he said as he held up the key then finished with, "in her coat." He motioned to the pocket of his jacket. Adele watched, impressed.

Then Saint-Exupéry continued. "The car," he said as he motioned using a steering wheel with his hands, "is blue." He then grabbed the watercolor of the king that Adele had been staring at, pointed to his long, blue cloak and said, "*Blue.*"

"Most impressive, Monsieur. Very, very good."

Getting the acknowledgment he expected earlier, Saint-Exupéry softened and held out the watercolor to her.

"You like him? It is yours."

Adele's eyes widened, pretending she had no idea what he was talking about. Saint-Exupéry stared at her, as if daring her to deny it.

"You do like him. I saw," he said.

Adele blushed realizing he caught her looking at it. Saint-Exupéry continued to stare at her, waiting for a response. She gently took the watercolor from him, touched by his generosity.

"He is the King," began Saint-Exupery, explaining one of his book's characters. "He insists his authority be respected, and tolerates no insubordination."

"He is rigid," said Adele, understanding.

"Ah-ha, yes! You would recognize that," Saint-Exupéry responded with a clever grin.

Adele shot him an offended look, but she wasn't really offended since she was getting used to his playful teasing. She looked back at the watercolor, liking how bright and imaginative it was, then at all the others on the table.

"When did you do all of these?" she asked.

Saint-Exupéry's softened, appreciative of her interest.

"At night. When it is quiet. This house…it has been a sanctuary for my writing. It is the best place I've written anywhere in my life."

"Home of your little prince," Adele said softly, not expecting those words to come out so loud and clear. She looked at Saint-Exupéry, embarrassed.

Saint-Exupéry heard them and smiled. His large, dark and watchful eyes that missed nothing stayed on her. Adele lost herself in them until she suddenly felt her knees quiver and her face become warm.

"You did very well with your verbs, Monsieur," Adele said, snapping to attention and changing the subject in hopes it would divert attention from the unwelcomed blush to her cheeks.

"Thank you," said Saint-Exupéry. "And now I must ask you to leave."

Leave? Adele shot him a confused look. "But we didn't have our lesson."

"I just showed you what I've learned," he said, confused that she expected more.

"All the more reason to continue," Adele argued.

"Mademoiselle, to be honest, I am bored by these lessons. I have important work that I need to finish," he said, not wanting to hurt her, but his writing and art was his priority. He began moving the watercolors around in a specific order, known only to him to emphasis this.

Adele watched as his fingers delicately touched each piece of work. She saw how intently he stared each one, contemplating its beauty and suddenly felt guilty for even trying to pull this artist away from his tiny masterpieces. Without saying a word, she rose from her chair and reached for her coat. Saint-Exupéry saw this, and was relieved she understood.

"Next time I'd like for you to read some pages from my story. Will you?" he asked.

Adele nodded. Saint-Exupéry smiled then held out his hand. Adele, moved by his gentle manner and strength, slowly took it. He gave the back of her hand a soft, appreciative kiss, and then helped with her coat.

He took the watercolor of the king and rolled it as he went over to the door and opened it for her. Adele walked out and he followed. He moved one-step close behind her down the hall toward the front door. She felt the magnetic pull of his masculinity, which caused a sense of tingling delight to flow through her.

Adele clutched the front of her coat as soon as she stepped outside. The cold beach air stung her cheeks and blew back her hair. Saint-Exupéry appeared immune to the weather as he marched down the front steps with the rolled up watercolor tucked under his arm.

When they got to her car, Saint-Exupéry stepped in front of Adele, brushing close to her as he reached for the door handle. He stopped suddenly and shot her a surprised look.

"What is your cologne? It smells so sweet."

Adele looked at him, startled. She was not used to that sort of attention or remark from a man and answered, "I'm not wearing any."

Saint-Exupéry smiled flirtatiously. "Ah. Then it is natural. It is *you*."

Adele blushed at his words, spoken in such a sincere yet daringly sexy manner. She nearly melted. But the moment disappeared in a snap as Saint-Exupéry opened the car door and helped Adele get in. He pulled the rolled up watercolor out from under his arm and handed it to her.

"Au revoir, Mademoiselle," he said with a seductive smile then closed the car door and started back toward the house at a fast clip, the cold air finally piercing his skin.

Adele watched his every step. She found herself extremely conscious of his virile appeal, how he lumbered up the stairs and into the house, closing the door behind him. Her heart was hammering foolishly as she fumbled blindly to get her keys into the ignition...

తకూ

WHEN THE MEMORY ENDED, Adele "came to" and was startled to find herself sitting in her car in the high school parking lot. When the memory first came to her she was standing in the school hallway. How did she get outside she wondered. She looked at the small groups of students that mingled out front and could not recall passing any of them. She let out several slight giggles that turned into sporadic chuckles at her own expense for allowing herself to get so swept away.

"Oh, Monsieur," she sighed as she shook her head, then removed her keys from her purse and started the car.

Chapter 13

Grounded

Norman was in front of his classroom reading from a book of poetry.

"Than ours, a friend to man, to whom thou say'st –"

Suddenly, he was interrupted when the classroom door opened. Principal Allardice stepped inside then held the door open for the shy, yet troubled looking Jack Doleman. He was a lanky sixteen year-old with floppy brown hair. His shoulders were hunched as he made his way to the back of the room and took a seat near the window without making eye contact with anyone.

Principal Allardice gave Norman an affirmative nod then walked out, closing the door behind him. Norman glanced at Jack for a moment before he returned to the poem.

"To whom thou say'st, beauty is truth, truth beauty – that is all ye know on earth, and all ye need to know."

Norman looked up and took another quick glance at Jack who was staring out the window, apparently more interested in what was happening outside than a poem by Keats. Norman decided not to embarrass Jack with a comment and continued with his lesson.

After class was over and the students were walking out of the room, the last one to leave was Jack, who walked past Norman with his eyes to the floor.

"Jack?" Norman called out.

Jack stopped. He glanced at Norman for a second then looked away.

"I had you listed in my class last semester, but we never had a chance to meet. What happened?"

"I took some time off," Jack muttered.

"That was a lot of time," said Norman with a friendly smile. "Plan on sticking around this semester?"

Jack eyed Norman suspiciously, shrugged and walked out. As he did, Norman noticed Jack's pants were rumpled, his shirt, too. He began to feel sorry for the kid when suddenly Adele appeared at the door, holding her file folder.

"Hello, Norman," she said as she confidently breezed into the room.

Before Norman could return the salutation, she got right down to business and pulled out a small stack of pages from her file folder.

"Here are the first chapters of my book," she said handing them to him.

"Terrific. I'm looking forward to reading it," Norman said as he flipped through the pages, catching snippets of her writing.

Adele pushed back her shoulders and said haughtily, "Thank you for taking the time. I would stay and chat, but I need to get back to work now. We will be in touch," and headed out the door just as students began to walk in.

Stay and chat? Norman chuckled at her pretentious attitude, then glanced at her pages one more time before placing them into his briefcase. He grabbed his book of poetry, waited patiently as his students took their seats then closed the class-room door.

That evening, Norman was relaxed in his chair, at his dining room table, reading Adele's pages. The table was littered with student papers waiting to be graded, but he was too engrossed in Adele's words than those of a teenager. He didn't even notice his wife, in her bathrobe, standing in the doorway.

"When are you coming to bed?" Josephine asked sweetly, although there was a hint of frustration in her voice.

"Soon," said Norman, not looking up as she entered the room.

This was something she's had to deal with, being married to a teacher. She was used to the competition between her and all those term papers, but it didn't mean she liked it. Nor did she like the answer she's heard hundreds of times either. Josephine eyed the student papers with a good balance of understanding and contempt.

"When we bought this table I thought we'd actually eat off of it," she said with mild sarcasm.

Norman looked up briefly, smiled then went back to Adele's pages. Frustrated, Josephine glanced at the handwritten papers of the students then noticed several that were typed. She peered over at what Norman was reading. It was also typed. She picked up one of the pages and looked at it. After reading several lines, she looked at Norman.

"What is this?" she asked.

Norman looked at the paper in her hand. "It's Adele's book, the first few chapters. I told her I'd proofread them," he then went back to reading.

Josephine put the paper back on the small pile, aggravated, and said, "As if you don't have enough work to do."

Norman, hearing the irritation in her voice, looked up at his wife. "Don't worry, it won't take a lot of my time. I promise."

Josephine looked at her husband, unconvinced and left the room without saying another word. Norman watched, knowing she wasn't happy with him. He thought of turning in to appease her, but was already immersed in what Adele had written, so he went back to her pages and continued to read…

୧⤫୧

IT WAS ANOTHER LATE afternoon at the Bevin House. Adele and the maid were standing outside the doorway of the parlor. The door was closed; however, the voices of Saint-Exupéry and another man's voice could be heard behind it. They were arguing about something in French. The maid kept her head down, pretending she didn't hear. Adele, understanding every word, stood there, stoically waiting, not pretending.

Suddenly, the door swung open and out stepped Saint-Exupéry with Commander Bessette, a handsome yet serious looking military man in full uniform. The maid curtsied and made her way down the hall, back to her chores. Saint-Exupéry had a strained look on his face, but quickly masked it with a polite smile when he saw Adele.

"Mademoiselle Breaux! Sorry for the delay. Let me introduce to you, Commander Bessette."

Commander Bessette smiled warmly as he took Adele's hand and gave her a slight bow. Adele was greatly impressed and thrilled by the regal formality.

"Mademoiselle Breaux is my English instructor. She's very good," Saint-Exupéry said with friendly sincerity.

Commander Bessette looked at Adele, surprised. "A compliment from Antoine is rare – especially for a teacher. You should be flattered."

"I am," responded Adele, charmed and beaming with pride.

Commander Bessette's tone suddenly turned impersonal when he gave Saint-Exupéry a serious look and asked, "Will we speak again?"

Saint-Exupéry shrugged as his polite smile faded. It was obvious he made his point just moments earlier and was no longer interested in any future arguments with his irritated colleague.

Commander Bessette said with all the graciousness he could muster, "I'll show myself out."

He nodded politely to Adele as he said stiffly, "Mademoiselle," then walked down the hall.

Saint-Exupéry watched with a stern eye, though there was sadness in his expression. He then quickly motioned for Adele to enter the parlor. She did. Once both were inside, Saint-Exupéry closed the door. Adele went directly to the table, put her satchel down and began to take out a sheet of paper. As she did this, she watched Saint-Exupéry light a cigarette, walk over to a window and stare out.

"I'd like to work on more verbs today. I've made a list that you can practice with," she said as she held it out to him.

Saint-Exupéry didn't respond. He continued to stare out the window, puffing slowly on his cigarette. Adele, not wanting to disturb his thoughts, but having a job to do, spoke a little louder.

"I said I made a list of verbs."

Saint-Exupéry was still lost in his thoughts and continued to stare out the window.

Adele, frustrated, nearly shouted, "A list of verbs, Monsieur!"

Saint-Exupéry suddenly snapped to. He walked over to Adele muttering impatiently, "Yes, yes. Verbs," then snatched the list from her hand and glanced at it. A look of disgust came across his face.

"It's in English!"

Adele, just as impatient, replied in a snippy tone, "Yes. The language I've been hired to *teach* you."

Saint-Exupéry looked at her, annoyed. Adele, just as annoyed, took the list from him.

"This will not work if you're unwilling to learn," she said as she started to put the list back in her satchel.

Saint-Exupéry was surprised by her attitude, but knowing he was the cause of it, softened and sighed, "Forgive me. I am upset over my conversation with Commander Bessette. He knows how important it is for me to fly, yet he refuses to let me, again, saying I am *too old*."

"Why, that's just *absurd*," Adele angrily blurted out.

Saint-Exupéry was taken aback. Adele realized she let her emotion slip. It was none of her business and she was the last person who would give any advice or make comment on anything of such importance to this man.

Embarrassed, she looked down at the floor, then, feeling the need to explain said, "I'm sorry. It's just...I know it would *infuriate* me if I was told I could no longer teach due to my age."

Saint-Exupéry was awestricken by her passion and smiled. Sensing his appreciation on what she thought, she decided to say more of what was on her mind.

"You're of sound mind and you're definitely not old. It's an insult that they treat you as some sort of invalid. For God's sake, we have movie stars flying in our Air Force...Jimmy Stewart, Clark Gable...if *they* can do it –"

Before she finished, Saint-Exupéry let out a slight chuckle. Adele didn't think she said anything amusing.

"I'm very serious," she demanded.

"Oh, I know you are," Saint-Exupéry said again with a chuckle, then his tone changed to one of defeat. "But General De Gaulle is doing everything to keep me grounded."

This enraged Adele. She deeply respected the French and its leader, but what she respected more was everyone's right to do and be all they can be with no limitations. This is what she spent her days in the classroom stressing to her students, and resented anyone telling them to the contrary.

"Don't let him!" Adele demanded. "Write letters, make phone calls. You should be in the sky. That is where you belong," she said loudly with passion and authority.

Saint-Exupéry stared at her, profoundly moved. He then smashed out his cigarette in a nearby ashtray and asked with a slight smile, "Tell me, is this how you are with *all* your students?"

"Encouragement is a vital part of my job," Adele said with strong conviction.

Saint-Exupéry looked at her carefully then straightened his back with confidence.

"Then you have succeeded. I will not let De Gaulle or anyone keep me from the sky." He then smiled, adding, "Where I belong."

He walked over to her, gently took the list from her hand and said respectfully, " Let us begin…"

ক৯০৯

NORMAN FINISHED READING AND carefully placed the page on top of the rest and retired to bed. As Josephine lay sound asleep, Norman lay awake thinking about Adele and Saint-Exupéry. Although he only read several chapters, something piqued his curiosity. What was the point of her book? Although the facts were interesting, it seemed there was more to her association with him than she was revealing.

How Adele spoke of him, which was almost always, and with such affection, didn't match at all what she was putting to paper. Did she have feelings for him? If she did, it was obvious she was purposely leaving it out of the book...but why? Did her friendship with him go deeper than she was letting on, or was she simply just a good teacher encouraging her student to fly?

Norman decided to wait for more chapters. Perhaps his answers were yet to come.

Chapter 14

An Unmarried
School Teacher

Several days later, Adele was walking up Woodbine Avenue, a road close to the waterfront that led to Main Street. She was carrying a stack of large mailing envelopes and was on her way to the local post office, which was quite a distance away. But she purposely parked close to the docks to catch the harbor's view and enjoy the scenic walk. Plus, the exercise was ideal.

She smiled appreciatively at her quaint and picturesque environment. She especially enjoyed the smell of the salty air mixed with the faint whiff of home style cooking that emanated from the local diners, as well as the squawking sounds the seagulls made as they circled above the boats.

When she approached the end of Woodbine Avenue, she stopped and stared at the spot that, to her, was the most treasured in the town – the corner of Bayview Avenue and Main Street. Whenever she came upon it, or purposely sought it out, she gave pause. Today was no exception. She held the mailing envelopes close to her chest, closed her eyes and allowed herself to drift momentarily to one of her fondest memories…

ADELE AND ANN WERE window-shopping along Main Street. Being late October, both were bundled in their coats and scarves, though Adele's scarf hung more feely around her neck. The harbor wind blew fiercely at their faces. Ann winced as it struck hers, but Adele enjoyed it. She smiled as it whipped back her short hair. Ann clutched tighter to her coat, teeth chattering, as Adele savored it and carefully surveyed everything around her.

"You know," she began, uncharacteristically upbeat, "this town does have a real *charm* to it."

"Since *when?*" Ann asked Adele as if she'd lost her mind. "As long as I've known you, you've only complained about how barren and lonely it is."

"I've been too harsh. It's actually quite lovely.

Ann bound her scarf tighter around her neck and replied shivering, "Right now, it's *freezing*.

"It's crisp," Adele said, correcting her. Ann stopped and looked at her friend, confused.

"What's gotten into you? Every year around this time you usually get all sentimental and homesick for Oregon. Going on and on about your friends back home and wondering why you ever…"

Ann stopped in mid-sentence when she saw Adele wasn't listening. Instead, she was staring raptly at something off in the distance. Ann slowly followed Adele's gaze. Near the end of the street, on the corner of Bayview Avenue and Main Street stood Saint-Exupéry with a distinguished looking gentleman in a military uniform in front of a parked car. Saint-

Exupéry looked movie star handsome in his thick overcoat and cream-colored scarf that waved softly in the wind.

Saint-Exupéry put his hand on the other gentleman's shoulder and let out a hearty laugh. He then glanced up the street and did a double take when he spotted Adele. His dreamy, heavy-lidded eyes locked with hers, and for the briefest of moments, time stood still, as if nothing else existed for either of them.

Adele felt the sincere affection that came from him, especially when that captivating smile stretched across his face. He gave her a slight wave before he and the other gentleman made their way around the car and got inside.

Ann looked back at Adele who was staring happily transfixed.

"Now I see where the *charm* comes from," Ann said with an I-see-what's-going-on-here tone in her voice.

Adele shot Ann a guilty look. Ann grinned and winked. Adele made feigned ignorance as they continued to slowly stroll past more windows.

"So, how are the lessons coming along?" Ann asked in a playful, hinting sort of way.

Adele decided to play along. She answered in honest, mockingly exaggerated French, "*Il m'enseigne plus que j'ai jamais rêvé avec un chuchotement simple à mon âme.*" (He is teaching me more than I ever dreamed possible with a simple whisper to my soul).

"That's not fair! You know I don't understand French," Ann whined.

"I know," answered Adele, smiling mischievously.

Ann stopped, frustrated as Adele kept walking, chuckling to herself.

"Adele! What does it mean?" she shouted as she limped after Adele, eager to know her secret…

ﾇﾟ∝ﾟﾌ   .

ADELE HELD TIGHT TO her mailing envelopes when she opened her eyes and looked at the spot where Saint-Exupéry stood all those years ago. The memory brought again the warm glow she felt then and every time since. She was also proud of herself never revealing what she said in French to Ann and headed gaily up the several blocks on Main Street to the post office.

When Adele arrived, she climbed the steps, opened the large, thick door and entered. She was relieved there were no lines, and approached a counter dropping the envelopes on top of it. A friendly, middle-aged postal clerk with glasses and thinning hair grabbed automatically grabbed them and began weighing and putting postage on each one. As he did this, he glanced at the addresses.

"I see these are all going to publishing companies."

Adele answered with pride. "It's the first several chapters of a book I am writing. I hope to solicit interest. This is an important project that I started last summer…"

Adele saw that the postal clerk wasn't listening. There was something at one of the other stations at the end of the long counter had grabbed his attention. Adele followed his stare and saw an attractive woman in her mid-40's approach another clerk with several packages to be posted.

The postal clerk looked back at Adele, leaned forward and in a gossipy whisper said, "That's Brenda Powell. You know, I've heard she's been seen going out with a dentist from Huntington. He's a married man with a coupla kids, but his wife has no clue…"

"Enough!" Adele snapped; her eyes narrowed in anger. "That is neither yours, mine, or *anyone's* business."

The postal clerk was taken aback and watched stunned as

Adele grabbed the stack of newly stamped envelopes from the counter.

"Hey, let me put those over here..." the postal clerk began as he reached for them, but Adele snatched them away. She spun around, walked to the door, pushed it open with her shoulder and walked out.

She stomped angrily down the steps carefully balancing her purse with the envelopes in her arms. Realizing she had them, she went over to an outside mailbox and started to shove them into it one at a time. As she did this, she looked up and saw the attractive woman come out of the post office and make her way across the street. A look of pained commonality was on Adele's face as she continued to frantically stuff the mailbox as if trying to outrace a memory...

IT WAS A COLD morning in mid-November, 1942. Adele was in her classroom sitting at her desk as her students were quietly taking an exam. The door slowly opened and a submissive looking administrative assistant entered. She approached Adele and handed her a folded note. Adele opened it, read it then stood and addressed her students.

"Class, I need to step away for a short while. Continue with your exam." She then turned to the assistant. "Please monitor until I return."

The assistant nodded and Adele left the room.

Principal Adelheid Kaufman was an older, severely strict looking woman with greying hair, glasses and a very uncompromising disposition. The students feared her, as did most of the teachers. Adele sat anxiously across from her as Principal Kaufman spoke authoritatively and with a hint of suspicion.

"You've been seen going in and coming out of the Bevin House several times by colleagues."

Adele was suddenly aware of an unknown dread. Was she being watched? All of her inner warning-systems went off at once, but managed to show no sign of it outwardly.

"Yes. I've taken a part-time assignment as language instructor to Monsieur de Saint-Exupéry. I can promise you it does not in any way take time away from my duties here," Adele admitted honestly.

Principal Kaufman stared at her with penetrating eyes. "It isn't your duties that concern me. I am merely warning you to be discreet in what it is you do outside of the school."

Adele's eyes squinted in confusion. What was she implying? In hopes to keep the conversation professional and brief, she responded, "I assure you, nothing that I am doing calls for anything outside of my usual, trained discretion."

"Miss Breaux, you are spending time with an outsider...a *foreigner*. It's a very small town and you must be careful with your reputation."

Adele chuckled, hoping that would lighten the tension that was steadily building. "Surely, people have better things to discuss than the goings on of a school teacher..."

Principal Kaufman corrected her. "An *unmarried* school teacher who should be cautious of jeopardizing her position," she stated firmly then added more judiciously, "He has a reputation. Everyone knows this, even his wife. Don't allow a temporary assignment to become anything more. No flights of fancy. Devotion to profession is where true reward is. Keep that in mind. "

Adele nodded, sobered by the frightening possibility that the rest of her career, and life, was going to mirror that of this rigid, homely administrator.

What Principal Kaufmann said haunted Adele as she

drove down the stretch of road in Asharoken to the Bevin House later that afternoon. She felt her dreams being under attack by common sense as she pulled into the driveway, parked and sat contemplating whether or not to go inside. At that moment, a car passed. Paranoid, Adele slid down in her seat and strained to glance in her rearview mirror.

Has it come to this? She asked herself as she sat back up and peeked nervously outside for any snooping colleagues. She then collected her satchel and got out of the car. Wasting no time, she sprinted up the stairs to the house and rapped on the door praying it would open fast. It did.

Once inside the house, Adele composed herself and followed the maid down the hall, walking now with a stoic air of respectable professionalism, to the parlor. The maid opened the door and stepped aside for Adele to enter. After Adele was in, the maid quietly closed the door behind her.

Adele took several steps forward then stopped when she saw Saint-Exupéry at a table tinkering with a radio. The back of it was open, exposing the wires. He was completely engrossed, committed to figuring out the mechanics of it, when suddenly he broke his focus, looked up and saw Adele. He beamed, happy to see her.

"Ah, Mademoiselle – come look! I am close to making it work," he said in playful excitement.

Adele stood there, paralyzed by the warnings of Principal Kaufman spinning in her head. She was apprehensive about being close to Saint-Exupéry at all. He waved his hand in a friendly manner, encouraging her again to come closer. Adele took several steps, but made sure to keep a safe distance. He looked at her puzzled by her suddenly strange reserve then went back to his tinkering. Adele watched, impatiently.

"Monsieur…I am here to teach you English," she said trying to maintain her professionalism.

Saint-Exupéry didn't look up when he said, "Of course."

Adele then added in a severe tone, "Not to waste time watching you play with a radio."

Saint-Exupéry glanced up not liking her words of contempt. He chose to ignore them by going back to his work. Moments passed. Adele watched growing more impatient when suddenly the sound of static came from the radio mixed with faint notes of music. Saint-Exupery's eyes lit up and he shouted, "Voila!"

He quickly started to rotate the dial, trying to get a clearer sound. He looked at Adele, wanting and waiting for her to share in his excitement.

Adele, fighting his infectious charm, demanded, "Monsieur...we have work to do."

Just then, the music came in perfectly clear. Marlene Dietrich singing Cole Porter's "You Do Something To Me" in a seductive, sultry voice drifted from the small speaker. Saint-Exupéry smiled, the sort of smile that forced one to grin back, turned the radio way up and, oozing French charisma, turned to Adele and held out his arms.

"Dance with me."

Adele was dumbfounded. Dance? She hadn't danced in years, let alone remembered the last time a man had asked her to. She blushed and stammered, "N-no. I-I don't..."

Saint-Exupéry chuckled. "Yes, you do," he said then gave a playful order, "You will."

He moved close to her, removed the satchel from her shoulder and placed it on the table. He then took her hands in his and stroked them gently as he led her to an open area of the room.

Adele tried to resist, but it was impossible. He was so *damn* enchanting. Knowing she was nervous and shy by the way she trembled, he tenderly held her in his arms and they started to step to the music.

Adele moved clumsily, and he was a bit stiff due to his many flight injuries, but they managed. The Porter lyrics became more relevant, about being under the mystifying, hypnotizing spell of seduction. Saint-Exupéry pulled her close and stared into her eyes.

Adele couldn't resist his potent brand of sensuality. She closed her eyes, too shy to keep staring into his, and overcome by this moment of romantic reverie. Saint-Exupéry smiled, warmed to see her under his "spell." He pulled her even closer and closed his eyes, enjoying the scent of this woman, then pressed his cheek to hers. Feeling the brush of his face, Adele quickly opened her eyes.

Coming to her senses, she pulled away and nervously composed herself, embarrassed at how happy that made her. Saint-Exupéry looked at her, confused, but still smiling. She was endearing when she was self-conscious and disarmed.

Then Adele said with a harsh and serious voice, "We have a lesson to do."

This took Saint-Exupéry by surprise. He thought she was playing, so he became just as rigid as she and, in mock imitation, replied, "Yes. Our lesson."

Adele brushed passed him as if he wasn't there, went to her satchel and removed a notebook. Saint- Exupéry playfully took his seat, and sat like a reprimanded schoolboy with his knees close together and clasped hands on his lap. He enjoyed this role-play and was happy to see where it would lead.

Adele pointed to the radio and barked, "Turn that music off."

Saint-Exupéry jerked back, shocked by her order. Seeing she wasn't kidding, he looked at her as a little boy would, wondering where his friend and playmate disappeared to then reached over and sadly turned the radio off…

ADELE, CRUSHED BY THE MEMORY, slowly shoved the last enve-
lope in the mailbox. By then, the sky had turned grey; it
looked like it might snow. As she headed back down Main
Street, the cold, wintry air made her eyes tear. At least that's
what she tried to convince herself was the cause.

Chapter 15

Been So Long

Several weeks passed before Adele completed another chapter of her book. She was eager to get it to Norman, so instead of waiting until he got home she made another trip to the high school. As she walked down the hall toward the English Department, hoping to find Norman during one of his free periods, she passed the main administrative office. Suddenly, from behind, she heard a female voice shout, "I don't believe it!"

Adele stopped and turned around. Her eyes widened in stunned disbelief at the sight of her old friend, Ann, who was heading in her direction. It had been a long time since they had seen each other. Ann left Northport many years earlier to be with her ailing mother in another state. This choice was the reason she had to quit her teaching career.

Ann and Adele had left on good terms and kept in touch frequently with letters and a weekly telephone call for the first few years, but as time wore on, the letters became sporadic; eventually reduced to one correspondence a year found tucked inside a Christmas card. The phone calls had stopped all together.

But here they were now, walking slowly toward each other with warm, welcoming smiles on their faces. Ann still had the limp and her hair was starting to turn grey, but she was still the friendly and kind woman Adele adored. To Ann, seeing Adele at seventy wasn't all that shocking. Sure there were more wrinkles and her once dark hair was now completely grey, but other than that she hadn't changed a bit from the woman she knew in the 1940's. She could tell by how Adele walked stoically toward her.

"Ann!" Adele exclaimed as she approached her friend and gave her a heartfelt embrace. "It's been so long."

They held each other for several moments before releasing to check each other out more carefully with huge grins on their faces.

"How are you, Adele?" asked Ann, beaming.

"I've been good," replied Adele. "What about you? What brings you back to Northport?"

"I just had a meeting with David Allardice," replied Ann. "I heard they were building a new high school and might need more teachers, so I thought I'd give it a shot."

A twinge of jealousy stung Adele. How she longed to be a teacher again, but didn't dare say it. She had to change the subject to hide her envy. "And your mother?"

"She passed a year ago," Ann sighed, then said quickly, "Hey, I heard you retired."

Adele, not wanting to discuss the forced retirement issue, simply nodded yes.

"What have you been doing with all your free time?" Ann asked, eager to hear.

"I'm writing a book," answered Adele with her chin in the air, proud.

"Wow, Adele, that's fantastic," exclaimed Ann. "What's it about?"

"The time Saint-Exupéry was here."

"Of course you are! I should have guessed. What a wonderful idea. You knew him pretty well, so of course you have a great deal to share."

"Yes, I think it's important for people to know the facts," Adele said with a sudden air of rigidity.

"The facts? Hopefully that means you'll be telling the whole story, right?" Ann asked with a look of knowing interest.

"I'm not sure to what you're inferring," said Adele as she looked passed her friend, as if already bored by the conversation.

Ann chuckled. "It's OK, Adele, it's *your* book. Write what you want. Either way, it is history and should be told."

Adele was relieved by Ann's amiable attitude and gave a slight smile. Just then, she saw Norman coming down the hall and called out to him, waving excitedly.

Norman walked up to her wearing a friendly smile. "Hi, Adele. Got more pages for me?" he asked.

"I do," said Adele. She opened her satchel and began pulling out a small stack of paper as she tilted her head toward Ann. "Norman, this is Ann, a very dear friend of mine. We've known each other for years. Ann, this is Norman Orenstein. He teaches English here."

Norman shook Ann's hand and said hello.

"Nice to meet you, Norman," said Ann. "I used to teach Home Economics here. That's when Adele and I used to be roommates. We go as far back as that old satchel she's still carrying."

Adele looked at her satchel then back at Ann as if insulted by the remark.

"Hey, remember that rickety boarding house we used to live at?" Ann asked Adele with a giggle.

"They tore it down about ten years ago," said Adele flatly,

not in the mood to stroll down memory lane as she handed her pages to Norman.

"Did you two know each other when you were seeing Saint-Exupéry?" asked Norman to Adele, interested.

"I wasn't *seeing* him, Norman, I was instructing him in English," Adele sternly corrected him.

Ann let out a playful cough as if indicating that wasn't all together true. Norman caught it, but acted as if he didn't and said apologetically, "Sorry, that's what I meant."

He then turned to Ann and mentioned innocently, "Adele's book is pretty good. Hey, maybe you can help fill in some of the blanks." He then added quickly, not intending to insult Adele, "That is, you know, in case there is anything Adele might have missed."

Adele looked at Norman, perturbed. Ann noticed and playfully toyed with her by saying, "Maybe I could."

"That won't be necessary," Adele firmly interjected. "I have my outline and all the notes I need," then, slightly on the defense, she changed the subject. "Ann is thinking of returning to teaching, Norman."

"Oh?" asked Norman, smiling at Ann.

"Well, it's not up to me. I just had a meeting with the *powers that be*. It seemed to go well, though. Fingers crossed. I'd love to teach again."

Adele, feeling again that twinge of envy again, asked, "Don't you have class, Norman?"

"Actually, no. It's my free period," replied Norman.

"Oh," said Adele, hoping the conversation was ending.

"Well, I'd love to stay but I have to run," said Ann, noticing the look of relief on Adele's face. "It was a pleasure meeting you, Norman. And Adele, let's get together soon. There's so much to catch up on."

"Yes, let's," agreed Adele with a smile.

Ann gave Adele another quick hug before heading down the hall. Adele watched then looked at Norman who was flipping through her new pages.

"Maybe you and I can get together soon, Norman, to discuss what you think of my work so far."

"OK," said Norman. "I actually have some questions."

"Questions? About my writing technique, I hope," said Adele in a tone implying she wasn't interested in discussing anything beyond that.

Getting her implication, Norman said, "Uh, yeah. Stuff like that."

"I'll call to set up a time when you can come to the house," she said in a formal manner. "I'll be happy to answer your questions then."

Adele then straightened the satchel on her shoulder and walked away. Norman watched her. Once she turned a corner, let out a relieved, "whew" as he slapped the pages against the palm of his hand and headed in the opposite direction.

Chapter 16

The Watercolor

Later that afternoon, Norman was reading a passage from Shakespeare's *Romeo & Juliet* to his class. Each student had their copy and followed along.

"By a name I know not how to tell thee who I am. My name, dear saint, is hateful to myself, because it is an enemy to thee. Had I it written, I would tear the word."

Norman glanced at his students and was pleased they were engrossed in the story. Even Jack was in the back of the room flipping through the pages, looking somewhat interested. A hopeful, satisfied smile spread across Norman's face as he closed his book and addressed the class.

"I want you to read the rest of Act 2 by Monday. Be ready to discuss it. Oh, and there may be a quiz."

Most of the students groaned at the thought of being tested.

Norman chuckled at this. "I said there *may* be a quiz, I'm leaving it entirely up to you to be prepared or not."

Some of the students chuckled at this, then the school bell rang.

"Have a great weekend," Norman called out as they left the room.

Norman went around his desk, opened his briefcase and tossed his book inside. Once the room was empty, he snapped his briefcase shut and took one last look around. He saw that Jack's copy of *Romeo & Juliet* was left on top of his desk. Norman quickly made his way to the desk, grabbed the paperback and rushed out of the room.

He looked up and down the hall hoping to see Jack, but he was gone. Norman's heart sank as he walked back into the classroom and grabbed his briefcase, discouraged.

Norman was hoping to find Morris to talk with him about Jack, but the English Department office was practically empty. Since it was late afternoon, and Friday, most of the teachers had already gone home. One of his colleagues was standing in a corner, opening his mail and noticed Norman's downcast expression.

"Everything all right, Norm?" asked the colleague.

"I was hoping to talk with Morris. Guess he left for the day."

"Yeah, about ten minutes ago. But if it's something urgent you can always phone him at home."

Norman gave him an odd look. Call his supervisor at home? The colleague noticed Norman's concern.

"He welcomes it. It's never an intrusion with Morris," he added smiling.

Norman nodded appreciating the tip and left the office. As he walked outside to his car, he thought about phoning Morris when he got home, but felt uncomfortable to bother him in a weekend. It was something that could wait until Monday he told himself.

On the way home, Norman came to a red light on Route 25A, the main road that ran through Northport. As he waited for the light to change he saw across the street, in the distance, Jack walking at a dawdling pace and smoking a cigarette. He was a sad and forlorn figure, with his hunched shoulders and eyes to the ground.

Norman rolled down his window, hoping to call out to him, but he was too far away. Instead, he watched as Jack approached a high, chain-linked fence, climbed it effortlessly and jumped over. Norman tried to see what was behind the fence, but other cars blocked his view. A car horn blared causing him to look ahead and see that the red light was now green. He quickly put his foot on the gas and drove off.

Norman couldn't stop thinking about the troubling image of Jack. He was not far from his home when he decided he didn't want to wait until after the weekend to talk to Morris. Remembering what his colleague said, he decided to speak with Morris in person. It would be easier than talking on the phone, so he quickly made a U-turn and drove in the direction of Morris' house.

When Norman pulled into Morris' driveway, he didn't see Morris' car, but thought perhaps it was in his garage. He began to have second thoughts when he parked and walked to the front door, feeling odd about disturbing his supervisor like this, but when he thought about Jack he knew couldn't turn back.

Norman rang the doorbell and waited a few moments before the door finally opened. Standing before him was Morris' wife, Harriet. She was an attractive woman with an open and hospitable personality. Norman liked her instantly.

"Hello," she said with a big smile.

"Hi, I'm Norman Orenstein, the new English teacher at the high school. Is Mr. Saxe at home?"

"Norman!" exclaimed Harriet, as if he were a long lost friend, "Of course. Morris told me all about you. I'm Harriet."

She opened the door wider for Norman. "Morris isn't here right now. He went to run some errands, but come on in."

Norman hesitated. "Well, if he's not in, I can come back another time."

"No, come in. Come in. He shouldn't be long," she said waving her hand for Norman to step inside.

Norman entered feeling a bit awkward until Harriet touched his arm and motioned for him to follow her.

"I'll make some coffee. We'll wait in the kitchen," she said disappearing into another room.

Norman peered around the corner and slowly followed her. When he entered the kitchen, Harriet was already setting out cups and saucers on the table. Norman glanced around taking in the cozy, friendly ambiance of this charming home.

"Please, sit. Coffee will be ready in a coupla minutes," said Harriet, her smile never leaving her face.

"I really don't mean to bother you, and I hope Morris won't mind," Norman said as he took a seat at the kitchen table.

"Oh, no, not at all. Morris will be glad to see you. I know I am. I only get to meet Morris' colleagues at teacher functions, but even then I only get a coupla minutes of chitchat and never get to know the whole person, ya know? Morris told me that you just moved here from New Jersey, and you have a baby boy?"

"Yeah. His name is Adam. He's a year old now."

"That wonderful. We have three kids, two sons and a daughter. A full house – except, not right now," she said with a chuckle. "It's nice to have the place to myself sometimes. So rare. You came at the perfect time."

She grabbed the coffee pot, brought it over to the table and placed it down. "Would you like some cookies, Norman? I also made a Bundt cake. That is, if the kids didn't eat it all," she said, again with her infectious smile.

"No, coffee is fine. Thank you," said Norman. He watched

as Harriet poured him a cup, then one for herself. She took a seat across from him when she finished.

"So, tell me, how do you like Northport so far? Let's start with the high school," said Harriet eager to hear.

"I like it a lot. Much better than where I just came from," said Norman feeling more comfortable.

"There's a lot of good people at the high school. I'm always impressed by who they bring in," said Harriet. "And what about Northport? Are you settling in all right?"

"Yes, my wife and I love it. Just minutes away from the beaches and the town itself is very friendly," said Norman. "We like our new home, too, and our neighbors."

"Oh, that's right!" exclaimed Harriet, as she was just about to take a sip from her coffee cup, "You live across the street from Adele Breaux. Morris told me."

"Yeah, that's right," said Norman.

"We've known Adele for...oh, let's see...since 1950, so about fifteen years now," Harriet said then took a sip from her cup.

"She's writing a book, so I'm helping her with grammar and spelling."

"How is it so far?" asked Harriet, leaning forward as if ready to be told a secret. "Be honest."

"It's pretty good. I mean, I don't know her too well yet, only that she used to teach at the high school and knew Saint-Exupéry."

"And talks about him constantly," added Harriet, her smile widened.

"Yeah," chuckled Norman. "I get the feeling that, although she's telling an interesting story, and he's a fascinating guy – it's just loaded with facts. It's not much of a *personal* story, you know?"

Harriet nodded and answered quietly, "I know."

"I wish she would write about what went on between the two of them. The association they had. I may be wrong, but I get the feeling there was more to it. He gave her one of his watercolors. That's kind of personal, don't you think?"

Harriet took a sip of her coffee then grinned. "Ah, the watercolor. Her prized possession."

"She treats it like gold," said Norman.

"Tell me about it," Harriet laughed. "Several years ago, Adele was taking a trip to Europe, so she came over one afternoon with the watercolor. She asked if I would keep my eye on it while she was away. She was afraid someone might break into her home and steal it."

"Steal it? I think if anyone was going to take anything it would be those antiques she has everywhere," said Norman, perplexed.

"Exactly. But to Adele they don't come close to that watercolor. I was surprised she entrusted me with it, but I said I'd look after it."

"You're very trustworthy," Norman said with a smile as he took a sip of coffee.

"Well, yes and no. I mean, with three kids I was afraid one of them would get to it and draw all over it or ruin it somehow, so I had to find a good hiding place for it. I decided to put it in between several of our old record albums. You know, Glenn Miller and Tommy Dorsey – music my kids would never listen to or go near," she said with a slight laugh. "Anyway, Adele was in Europe for a long time, well over a month, and I had forgotten about the watercolor, and Adele for that matter, until she returned.

"The second she got home she phoned me and said she wanted to come by the next day for the watercolor, but by that time I had forgotten where I placed it. Knowing what that watercolor meant to her, I went into a panic. Morris and I searched this entire house from top to bottom, even the garage, looking for it. We were up until three in the morning tearing the place apart, but couldn't find it. So, I finally had to call Adele and tell her I'd lost it."

"How did she react?" asked Norman, engrossed in the story.

"Surprisingly well," replied Harriet. "At first Morris said he'd phone her and take the blame, but I told him I was the one who lost it so I'd be the one to take the blame. It was my fault, after all. So, I phoned her and told her. I was expecting screaming from the other end, so I held it away from my ear, but instead Adele said she understood and believed it was in my house somewhere and that one day it would turn up."

"Wow," said Norman as he sat back in his chair, impressed.

"Then, three years later..." Harriet began.

"Three years later?" exclaimed Norman.

"Yes, three years later," Harriet continued, smiling. "I was cleaning house, and was near the record collection. I saw dust on the albums. I guess the kids weren't the only ones not listening to Glenn Miller anymore," she laughed, "So, I pulled out the albums and began dusting them one by one. When I pulled out a few more, the watercolor was shoved between them and fell the floor! I literally screamed at the sight of it because I always felt guilty about it, knowing how important it was to Adele."

"What did she do when you told her you found it?" asked Norman.

Harriet laughed again. "I called her immediately, of course, and right after I said, 'Hello, it's Harriet,' Adele said, 'You found it, right?' It was as if she knew that's why I was calling. She never even said what 'it' was, and neither did I, but I told her yes and she said, 'I'll be right over.'"

"Wow," said Norman, again impressed. "She did trust the right person."

"She trusted the watercolor. She believed it wasn't lost and would show up again. Like how, I think, somewhere deep down inside she believes Saint-Exupéry will show up again, too."

Norman looked at Harriet, worried.

"Not that she's delusional. She's too intelligent to actually believe that, but I think her heart still holds out for that kind of miracle. I guess anyone would when a loved one goes missing, right? Are you sure you don't want any cookies or anything, Norman?" Harriet asked sweetly.

"I'm good, thank you," he answered then went back to the subject of Adele. "That's kind of what I was getting at when I said I wish she'd get more personal in the book."

"That's not Adele, Norman," Harriet said shaking her head. "She won't ever come out and share her feelings. She does it more in her actions. For instance, what she did *after* she got the watercolor back."

"What happened?" asked Norman, interested.

"Well, seeing that she nearly lost it for good after giving it to me, she decided she wanted to do something special with it, so she got it framed. And, again, it's all in her actions. She didn't take it to just any local frame store, no, she brought it into Manhattan and had it professionally framed at Sotheby's and spent a fortune for it. She showed it to Morris and me after. It was beautiful. Then she flew to Oregon with it to donate it to Reed College, her alma mater."

"That's a good place for it," said Norman.

"We thought so, too, but she didn't just hand it over to them, it came with conditions."

Norman let out a laugh upon hearing the word "conditions." That sounded like Adele. "And what were those?" he asked, wanting to know.

"When she brought it to Reed, she insisted it be hung in

the library, so Adele went with several of the administrators to find the best wall to hang it on. They must have tried every wall of that library until Adele finally settled on it being hung directly in front, so it would be the first thing people saw as they entered."

"Of course," said Norman half mocking Adele's choice. Then it suddenly occurred to him. How was it back in her possession? He asked Harriet.

"Well, a year later Adele decided to make another trip to Oregon and to Reed to 'visit' the watercolor. When she arrived, *unexpectedly*, mind you, she walked into the library and the watercolor wasn't on the wall. It had been replaced by another piece of artwork. Adele was furious. She demanded to know where the watercolor was. The head librarian told her it was in the back room. Adele insisted she be taken to the back room to see it. Once inside, Adele saw that the watercolor had been taken out of it's expensive frame and was now in a cheaper frame and was leaning against a wall among stacks of books and other library discards."

"Uh-oh," said Norman, fearful of what was to come next.

Harriet nodded then shook her head, preparing to tell Norman a doozy.

"Adele saw that and went into a rage! She began ranting and raving about how important that watercolor was, and how important Saint-Exupéry was, and how *dare* they disrespect him and his work."

Norman cringed.

"Then she grabbed the watercolor that was still in the cheap frame, and started for the door," added Harriet. "The library staff told her she wasn't allowed to take it since she had already donated it to the college, but Adele wasn't about to leave it there, and told them that. If they didn't know how to treat precious work then they didn't 'deserve' to have it."

"I have to agree with Adele on that one," said Norman with a shrug.

"Me, too, but when they tried to take it away from Adele, she made a run for it."

Norman's eyes bulged from his head as his mouth fell open. A *run* for it?

Harriet laughed. "Yeah, she ran out of the library and out into the parking lot! They chased her, but she outran them. She threw the watercolor into the backseat, got in her car and peeled out!"

Norman burst out laughing at the image of the straight-laced Adele on the run. "So, basically she stole it," he said with a chuckle.

"*Technically* she stole it, yes, but it was a gift. They never pressed charges or anything. I think they understood they made an error," said Harriet.

Norman shook his head, reeling from the story. "Wow," he began, "She's really in love with that watercolor."

Harriet smiled at Norman, titled her head slightly and said, "It's not the watercolor she's in love with, Norman."

Just then, the sound of the front door opening was heard with Morris shouting, "Harriet, I'm home!"

Harriet shouted back, "I'm in the kitchen, Morris...with Norman." She then gave Norman a friendly wink.

Chapter 17

You Do Something To Me

A fter the weekend, Norman was back in class passing out a quiz to his disgruntled students. "If you read Act 2 as I've asked, this should be a breeze," he said with a grin.

He approached Jack's desk. Jack kept his eyes down, waiting for the quiz paper to be put in front of him. His paperback copy of *Romeo & Juliet* was put there instead. Jack looked up. Norman gave him a dissatisfied glance as he moved on to the next row of students and continued to pass out the quiz. Jack watched, outraged and embarrassed as his classmates began jotting down their answers. He glared at Norman, then sat back in his seat with arms folded and a scowl on his face.

After class, as the students were leaving, Norman leaned against his desk and waited for Jack to pass him. Jack made his way to the front of the room with his eyes to the floor.

"Jack, let's talk about..." Norman began, but Jack didn't stop. He stomped past Norman in angry defiance and walked out. Norman watched, then let out a long sigh. As he began to make his way around his desk, he noticed Jack left the copy of *Romeo & Juliet* on his desk.

Later that evening, Norman was home with Josephine having dinner. It was a simple yet hearty stew that Josephine had prepared. She watched as Norman happily devoured his second helping then looked at their infant son in his high chair, playing with his bowl of peas.

"You think on Saturday you can take time out of your busy schedule and mow the lawn?" she asked with a slight hint of cynicism.

"Yeah. I can do it in the morning," said Norman, without any firm commitment behind it.

"Are you sure?" Josephine asked, looking at him unconvinced.

Norman looked at his wife. "Yeah. Why are you looking at me like that?"

"I've asked you two weeks in a row now, that's why."

Norman stopped chewing. He looked caught and guilty. He swallowed as he wiped his mouth with his napkin and said, "I'm sorry. The weekends fly by so fast, it's Monday before you know it."

"I know. It's not easy squeezing anything into your schedule," she said, resigned.

"I don't have a schedule, Jo," said Norman. "I have papers to read and grade. It's part of my job."

"I'd just like you to consider me, Adam and this house as part of your job, too," she replied.

Norman looked at her. "You and Adam are more important to me than anything. I'll mow the lawn Saturday morning, and then we'll go out after."

"Where?" Josephine asked.

"Anywhere you want. We'll go for a drive. You could use a break, too," he said, understanding.

"We don't have to go for a drive," Josephine said softly. She wanted him more to get her point than placate her.

Norman touched her arm gently and said with all sincerity, "I want to go."

Josephine relaxed. It was nice to be on the same page again with her husband. She began to finish her meal, but the blissful moment was soon interrupted by the sound of the doorbell. Norman froze midway from putting a spoonful of stew into his mouth. Josephine shot him a perturbed look as he put the spoon back in his bowl, got up and left the room. He went to the front door and opened it. Adele was on his doorstep holding a small stack of papers.

"Sorry to disturb you, Norman, but here is one more chapter," she said as she held it out to him. He took them with a slight hesitation. "When you're finished reading it, please come over so we can edit it together."

Norman, hoping Josephine didn't overhear this, was about to say something to the contrary, when Adele added, "When you have the time, of course. I know how demanding it is to be a teacher, so only when it's convenient for you."

Norman, gave in and said, "Yes, Adele. I'll be happy to."

Adele said goodnight and turned to leave. As Norman was closing the door, she made a backward glance and caught a glimpse of Josephine stepping up behind Norman looking displeased. The door closed. As Adele began to step away she heard the muffled sound of Josephine's irate voice.

Adele stopped and listened for a moment. She heard Josephine complain, "You spend enough time away with the work you already *have*. We can't even have a quiet dinner without her showing up..."

Embarrassed, Adele walked quickly back to her home. As she did, a specific memory came to mind, one she would rather have forgotten...

ঔৎঙ

ADELE, IN HER COAT and scarf and holding her satchel, was standing stoically at the parlor room door in the Bevin House. The maid slowly opened it and said quietly, "Monsieur will be with you soon."

Adele entered the room. The maid closed the door. All was still and quiet in the room except for the crackling logs in the fireplace. Adele approached the table where Saint-Exupéry's sketches, watercolors and papers were strewn about. She put her satchel on a chair then unraveled her scarf and unbuttoned her coat as her eyes roamed the creative brilliance before her.

She smiled wondering what the story could be about as she studied the wonderful watercolors. One was of a clown; another was of a drunk. Then there was a lovely one of a small blonde haired boy with a fox. What did it all mean?

As she placed her coat and scarf across her chair, she saw Saint-Exupéry's jacket hanging on the back of another. The sight of it caught her off guard. She couldn't understand why seeing it made her heart skip a beat. Adele took a step toward it, as if it had a magical, magnetic pull, yet felt so forbidden. She put out her hand, wanting to touch it. Her fingers trembled as they inched nearer. When her fingertips brushed the shoulder of it the entire room suddenly transformed into the most enchanted fantasy her mind could conjure.

Marlene Dietrich singing, "You Do Something To Me" began to play and the fireplace burst into bright, sparking light. Her hands were now on Saint-Exupéry's shoulders as he held her close and both danced perfectly, cheek to cheek to the rhythm. The watercolor characters of the Fox, the King, the Little Prince, and all the others became vibrant and bounced in slow, twinkling beauty on the table. They danced just as wonderfully, the colors swirling beneath them.

Adele closed her eyes as Saint-Exupéry whiffed her hair

and nuzzled her neck. She felt a warmth rush down her body. As he moved his lips closer to hers she heard him murmur, "Mademoiselle" softly. It made her swoon. She heard it again in a more stern tone. Confused, Adele opened her eyes and lifted her hand from his jacket on the chair. As soon as she did this, the room went back to being still again with only the sound of the crackling fire.

When she turned around, she was surprised to see Saint-Exupéry approaching her, looking anxious and worried.

"Mademoiselle, my apologies," he began. "My wife...she is not feeling well. She needs my attention. Can we have our lesson another day?"

It took a few seconds for Adele to adjust from fantasy back to reality, looking utterly disoriented. She nodded in agreement without making eye contact with him. Saint-Exupéry watched her, concerned.

"Mademoiselle, is everything all right?"

Adele stammered as she started to button up her coat, "Y-yes. I – I'm fine."

She wrapped her scarf securely around her neck and grabbed her satchel. Saint-Exupéry held open the door as she walked out of the room.

In the hallway, Saint-Exupéry gave a nod to the butler standing nearby, as if to say please see her out. The butler approached them as Saint-Exupéry again gave Adele his apologies. Adele, embarrassed by her elaborate fantasy, still couldn't look at him. He tilted his head, trying to see her eyes. Adele gave him a quick glance to "prove" she was fine, blushed, then looked away. Saint-Exupéry smiled then headed up the stairs to his waiting wife as Adele headed toward the door with the butler. He opened it and she stepped outside.

When the door closed, Adele went to the porch railing and grabbed it as if he legs were going to give out, wondering what had gotten into her. She touched her face. It was still warm with arousal. Suddenly, from inside the house, she heard the muffled sound of Consuelo shouting angry obscenities in a mixture of French and Spanish.

Adele turned and looked up at the windows, trying to see where in the house it is coming from. Then the muffled sound of Saint-Exupéry shouting was heard, though not in anger, but as if pleading for peace. Then there was silence. Suddenly, the sounds of plates smashing and breaking were heard. Startled and frightened, Adele quickly made her way down the porch steps and to her car...

ADELE WALKED JUST AS fast away from Norman's house as she did from the Bevin House that afternoon back in 1942. When she reached her front door, she pushed it open and entered. The vividness of that memory mixed with the irate tone of Norman's wife behind their door caused her to stand frozen in her foyer and hold her face in worry.

Chapter 18

What Frenchmen Do

It was early Saturday evening when, long after Norman mowed his lawn and returned from the promised drive with his wife and son that he sat with Adele at her dining room table. In front of them were the chapters she had written so far. Opera music played softly in the background, as usual.

"I made corrections in red," said Norman as he passed several pages to Adele. "There were some typos and a few run-on sentences. And here," he pointed to the top page, "I noted that you may want to restructure these paragraphs, just for more clarity."

Adele looked at his notes and smiled. "Thank you, Norman. I'm so fortunate to have your expertise and keen eye. Tell me, are you finding the book interesting?"

Norman froze. He wasn't sure how to answer, and wasn't any good at lying. He cleared his throat and said simply, "Uh...yeah."

"That didn't sound very convincing," Adele said, eyeing him carefully.

Norman didn't think he would have to critique the book's contents, only the grammar. She made that clear. He stammered again, trying to find the right thing to say. "Well, I-I think it's pretty good," he said, which wasn't exactly a lie.

Adele reached for a folder, opened it and removed several letters. "You seem to be the only one to think so. I received these this week," she said as she handed them to Norman. "Rejection letters from publishers."

Norman looked at the letters as Adele sighed in defeat. "I'm afraid I've been wasting your time. And been an intrusion to your family...for nothing."

"No, no. You're not wasting my time, and you're not an intrusion," said Norman, feeling bad. "And this isn't for nothing."

Adele asked in almost a plea, "Then tell me why these letters? What does my book need?"

Feeling on the spot, Norman hesitated, trying to find the right words. "Uh, maybe it could use...more about...I don't know. Maybe you focus too much on describing things such as the landscape and the Bevin House."

Adele quickly replied, "I can easily fix *that*. Tell me what it's missing."

Again, Norman struggled to answer her honestly. "Well, in my opinion, when you write about Saint-Exupéry, it's a lot different from how you *talk* about him."

"For example?" asked Adele.

"Uh, it seems, at least to me," he began, "that maybe there is more to the...I mean maybe there was more..."

He stopped, not knowing how to address a possible affair of some sort between Adele and Saint-Exupéry. He didn't want to imply an affair if it weren't true, and didn't want to get into it if it were. Adele looked at him with intensity, waiting for an answer. Norman chose his words as delicately as possible.

"In regard to your rela..." he started then quickly chose a better word, "association with Saint-Exupéry. When you speak of him, there's more pass...infatu...uh, *enthusiasm*, in regard to the obvious impression he's made on you. You know, maybe you can elaborate on...that is, if there was any kind of...that the two of you might had...that is, *if* you two..."

Adele was now staring hard at Norman as if daring him to make the insinuation. Norman swallowed hard. Unable to stand it, he quickly changed the subject. "I notice you like opera."

Adele lost her stare and was touched that he noticed the music. "Yes. I used to sing opera," she said proud of the fact. "When I was younger, I was with a small company. We toured Europe," she smiled, "I was good. Quite good."

Suddenly, her smile faded. "Then the stock market crashed and the depression came. Our small company folded. I needed work, and because I knew French I decided to teach. That's how I came to Northport. They were hiring." She added, sadly, "Such became my vocation."

The memory of her failed aspirations put her in a melancholy mood. She began collecting the letters back from Norman and said, "I will consider your *suggestion*, Norman, and write more about Saint-Exupéry. The book is about him after all."

Norman nodded. "Right. He's the central theme. Not that what you wrote wasn't interesting. I guess as teachers we don't lead very eventful lives."

Adele slammed the folder shut and glared at him, insulted. "Excuse me?" she snapped. "Norman, I may have ended up a provincial school teacher, but *I've lived*!"

Norman was taken aback. He slowly nodded his head to let her know he got the message and watched as she shoved the letters into the folder in frustration. When he looked at her face, he could see that she was fighting back tears.

Feeling bad, Norman tried encouragement. "You'll find a publisher, Adele. I'm sure you will."

Adele managed a smile, appreciating his optimism. "You're very dear," she said sincerely. Then she recalled the other evening and added, "Now go home to your wife. I've taken up enough of your time."

They both rose from their chairs and walked to the front door. Norman wanted to leave on a happier note, so he said with enthusiasm, "They're close to finally finishing the new high school on Laurel Hill. It's very big. You should go by and see it sometime."

"Yes. Perhaps I will when I find the time. Thank you again for your help, Norman."

He sensed his attempt did little good for her mood and didn't know how else to help, but to leave. She opened the door. Norman stepped out, gave a slight wave and headed home. After closing the door, Adele leaned against it. Tears of disappointment filled her eyes.

৩৯০৫

AT SCHOOL, THE FOLLOWING week, Norman and Morris were walking down the hall together. It was late afternoon and both were heading toward the English Department to wrap up their day.

"So, any improvement with the Doleman kid?" Morris asked.

"No. He's shut me out," Norman said with a despondent sigh, "But I'll keep trying."

"Do you want me to have a talk with him?"

Norman thought about it. He wasn't ready to resort to bringing in another administrator, even if it was Morris. He felt that might scare Jack away.

"Not yet," he said, "Give me a little more time."

"It's your call," said Morris, "But if there's no getting through, and he's not participating, you need to let me know."

"I will," promised Norman with a worried look on his face. Just then, he saw Ann coming out of Principal Allardice's office. Seeing her made him smile with excitement.

"I need to go, Morris. I'll see you tomorrow," he said enthusiastically as he headed off in Ann's direction. Morris watched, puzzled by his sudden mood shift.

Principal Allardice had just shaken Ann's hand and went back into his office by the time Norman walked right up to her. "Hello, again," he said, smiling.

Ann looked up, startled. "Oh, hello! So, we meet again," she said with a chuckle. "Norman, right?"

Norman nodded. "Yeah. Hey, I was wondering if I could speak with you? Do you have time?"

"Right now?" asked Ann, sensing his urgency.

"Yeah. It's about Adele."

Ann looked worried. "Is she all right?"

"Oh, yeah. She's fine. I just – I'd like to discuss her book with you."

Intrigued, Ann said, "Sure."

"Let's go where we can talk privately," Norman said, as he led her down the hall.

A short time later, Ann and Norman were sitting at a small table in the empty teacher's lunchroom sipping coffee they wrangled from the kitchen before it closed.

"I want to help Adele. I think she has a great story to tell," said Norman. "But her writing could be better."

"You do *know* this is her first book," said Ann, gently defending her friend.

"I know, and that's apparent, but it's not so much her writing style. She *can* write; it's the content. It's very…stale.

The facts, I mean. I think it could be a lot better if she went deeper."

"Have you told her this?" asked Ann.

"No. I'd like to, but I'm not sure how. I don't want to hurt her feelings, and I don't want to encourage her to write any-thing that might, I don't know...embarrass her," said Norman, looking intently at Ann. "Do you know what I mean?"

"I do," said Ann, as she took a sip of coffee.

"Here she was with this great author and pilot, who wrote one of the world's most famous books ever, and...well, you were there, so I thought maybe you could tell me what she was like back then, and how I might be able to get Adele to be more revealing."

Ann looked at Norman with raised eyebrow.

"Oh, I don't mean...I'm not implying...I just want her book to get published," Norman said quickly. "She's gotten rejection letters from publishers already, and I don't want her to get discouraged. I'd just like her to write something more worthwhile. I want to help."

"It's nice that you care, Norman, and I wish I could tell you what transpired between Adele and the French guy...that's what I called him," she said with a laugh. "I never did learn French...and I only saw him once briefly. I never met him, and I never saw them together, but I will say that she definite-ly had a big infatuation for him. And when he was here? Oh, boy, was she over the moon most of the time. And then there were times when..." her voice drifted.

Norman looked at her, his eyes encouraging her to keep going.

"She would be very withdrawn and sullen, even sad," said Ann. "But she would never confide in me about why. I was always trying to guess myself what was going on. I have my own theories, but they're just theories."

Norman looked at Ann hoping she would share them, but didn't want to pry. Ann must have picked up on this since she moved her chair closer as if about to tell a secret.

"OK, for instance, there was this one time when I was in our apartment by myself. I had just come home from school and was preparing a lesson plan for the next day. I used to do that during the times Adele would be at the Bevin House, when I had the place to myself..."

∾৹৵

IT WAS 1942. ANN was at a small desk in the living room carefully creating a lesson plan for her students. Suddenly, the door of the apartment swung open. Adele entered out of breath, looking unraveled. She tossed her satchel on the couch and began frantically unbuttoning her coat. Ann immediately stood up, concerned.

"Are you all right?" she asked.

"Y-yes," said Adele, near tears as she went the closet by the door, opened it and reached in for a hanger. It took her several attempts to get her coat on it; she was that distracted.

"No, you're not," said Ann as she went around to help Adele, but Adele already hung her coat and closed the closet door. She breezed past Ann, wringing her hands, looking distraught.

"Did you have your lesson with the French guy today?" Ann asked.

Adele shot her a disturbed look and replied, "Yes."

Usually she would correct her friend, saying sternly, "Monsieur Saint-Exupery," but not on this day. That was a huge signal to Ann that her friend was in some sort of trouble.

"What did he do?" Ann asked.

"He didn't *do* anything," answered Adele, unconvincingly, as she made her way to the couch and sat down.

Ann sat next to her. "Hey, did he *try* anything with you?"

"No!" said Adele, put off, as she moved an inch away from Ann.

"Well, I had to ask. You're acting strange and, after all, he is French."

Adele shot her another disturbed look.

"What?" asked Ann defensively, "That's what Frenchmen do. We've seen Charles Boyer do it a million times in the movies. Right?"

Adele shook her head, not in the mood for this sort of conversation.

"Did ya get fired?" Ann asked in a hushed tone.

"No. Will you please stop asking me all these questions," Adele asked, now annoyed.

"All right, all right," Ann said as she reclined back on the couch. "You're just worrying me, that's all."

Adele thought carefully for a moment then admitted, "I was called into Principal Kaufman's office today."

"You were? Why?" Ann knew that meant something serious.

"She wanted to remind me that I had a reputation to uphold. Some people, or someone, commented on my being at the Bevin House."

"So?" asked Ann not understanding.

"She made it sound as if I was involved in something illicit," Adele answered, worried.

Ann laughed. "*Illicit*? What is she talking about? And who would say such a thing?"

"I don't know, but it's no laughing matter, Ann. This is serious," she said as she stood and nervously paced the room.

"Adele, you're only teaching the French guy English. Don't pay attention to stupid gossip. Principal Kaufman shouldn't have either. You've got nothing to hide."

Adele stood near the corner of the room nervously chewing

on her thumbnail. Ann noticed. Her suspicion began to rise. She's never seen her friend acting so agitated.

"Or *do* you?" Ann asked with raised eyebrow.

"Of course not!" Adele snapped.

Ann looked relieved. "Right! Of course not! Then, what's the problem?"

"I don't know," Adele fretted. "Did I make the right choice?" she asked as she returned to the couch and sat.

"About what?" Ann asked.

"Everything. Teaching. This so called career," she said teary-eyed. "It never really felt like a choice to me. More like a life sentence."

"But you *love* teaching. What are you talking about?" asked Ann as she looked at Adele, confused.

"What if there's more? What am I missing?"

"I don't understand," said Ann.

Adele glanced at Ann as if wanting to say something. Instead, she looked away. She hesitated, then said both wistfully and timidly, "He asked me to dance."

"The French guy?" Ann asked, surprised.

"It was innocent," said Adele turning back to Ann.

"Did you?" Ann asked sitting up, very interested.

Adele nodded. "He's very...he does everything to avoid his lessons, so I indulged him...but only for a moment. I immediately put an end to it and we went back to work," Adele confessed, half ashamed about it, and half still thrilled by it.

"When did this happen?"

"Today," answered Adele as she looked down at the floor, confused. She was never good at expressing her feelings, let alone confiding them to anyone. "When we danced," she began, "it was brief; he was just being silly...as usual. But I'm a professional. I take my job very seriously, as you know."

"I do. So, what's the problem?" asked Ann.

Adele didn't answer. She looked away, as if trying to figure out what the problem was as well.

"OK, so you danced with the guy. So what? He's French and likes to fool around..." Suddenly Ann stopped and looked at Adele as if something just dawned on her. "Wait a second...you liked it."

"I didn't say I did! Don't be putting words..." Adele said defensively before Ann cut her off.

"You *liked* it. Oh, my God...Adele!" Ann shrieked excitedly.

Adele stiffened, trying to maintain her propriety, but it was a losing battle. She quickly stood and moved around the room trying to look like she suddenly had something more important to do.

"I will not engage in whatever it is you think I liked or didn't like," snapped Adele.

"Wow. You and the French guy!" said Ann sighed with surprise.

"There is no *me* and the French guy, Ann! Please!" shouted Adele.

"But you *danced* with him. Wow! It must have been... dreamy!" Ann said loving the idea of her friend being caught up in a romance with a foreigner. "And that's why all of a sudden you're questioning your career. Are you thinking of running off with him?"

"Oh, don't be absurd, Ann! You're sounding utterly ridiculous. I am *not* running off with him or anyone. I was only...my meeting with Principal Kaufman simply made me wonder if this was where I should be."

"And you want me to believe it had nothing to do with dancing with a Frenchman?" Ann asked, ready not to believe her answer.

"Not at all. If there are people snooping around trying to find gossip about *me*, then this town *is* too small and I no longer wish to discuss it," said Adele, irritated, as she went over to a table, picked up several letters of mail and began sorting through them.

Ann sat back on the couch and pondered all that had been said. After a moment, Adele slapped the mail on the table and turned to go into her bedroom. As she did this, Ann sat sideways on the couch and leaned over the back of it.

"Hey, Adele…"

Adele stopped and turned to Ann.

"Does he have a brother?"

Adele rolled her eyes and went into her bedroom, slamming the door behind her…

BACK IN THE TEACHER'S lunchroom, Ann let out a hearty laugh. Norman laughed, too.

"So, she *did* have a thing for Saint-Exupéry," said Norman.

"Whatever the 'thing' was, Norman, she never admitted it to me, or anyone that I know of. I think it's always been her curse."

"Curse?"

"Yeah. I don't think it was the small town that had her trapped. It was always her inability to allow herself to feel what she feels. I think if she did that with whatever it was between her and the French guy…she'd be free."

Norman pondered this as he watched Ann finish her coffee.

LATER THAT EVENING, ADELE was preparing dinner for herself. She had an opera playing in the background on her hi-fi set. She hummed softly along as she put on her large oven mitts, removed a small roasted chicken from the oven and placed it on top of the stove. Suddenly, the doorbell rang.

Adele removed the oven mitts and went to her front door, wondering who it might be. She opened the door. Seeing Ann on her doorstep made her smile.

"Hi, Adele," said Ann, friendly as ever.

"Your timing is impeccable. I just made dinner," Adele said as she pushed open the door wider and invited Ann inside.

Ann only took a few steps inside before she stopped. "It smells delicious, but I can't stay. I have to get to the airport. But I wanted to tell you I've been hired. Dave Allardice said I could start once the new high school is completed, which will be next fall."

"Oh, that's great news, Ann," exclaimed Adele, again feeling a twinge of envy, but she was sincerely happy for her friend.

"So, when I come back, I'll call you and we can pick up where we left off," Ann said with a giggle.

"Yes. I'd like that very much. It really will be nice to have my old friend return," said Adele.

"Well, I should get going. I'll let you know my plans."

"Yes, please do," said Adele as she hugged Ann goodbye. A hug they held longer than usual. When they finally pulled away, Ann turned for the front door, then stopped.

"Adele…" she began as she turned back around, "Good luck with your book."

"Thank you," said Adele, trying to hide the discouragement on her face. Ann noticed.

"Say, Adele, can I ask you something before I go? It's kind of been on my mind now for a lot of years."

"Certainly," said Adele, interested.

"Remember that afternoon you came home and told me about that meeting you had with Principal Kaufman regarding your reputation? It was the same day you danced with the French guy.

Adele winced.

"Sorry, I meant Saint-Exupéry," Ann said.

Adele looked up at the ceiling, acting as if trying to recall. "Yes. Yes, I remember," she said looking back at Ann.

"Did you dance with him before or after your meeting with Principal Kaufman?" she asked, wanting to put all the pieces together.

"It was after. I always had my lessons with Monsieur de Saint-Exupéry *after* school hours," said Adele, her memory apparently sharp as ever.

"OK. Well, my question is, if that meeting with Principal Kaufman had never occurred, would you have stopped dancing?"

Adele stared at Ann, caught off guard. Ann knew that would be her reaction, so she reached out and touched Adele's arm tenderly and said, "No one is snooping anymore, Adele. The past is just a lot of funny stories. Don't be afraid to share them." She then let go of Adele's arm, turned and walked out the door.

Chapter 19

Never Said Goodbye

"I've stopped writing. No one is interested in the book," Adele said with eyes downcast as she sat next to Saint-Exupéry in the cockpit of his plane.

Saint-Exupéry was flying steadily, staring straight ahead, but turned his head to look at her. He saw she was upset, but said nothing. He stared straight ahead again as Adele continued, "I suppose all that once was is now gone forever. I feel foolish thinking I could have easily recaptured it like a firefly in a jar."

Suddenly, the sky darkened and the plane hit nerve-rattling turbulence. It jerked several times, rocking the plane hard. Adele, terrified, clutched onto her seat and screamed, "We're going to die. We're going to die!"

Saint-Exupéry looked at her, surprised. "Who says we die?" he asked in a calm manner that made Adele feel strange, yet instantly comforted.

As the plane continued to bounce and shake with great force to the turmoil outside, Adele looked at Saint-Exupéry with sweet longing and reached out to touch is face when suddenly a loud thud was heard.

Adele opened her eyes at the same time she let out a sharp gasp. She quickly sat up and glanced around the room trying to get her bearings. It was daytime and the sun from the windows made her squint. She had been lying on her couch taking a nap.

The loud thud was heard again. She realized it was a knock at her front door. Trying to shake off the bad dream, she got up, went to the door and opened it. Morris was standing there holding a beautiful potted plant.

"Hi. This is from Harriet," he said as he held it out to her. "She sends her regards."

Adele blinking her eyes to focus said nothing. She robotically took the plant with both hands and turned back into the house. Morris followed after closing the door behind him. Adele entered her dining room where she looked around absent-mindedly for a place to set it.

"So, do you have any chapters for me read?" Morris asked, watching her.

"No," said Adele flatly, "I'm having a block. And I'm not sure I'm going to continue with the book. I've been wondering if it's at all worth it."

"Does this have anything to do with a few publishers turning you down?" asked Morris nonchalantly.

Adele looked at him, embarrassed. "How did you…?"

"Norman told me. He's a little worried about you."

"He needn't be," she said dismissively, looking harder for a place to put the plant.

"Give yourself a break, Adele. It's your first time at this," said Morris as he gently took the plant from her and placed it on an end table.

Exasperated, Adele broke down. "Saint-Exupéry was important, Morris. Don't these publishers realize? How can they reject not me, but *him*?"

"They're not rejecting either of you. They're rejecting the work. You're not an historian, Adele."

"I never claimed to be! This is a memoir, not a history book!"

"Then *write* a memoir. Screw sticking to the facts. Write what's in your heart."

"My heart has nothing to do with any of this," Adele said in her usual hoity manner.

Morris laughed and walked over to the table where her notes, papers and typewriter sat. He saw the watercolor of the King that Saint-Exupéry had given to her and picked it up.

"Why do you think Saint-Exupéry gave you this?" he asked.

"It was one of many. A throwaway," Adele said, brushing it off as such.

Morris had to stifle a laugh knowing full well that it was far from a 'throwaway' and, to Adele, the most valuable thing she owned, but he wasn't about to get into that with her. He wanted to make a more important point.

"Wasn't the King the first character the Little Prince met on his journey?"

Adele nodded yes, though bored by such an obvious question.

"Stubborn guy, the King. I've always liked the Fox, myself," Morris began, "Especially how he got the Little Prince to tame him." He looked at Adele, contemplative. "You know what I think? I think you wanted Saint-Exupéry to tame *you*. Funny thing is…he did. And like the Little Prince, Saint-Exupéry left…and now you're sad."

Adele looked irritated by the point he was trying to make. "If you read the book you'd know the Fox didn't mind being sad."

"Oh, I've read it, and you're right, he didn't mind, but *you* do. And that's *not* how Saint-Exupéry would want you to be. Would he?"

Adele looked at him, hating how right he was. She shook her head no then sat on a chair looking long-suffering, shouldering a heavy weight of regret.

"I never got to say goodbye to him, Morris," Adele said holding her fist to her lips, fighting tears.

"No one did, Adele. He disappeared," Morris said gently. "But I don't think you're sad because of that. I think it's because you weren't able to say something else. Something more important."

Adele looked at him. Her loneliness and confusion welded together in a devouring yearning she was incapable of expressing. Morris carefully placed the watercolor back on the table, knowing it wasn't the time to press the issue.

"I know this...*block*...is only temporary, Adele," he told her. "And I also know the book will be good because it comes from your heart. Whether you want it to or not."

Morris walked over and lovingly squeezed her arm. As he headed out of the room, he turned and pointed to the plant.

"Water twice a day with direct sunlight. Should live forever." Then he was gone. The sound of the front door opening, then closing, was heard.

Adele slowly rose and went over to the table. She looked down at the watercolor. Seeing the vibrant colors of the King caused her to recall one of her late afternoons at the Bevin House...

❧

SAINT-EXUPÉRY WAS SITTING near the fireplace when Adele entered, arriving on time, as usual. He grinned when he saw her and shot up from his chair like an eager child.

"Mademoiselle, come see what I've been working on," he shouted, his enthusiasm infectious.

As Adele removed her coat, happy to be received with such exhilaration, Saint-Exupéry led her to the table and gathered together several typed-written pages. He held them close to his chest, excited.

"I want you to read what I wrote. It's a fantasy. Do you like fantasy?"

Adele nodded yes. He handed her the pages. She looked at him, thrilled, though didn't show it and started to read.

"Wait! Not like this. Come. Sit," he said and led her to a more comfortable chair and helped her into it. Adele smiled, liking the attention. He then grabbed a floor lamp and pulled it closer to her for more light. Adele was touched by his hospitality and nervousness.

As she started to read, Saint-Exupéry wandered over to a window. He lit a cigarette and stared out. A moment passed and Adele chuckled. Saint-Exupéry quickly looked over at her.

"What? What is so funny?" he asked with an edginess in his voice.

Adele glanced above the pages and said, "The boa. The hat."

"It's true!" exclaimed Saint-Exupéry. "I drew a boa constrictor that swallowed an elephant when I was a small child," he said followed by a sad sigh. "But people saw only a hat. It discouraged me, so I gave up drawing."

The memory pained him as he looked out the window again and quietly puffed on his cigarette. Adele watched sympathetically then went back to reading. She put her hand to her heart at one point, deeply moved by his words. Then, after some time passed, finished and carefully shuffled the pages back into a neat stack.

"This is written by the boy you once were," she said softly. "You were not understood, were you?"

Saint-Exupéry turned and looked at her. Adele rose from her chair, embarrassed at having said something so personal. Saint-Exupéry approached her, but said nothing.

Adele asked boldly, "Would you allow me to translate your story into English?"

Saint-Exupéry smiled, appreciating her offer. "My publisher has already hired a translator," he said with regret.

Disappointed, Adele handed his pages back to him and spoke candidly. "It's a lovely story. There is a sadness to it, something seems unattainable for you."

She looked up at him and saw he was staring at her. She suddenly became self-conscious and said with a blush, "Oh, forgive me. I am so familiar with your other books that I feel I understand you. Your books, to me, they read like a series of wonderful letters from an understanding friend."

The look on Saint-Exupéry's face mingled eagerness with tenderness as he took a step closer to her. "Are you a writer?" he asked, his voice filled with hope.

"No," Adele answered, shaking her head.

He asked with longing, "Why don't you try it? Then I, too, may experience wonderful letters from an understanding friend."

He stared at her as if wanting, *needing*, to connect. Adele would have loved to say yes, yes to anything he would ask of her, but her sense of propriety got in the way and she answered with an air of detached directness, "Monsieur, I am not a writer. I am a teacher."

Saint-Exupéry's hope for a connection was dashed. It was obvious from the sorrowful expression on his face.

"Oh. I see," he said as he managed a smile, nodded and stepped away from her…

❧

TEARS FILLED ADELE'S EYES at the memory as she stared down at the watercolor King. A single tear of deep regret fell and hit it. The tiny splash startled her. Before it spread, she quickly dried it with her finger then held it close to her lips and blew on it to dry. Having it so close to her mouth she felt the urge to kiss it, and would have when suddenly the phone rang.

She placed the watercolor back on the table, composed herself and went to her kitchen to answer it. The voice of a young man at the other end, asked politely and directly if he was speaking with Adele. Adele suspiciously replied yes.

"Miss Breaux, I'm a representative from Knopf Publishers in Manhattan. We've reviewed your inquiry as well as the chapters you've sent and would like to see more of your work," the young man stated.

Adele couldn't believe what she was hearing. A major publisher was *interested*?! After a short pause of surprise, she replied, "Y-yes, yes, of course. I have a couple more chapters I can send to you.

"That would be great, Miss Breaux. Send us whatever you have. We'll look it over and call you to schedule a meeting."

Adele was trying hard to contain her sudden and unexpected joy as she bade the young man goodbye in return and hung up the phone. She stood frozen for several moments then, wanting to share the terrific news, rushed to the front door and opened it hoping Morris was still outside. But his car was gone. A moment of disappointment hit, but by the time she closed the door, she was smiling.

"I'll tell him later," she muttered happily and quickly went over to her table and sat down. She scanned her notes, seeing where she left off then gleefully scrolled a fresh piece of paper in her typewriter and began typing feverishly with renewed determination.

Chapter 20

The Story

A week later, Norman was pacing slowly between the rows of desks in his classroom as he read aloud to his students Juliet's soliloquy from Act 3 of Shakespeare's *Romeo & Juliet*. As he passed Jack's desk he stopped. The chair was empty. Norman paused for a moment, dismayed that he may have failed in reaching his student, then continued on with the soliloquy.

That evening, Norman sat at his kitchen table, hardly touching the food on his plate. Josephine was busy trying to keep a bottle of milk in her son's mouth, but noticed Norman's disheartened mood.

"Everything all right?" she asked.

"I guess I'm not that hungry. Something happened at school that has me worried."

Josephine looked at her husband, waiting for him to tell her.

"It's one of my students…Jack. Remember I told you about him?"

Josephine nodded, but wasn't much interested. She knew Norman was dedicated to his job and was supportive of it, but when it came to specific times of the day, such as whenever they shared a meal at the table, she preferred the discussion be about family or the house.

"He hasn't been in class for the past couple of days. I'm worried he's going to drop out again. I've tried talking with him, but nothing gets through. I thought about calling his parents, but I get the feeling if I did it would only alienate him more. I think there's a way to reach him, but I haven't figured it out yet. But I need to soon because I'm going to have to tell Morris what's happening and once it's out of my hands, I think the kid will just give up."

As Norman spoke, Josephine spent the time looking at her son. She glanced at Norman only once and simply nodded politely.

"I think the next time I see him, if I see him, I'm going to have to really talk to him, use my authority, but do it in a way that won't scare him off," Norman continued much to the chagrin of his wife.

"Norman –," began Josephine, "Can we talk about something else?"

"Sure. This is just something weighing on my mind."

"I understand," she said as she stood, lifted Adam and held him in her arms. "But while you're sitting here putting all your time and effort into this teenager, know that you've hardly paid any attention to your own son."

Norman felt that was unfair and told her so. Josephine bounced Adam in her arms and said, "What's unfair is you get to go to your job while I stay here all day with our son. Not that I'm complaining, but I'm getting tired of spending my days taking care of Adam only to have you come home and have to listen to you talk about school. Sometimes I'd just like to talk about something else."

Norman looked at Josephine, completely understanding

her position, but didn't know what to say. Josephine waited a moment for him to respond, but once she realized nothing was forthcoming, she said flatly, "I'm going to put Adam down for the night," and walked out of the room.

"I'll take out the garbage," Norman shouted, hoping she heard. It was the least he could do, but knew it wasn't going to really help the tension that was already there.

He got up and collected the few dishes that were on the table and placed them in the sink, then he grabbed the trash, rolled and sealed the brown paper bag it was in, and carried it outside to the end of the driveway where the garbage can was placed for the morning pick up.

After he lifted the metal lid from the can and tossed the bag inside, he sealed it shut and glanced over at Adele's house. He could see Adele washing her dishes through her small, curtained kitchen window. She appeared to be in a happy mood, smiling as she placed a water-dripped pan on the drying rack.

Something about seeing Adele in this mood caused Norman to grin, so he strolled casually toward her house. From a window of his house, Josephine peered out through a curtain and watched him with a resentful look on her face.

As Norman walked the small path that led to Adele's front door, Adele saw him from her kitchen window, tapped on it, caught his attention and waved. Norman gave a friendly wave back. Inside, Adele quickly dried her hands and headed for the door. She grabbed her sweater on the way, wanting to greet Norman outside for some fresh air.

When she opened the door, she stepped outside just as Norman arrived.

"I was putting out the trash and saw you," said Norman. "I thought I'd come over and say hi."

"I'm so glad you did," said Adele as she tucked her arms in the sleeves of her sweater then folded them to brace herself from the chilly night air. "It's much warmer than I thought it would be, being that it's still winter."

"Yeah, the weather has been a little odd lately," said Norman as he looked up at the sky.

Adele looked at him and sensed a hint of melancholy. "Is everything all right, Norman?" she asked.

Norman feigned a smile. "Yeah. I'm just concerned about a student. The same one I've been telling you about...Jack."

"I thought he returned," said Adele.

"He did, but he's gone again. Or, he hasn't been to class. I don't know. Sometimes I think I care too much. Jo thinks I do," he sighed then shrugged. "Guess I can't help it."

"He's important to you, this student," said Adele with understanding.

"He is," said Norman without hesitation. "They all are."

"That's something your wife will never understand, Norman. Don't be upset with her. It's like any profession someone is passionate about. For instance, golf. I'll never understand why people play that silly game, nor do I have any patience to listen to two men going on about it, but they would have the same reaction if they had to listen to me discuss the workings of a classroom."

"I guess you're right," said Norman.

"We feel responsible for our student's lives, that's why we get so fervent with their education. We understand the true value of it," said Adele talking like a true sage. Then she said confidently, "I'm not worried about Jack, Norman. I know he will be all right."

"How can you be so sure?"

"Because he has *you*."

Norman smiled. "Thanks, Adele," he said, feeling a lot better. Then he realized she was happier then the last time he saw her. "Hey, you seem in better spirits."

Adele smiled. "I have a publisher considering my book," she said with a sly smile.

"No kidding? That's fantastic!" Norman exclaimed, almost wanting to hug her, but didn't.

"It is, yes," Adele said proudly.

"See? You just had to keep at it," Norman said nodding his head and grinning.

"I did, thank you," Adele said sincerely.

Norman looked at her, very pleased, then it occurred to him time had passed. "Well, I better get back inside. It's getting cold, and Jo is probably wondering where I am."

"Yes. Good night, Norman. I'll see you soon," she said as he began to walk away. He turned and looked back at her. She gave him a small wave then tucked her hand back under her folded arm. She watched him cross the street, walk up his short driveway and go inside.

Before going into her own house, Adele looked up at the sky and studied the stars that twinkled brightly. A smile came to her lips thinking about Norman's dedication to his rebellious student because it reminded her of one of her own...

৩৯৵৻

ADELE ENTERED THE PARLOR room of the Bevin House ready to get to work. She walked right up to the table and noisily plopped down her satchel. Saint-Exupéry was on the other side of the table, busy working on his watercolors. He glanced up and watched, silently perturbed, as she unraveled the scarf from around her neck and took off her coat.

"Mademoiselle, must we have a lesson today?" he asked sounding like an impatient schoolboy.

Adele smiled, now used to his foot-dragging attitude.

"Yes. We must complete our verbs," she answered.

Saint-Exupéry shook his head and, ignoring her, went back to his water coloring. Adele walked around the table and stood next to him. She peered over his shoulder, purposely making it uncomfortable for him to work.

"Mademoiselle…" he said gruffly, and moved a few inches away from her.

Adele wasn't offended. In fact, she tried not to chuckle. She looked again at the watercolors and began studying them. Suddenly, her eyes widened, inspired. "Monsieur, I have an idea!" she said excitedly.

This caught Saint-Exupéry's attention, having never seen her become so animated before.

"Please, lay out your watercolors and sketches in the order of your story," she requested.

Saint-Exupéry looked at her, perplexed yet intrigued, and did just what she asked. It took him several minutes to gather them and block them in their right order. Some of the artwork was completed, others not. When he was done, he looked at Adele as if to say, 'What next?'

"You will now tell me your story…in English," she said with a smile.

Saint-Exupéry shot her an odd look. "But I cannot speak English," he said.

"You will today," she responded confidently. "Let's start." She pointed at a sketch of the Little Prince. "First, explain this little blonde boy to me."

Saint-Exupéry was pleased to have her interested in his work, so he explained simply, "He is a little prince, from a distant planet."

"Where is he now? Earth?" asked Adele.

"Yes. A pilot crashed his plane in the desert and that's where he met this little prince."

"I see," said Adele. "So, the verbs we have now are…a pilot *crashed* his plane and *met* the prince. Repeat that."

Saint-Exupéry slowly repeated in English, "*C-crashed* the plane. *Met* the prince."

"Very good," said Adele very pleased. "Now, tell me more," she encouraged.

"The Little Prince fell in love with a rose, but he caught her lying one day and no longer trusted her and that is why he was on earth. To cure his loneliness."

"All right," said Adele, slowly putting it together, "So, the prince *fell*…that's the verb…in love, then caught her *lying* and no longer *trusted* her. The last verb is *cure*. Let's repeat those."

Saint-Exupéry looked at Adele. She pointed to the watercolors that matched his story as he repeated the verbs. The first one she pointed to was of the Little Prince.

"He *fell*," Saint-Exupéry repeated slowly in English, "And he *caught* her *lee-lying* and did not true-trust her. To *cue-cure* his loneliness."

"Very good," exclaimed Adele, proud of her student.

Saint-Exupéry grinned. "We continue?" he asked, enjoying this.

"Yes. What happens next?"

"The Little Prince meets narrow-minded grown-ups. First, a King," he said pointing to a newer, completed watercolor of the King. Then he pointed to each different water colored character and explained, "A man of vanity…a drunkard…a businessman…a lamplighter…a geographer. All alone in their occupations."

"*Meets* is the verb," said Adele, trying to keep up with the lesson, but being pulled into the engrossing story.

"*Meets* them individually," repeated Saint-Exupéry. "Yes. And the Little Prince cannot understand why they need to dictate to people, or be admired and to own everything."

"Dictate?" asked Adele. "Who dictates?"

"The King," replied Saint-Exupéry as he grinned at Adele, recalling the watercolor he gave to her several weeks earlier.

Adele eyed him, getting the message behind his grin. "I don't dictate," she insisted.

Saint-Exupéry laughed at this. "Dictate. Is verb?" he asked instead, as if only she would know.

"Yes. It's a verb," said Adele wanting to get off the subject, "Let's move along here."

Saint-Exupéry chuckled then looked at his watercolors. He pointed to the Geographer.

"The Geographer tells the Little Prince that flowers do not live forever, so the Little Prince begins to miss his rose," he said, as sadness reflected in his eyes.

Adele saw this and was touched by his sensitivity. She said softly, "*Tells* is the verb. *Live*...and *miss* are, too."

Saint-Exupéry repeats, "*Tells...live...miss.*"

Adele nodded, although she was beginning to lose interest in the lesson and wanted to hear more of the story. Saint-Exupéry pointed to the watercolor of the Geographer again.

"The Geographer tells the Little Prince to go to earth. This is how he lands in the desert and *meets* the pilot. Then..." Saint-Exupéry began as he reached for another watercolor, "He meets a snake."

He showed Adele a sketch of a snake.

"What does the snake do?" asked Adele.

"He speaks in riddles," Saint-Exupéry said in a whisper. "He tells of a poison that can send the Little Prince back to the heavens...if he so wishes."

Adele stared at the sketch of the snake; not liking the dark turn the story was taking.

"But the Little Prince ignores him," said Saint-Exupéry. "He leaves and finds a rose garden."

"I see," said Adele, looking relieved to hear this.

"But seeing the rose garden makes the Little Prince sad. His rose told him she was the only one of her kind."

"Oh," said Adele, shaking her head. "She lied."

"Yes," said Saint-Exupéry. "But then…" he began as he reached for a bright looking watercolor of a fox, "The Little Prince *meets* a fox. And the fox tells the prince that his love for the rose makes her unique and therefore he is responsible for her."

"Responsible?" asked Adele.

"Yes. We are all responsible for whomever we love and care for, are we not?"

Adele was wordless by this point, her lesson forgotten; she was now being taught by her student. Saint-Exupéry placed the watercolor of the fox back on the table and told her the pilot and the Little Prince agreed that too many people did not see what was truly important in life.

He then held up a smaller watercolor of the Little Prince. In the watercolor, the Little Prince was looking up at a star in the sky with his arms covering his face.

"The Little Prince," said Saint-Exupéry softly, "Made plans with the snake to return to his rose as the pilot fixed his plane and prepared to go home. Then…" he said even softer, "The snake bites the Little Prince and…he falls to the sand…without making a sound."

Adele was moved beyond measure as Saint-Exupéry placed the watercolor of the Little Prince with the others and said with a sigh, "The pilot misses the Little Prince, but takes comfort when he cannot find the body of the Little Prince anywhere. He believes the Little Prince has returned to his planet, and to his rose. He also believes that one day he will hear from someone that the Little Prince has returned."

Saint-Exupéry then placed both hands on the edge of the

table and leaned forward, staring at his watercolors and contemplating the story he just shared. Adele saw this and stood in awe, realizing fully that not only did her feelings for him deepen but that she was in the presence of greatness.

Chapter 21

New School

The new high school on Laurel Hill Road was still under construction with bulldozers on the property and dozens of workers moving about. At the center of all the activity was a small group of teachers, dressed in sweaters and overcoats, waiting to be given a special tour of the nearly completed building by Principal Allardice.

Carmen was among the group. She stood out, as usual, the center of attention, boasting about something regarding herself. Unbeknownst to her, she was being carefully eyed by Adele who was sitting with Morris in his car in the parking lot.

"Are you ready for this? Morris asked, unsure.

"Yes. I like to see progress," Adele answered without taking her eyes off of Carmen.

Morris saw Adele staring at Carmen and started to have second thoughts about bringing her. It wasn't so much Adele's attitude toward Carmen that worried him, but what inspecting the new school that she would never be allowed to teach in might do to her spirits. Adele looked at Morris and saw his worried expression.

"I'm OK, Morris," she said, bothered by his overprotectiveness. "Let's go."

Morris nodded and they got out of the car, though neither rushed to approach the group, and made sure to hang in the back as Principal Allardice led them all into the building. After first showing them where the administration office will be, as well as the gymnastic facilities and music rooms, Principal Allardice introduced them to the expansive "commons" area.

"This space will be for students to socialize, and move more freely to and from classes," he said proudly as he held his arms out wide emphasizing the large space, and grinned. "Quite a contrast from the narrow hallways we've all been used to, and a better way for the staff to monitor."

The teachers nodded in agreement, liking very much what they were seeing.

"Now, come this way and I will show you where the students' and teachers' lunchrooms will be."

As the group began to follow Principal Allardice into a large dining area where workers were plastering drywall, Adele grabbed Morris' arm, held him back and whispered, "Let's go see where the language department will be."

Morris and Adele waited until they all entered the cafeteria then "ditched" the group and headed in the opposite direction. They walked carefully on papered floors, down a half finished wing, passing construction workers to a freshly painted part of the building.

"It's over here," Morris said as he guided Adele into a large classroom, bigger than the ones she had been used to. The room was empty except for several power tools on the floor and taped windows. When Adele stepped inside, she was instantly in awe. Morris entered and watched as Adele looked around in wide-eyed wonder.

"Not too shabby, eh?" he asked as he looked up at the ceiling.

"It's fantastic, Morris! Oh, what a thrill it was to be on the committee for this. A school designed by teachers, not architects, as it should be, and it turned out splendidly. Although it will never belong to me, it's nice to know I was a part of it in some way," she said with a sincere, wistful smile.

As Morris stepped up to her, ready to her take her arm and give it a tender, supportive squeeze, Carmen appeared in the doorway, shattering the mood.

"Oh! I see you've found *my* classroom!" she exclaimed, obnoxiously.

Morris held his breath, hoping there wouldn't be a showdown. Adele, biting her tongue, feigned a gracious smile and said, "Yes, it's a beautiful room."

Carmen entered, acting like the queen of her castle, and continued to boast, "It is! I was wondering, should my desk go over here, on this side...or over on that side, by the windows?"

"It's entirely up to you," Adele said dismissively.

"Morris?" Carmen asked, doing her best to engage him in her little game.

Doing *his* best to be polite, Morris said weakly, "Uh...by the windows, I guess."

"Yes," said Carmen in a grand manner, "I think you're right." She then turned to Adele, still acting superior. "So, Adele, what have you been up to? How's retirement?"

"It's been good," answered Adele with a strained smile, "I've been keeping myself busy."

"I heard you were writing a book."

"That's right," Adele replied, then turned her back to Carmen, seeming disinterested. Morris watched Adele, wondering why she wasn't taking the opportunity to boast about it.

"How's it coming along?" asked Carmen, being more a snoop than actually interested.

"Fine," answered Adele, not turning to look at her.

Morris was completely baffled watching these two women playing this passive-aggressive game.

"Well, don't keep me in suspense, Adele. Tell me what the book's about," huffed Carmen in frustration.

Adele slowly turned and said with hoity pride, "Well, if you must know, it's about my personal relationship with Monsieur de Saint-Exupéry."

Morris tried to hide his smile. *There's* the Adele he knew, and from her tone, also knew she was ready for battle.

"Oh, right," said Carmen, snidely, "You were his *help*."

Morris winced. That was a low blow, he thought, and worried this might get ugly.

Adele's eye narrowed. "I was his *language instructor*," she retorted trying not to let her annoyance show.

"For a few weeks," said Carmen flippantly.

"For several *months*," corrected Adele.

"Many, *many* years ago," said Carmen, doing her best to belittle any importance to Adele's association.

"We maintained a friendship," said Adele, looking ready to slug her.

"Then he died shortly after, didn't he?" Carmen asked in a cruel way with a malicious smile on her face.

Morris winced again. There went the knife.

Adele flinched slightly at Carmen's words, then responded delicately, "Yes, but not his books, nor his legacy, which I intend to preserve."

"Your own personal mission," Carmen said in a catty way. "I see."

Adele looked over at Morris. Her eyes pleaded for his help with this wretched woman. Seeing this he quickly interjected.

"Adele has interest from Knopf Publishing. Looks promising. Going from being a teacher to being an author...that's pretty darn impressive."

Adele smiled when she saw Carmen's deflated expression.

"Oh. Well...congratulations," Carmen said reluctantly. "You'll have to sign a copy for me once it's published."

"You'll be the first," replied Adele, now grinning. Revenge is sweet.

Knowing she had nothing to top Adele publishing a book, Carmen said in a tone that made it seem she was suddenly being called away, "Yes, well, I should get back to the group. It was good seeing you again, Adele. And you, too, Morris."

Morris nodded politely. Carmen hurried for the exit. As she was about to leave the room, her shoe slid on the papered floor causing her to lose her balance. She slid haphazardly; with her arms flailing about trying not to fall. She quickly regained her composure and, without turning around, trotted fast out the door. Adele put her hand to her lips, hiding her laughter.

Morris chuckled then let out a sigh of relief. "That went better than I thought it would." He looked at Adele and asked, "How'd I do?"

"Just as you promised, mashed potato right in the eye. A direct hit!" she answered, giving him an appreciative "thumbs up," then they both broke into laughter.

ॐ

THAT SAME DAY, NORMAN was at school monitoring a hallway during his free period. As he lazily strolled a busy wing, he would stop and chat with friendly students and remind late ones to get to class. While doing this, he saw Jack near the end of the hall at his locker. Seeing him made Norman anxious. He wanted to be sure not to make this kid turn away, and worried about how. As the hallway cleared, Norman gently approached Jack in a casual, non-threatening manner.

"Hello, Jack," he said.

Jack shot a sideways glance at Norman then quickly slammed his locker door shut. Norman flinched at this.

"Angry about something?" he asked.

Jack turned and looked at Norman. His right eye was black and swollen. Norman was quickly taken aback.

"My God! What happened?" Norman asked, shocked to see such a horrible bruise.

Jack looked away, shrugged and said nothing.

"Is it –" Norman began reaching out as if to touch Jack's swollen eye, though he wouldn't have. It was only a reactive gesture.

Jack flinched and took a defensive step back.

"Sorry, I wasn't going to –" Norman began then stopped. Seeing that Jack was on edge and ready to walk away, he quickly changed the subject. "Why haven't you been in class?"

"I don't know. I'm not learning nothing," Jack grunted, bored.

"*Anything*. It's, 'I'm not learning *anything*,'" corrected Norman.

"OK," said Jack, glancing quickly up then looking away again, "I'm not learning *anything*."

Norman smiled. "You just did."

Jack didn't return his smile. He looked away, resigned, and muttered, "I'm not gonna be here much longer. I'm thinking of dropping out for good," then added angrily, "And I'm not writing any stupid papers."

Norman kept a neutral look on his face even though inside he was panicked at the thought of losing his student. It was something he couldn't bear, and went against everything he stood for. He had to think fast, knowing this was more than likely his only chance to save this kid.

"Look, forget the papers, OK? Just come to class," Norman

said as he leaned on the lockers to put himself at Jack's physical level and looked him straight in the eyes.

Jack glanced at him, suspiciously. "Just come to class?"

"Yeah. Do you think you can at least do that?" asked Norman.

Jack didn't know whether or not to be insulted by the question. Did Norman think he was a moron? "Yeah, I can do *that*," he answered more out of anger than wanting to make a promise. "But what's the catch?"

Norman smiled and spoke sincerely. "There is no catch. I just don't want you to give up. And I'd also like you to get some ice for that eye."

Jack, confused by the whole exchange, said nothing and walked away. Norman watched, hoping he said the right thing. Just then, another student who was standing nearby, and overheard the conversation, walked over to Norman. He was more studious looking; the kind that made sure all of his homework was done on time.

"You wanna know how he got the black eye?" the student asked as he glanced around to make sure no one could overhear. "His father did it."

Norman looked at him, shocked. The student added, "He'll deny it, but we all know. Seriously, Mr. O., forget about him. He's just one of those guys."

The student turned and walked away. Norman stood there trying to process this information about Jack, and wondered what to do with it.

Chapter 22

Fluent French

Inspired by seeing the new high school earlier that morning and putting Carmen in her place, Adele neatly shuffled the most recent chapter of her book that she had on her dining room table, put on her coat and hurried out the door to Norman's house. It was late afternoon and surely he would be home, she thought. When she approached Norman's front door, she knocked. At first there was no answer. Adele stood and waited.

From a window, Josephine peaked out to see who was at the door. When she saw it was Adele, she rolled her eyes and moved away from the window.

Adele didn't see Josephine and knocked again. A long moment passed before Josephine finally opened it, looking bothered.

"Hello, Josephine!" Adele said gaily in a happy, sing-songy voice.

Josephine folded her arms and said in an icy tone, "I like to be called Jo."

"Oh, yes. Forgive me," said Adele, sensing, though confused by, her annoyance. "Well, *Jo*...is Norman at home?"

"No," Josephine flatly replied.

Adele, still smiling, held out her small stack of papers. "Well, would you be so kind and give him this? It's another chapter of my book," she said proudly. "I have an appointment in the city tomorrow with a publisher, which is why I have been diligent in getting these pages completed, and would like to be able to tell them there will be more coming."

Josephine didn't take the pages. She looked at Adele suspiciously. "You know, Adele, you've been spending a lot of time with my husband. Don't you think it's beginning to seem a little like, you know…"

Adele was surprised by her odd insinuation and said defensively, "I am spending time with your husband because…" she then stopped and smiled. Knowing Josephine meant, she decided to pretend she meant something else, something more *"illicit"* and said, "My dear, I am seventy, *not* seventeen."

Josephine looked at Adele, puzzled, then quickly realized the gross misunderstanding and stammered, embarrassed, "No. Oh, no…it's not *that*. I was just…I…what I meant was…"

Adele stared at Josephine, innocently. Josephine stammered for a few more seconds then quickly snatched the pages from Adele's hand as she sighed in defeat, "Oh, never mind. Just give me the pages."

"Thank you…*Jo*," Adele said with a slight grin.

Josephine muttered, "no problem" as she turned, went back into the house and closed the door. Adele stood there for a moment, trying not to laugh then started back to her house. As she did, the smile on her face grew when she began to recall a memory…

ADELE WAS SITTING IN her apartment preparing a quiz for her students when the phone rang. She got up and answered it with a cheerful hello then cringed when she heard Saint-Exupéry's wife, Consuelo, on the other end. Consuelo had phoned to tell Adele that her husband was in Washington and would not be back until that Friday, so there was to be no lessons that week. Adele hid her disappointment, said she understood and thanked Consuelo for calling. She was also relieved the call was a brief one.

As Adele was about to hang up, Consuelo stopped her and said in an accusatory tone, "Miss Breaux...you spend a lot of time with my husband. What is it that you are doing with him?"

Adele was taken aback, but answered carefully and truthfully, "I am teaching him English."

"What else?" Consuelo demanded.

What else? What did she mean by that, Adele wondered and was unsure how to respond, so she didn't. Thankfully, Consuelo was too caught up in her accusation to notice and said, "Tonio says these lessons interfere with his writing."

Hearing that wounded Adele, even though she knew to take whatever Consuelo had to say with a grain of salt. Then Consuelo added, "But he says when you are here, he feels at ease, and after his time with you, he is happier and able to write more freely into the night. Why is that?"

Hearing that quickly erased any hurtful feelings Adele was starting to have. It was also wonderful to know that she in some way inspired him to write. Adele smiled, extremely flattered, but didn't let on that she was. She made sure to sound perplexed when she told Consuelo, "I-I have no explanation. Perhaps I am simply being a good teacher."

"You are *hiding* something," Consuelo hissed. "You are doing something else with my husband, but not saying."

Adele didn't know how to respond to that, especially with the obviously hateful underlying tone Consuelo took, so she remained silent.

A moment passed before Consuelo broke that silence with a flippant, "Nevertheless…you will return next week?"

Adele was flabbergasted. The woman practically accused her of having an affair with her husband and yet was asking if she would return? Adele, tired of the chaotic conversation, said simply, "Yes."

Consuelo concluded with, "Very well. Goodbye," and hung up the phone before Adele could say goodbye herself.

Adele looked at the phone's receiver in shock then hung up. Rattled by the entire exchange, she held her hand to her chest to help settle her nerves. As she walked back to her desk, the corners of her mouth started to grin. No one had ever accused her of fooling around with any man, let alone someone as great as Saint-Exupéry. Where once such an insinuation would have appalled her, she now found it most flattering…

ADELE HAD REACHED HER front door by the time she finished recalling the memory. She paused thinking about what had made her invoked it and turned to look back at Norman's house. She suddenly felt bad playing such a game with Josephine, and putting her in an uncomfortable position. It was unfair. She liked Josephine very much, and needed to let her know that any inkling of romance in regard to Norman was the farthest thing from her mind. Just in case Josephine did have suspicions. She quickly turned and made her way back toward their house.

Adele approached the front door and knocked urgently. Within seconds the door sprang open. Josephine was startled to see Adele again and said "Hello," with a puzzled look on her face.

Adele had no preparation in how to assure Josephine that there was nothing was going on between herself and Norman, so she did what came best and easiest…she spoke in French.

"You need to understand that your husband, as considerate, kind and virile he may be, holds no interest for me romantically. And vice-versa, I'm sure, though I would consider myself quite the catch."

Josephine looked at Adele confused and shocked. Adele finished with a terse, "Bonjour," then turned and began to walk away.

As she did, Josephine shouted back at her, also in French, *"Thank you for putting my mind to rest on the matter."*

Adele stopped and froze. Josephine spoke French? Oh, no. She was too embarrassed to turn around, and thought about making a run for it, but knew that she couldn't and had to face the uncomfortable disgrace. When she did, she saw Josephine covering her mouth, trying not to laugh.

"You speak French?" asked Adele as she slowly walked back to the door, her face beet red.

"Fluently," replied Josephine.

"So, you understood what I…" began Adele.

"Every word," nodded Josephine, now unable to contain her laughter. "So, you're quite the catch, eh?"

Adele looked down at the ground, mortified. "I-I don't know what to say…"

"Well, whatever you say, first make sure the other person won't understand you," Josephine chuckled.

Adele looked at her; relieved she had a sense of humor.

"Would you like to come in for some tea, Adele?" offered Josephine.

Adele was touched by her offer and replied in French, *"Only if you have the time…Jo."*

Josephine answered back in French, "I do," as she held opened the door and Adele stepped inside.

Chapter 23

Recommendation

*A*dele sat comfortably in the cockpit, tapping her fingers against her seat's armrest and humming a happy tune. In the seat next to her sat Saint-Exupéry who stared straight ahead, silently flying his plane through baby blue skies and white, cottony clouds. He glanced at her momentarily, then looked ahead again without saying a word. Adele noticed this and began to hum a little louder, hoping to get his attention.

After a moment passed, Saint-Exupéry leaned forward, reached into his pocket and pulled out a crumpled pack of Gauloise cigarettes. He flicked one from the pack, placed it between his lips then shoved the pack back in his pocket. Adele watched how he then skillfully pulled out a small, gold lighter and lit the cigarette with ease. He inhaled, long and slow, then exhaled never taking his eyes off the skies in front of him.

Adele watched the smoke linger steadily for a moment, then disappear behind them. Once it did, she said with a smile, "I may have a publisher."

Saint-Exupéry didn't respond. He continued to stare ahead, taking small, lazy puffs on his cigarette.

"It's exciting, isn't it?" she asked.

Again, Saint-Exupéry said nothing.

"I suppose you're used to it. You've written enough books," Adele said with a sigh. "Still, don't you recall the first time you published a book? The thrill of it?"

"Mademoiselle," Saint-Exupéry began as he flicked ashes on the floor of the plane, "Your book is about me?"

"Yes, when you came to Northport...Asharoken...the Bevin House."

Saint-Exupéry looked over at her. "Are you in it?"

"Yes, of course," replied Adele, happily. "I was there."

"Then it is about us," he exclaimed.

"Well, no," said Adele, "It's more about what I remember...about you."

"And what is it that you remember most about me?" he asked.

"Oh, many things," began Adele, a smile coming to her face.

"Name the most important," he requested.

Adele was surprised by the question and looked out at the sky in front of her, thinking hard. Saint-Exupéry grinned.

"Was it my eyes?" he asked, looking at her dreamily.

Adele looked at him and said curtly, "No."

"My smile?" he asked grinning broadly at her.

"No," she said, trying not to give in to his playfulness.

Saint-Exupéry pouted, ready to give up, then shouted, "I know! It was my irresistible charm!"

Adele looked at him again and rolled her eyes disapprovingly.

Saint-Exupéry threw up his hands in defeat and said, "Then it can only be my skill in mastering the English language."

"That is most certainly not it," Adele said.

Saint-Exupéry laughed out loud. "What then? Tell me....please," he begged.

Adele turned, faced him, and spoke sincerely, "It was the moments when I sat in my car in the driveway of the Bevin

House…*right after I parked and before I went inside, knowing that when I did, I would be seeing you. Those few precious seconds."*

Saint-Exupéry looked at her, touched. Then he roared with laughter. Adele glared at him, wounded and insulted. "What's so funny?"

"That is the most important thing you remember about me? Being alone in your car? I was not even there!" he bellowed.

"Oh, but you were," argued Adele.

"How? Explain, please."

Adele opened her mouth to tell him, but she couldn't find the words. She tilted her head sideways trying to think how best to explain it. Saint-Exupéry watched her, waiting, when slowly an understanding smile drew across his face.

"Mademoiselle…" he began, his eyes looking deeply into hers, "I was in your heart, and always will be." He then placed his hand over his heart, and gently patted it.

Adele's heart melted, her face blushed. She moved forward in her seat to get closer to Saint-Exupéry when suddenly the plane shook violently and dropped straight down, as if it was falling, then pulled back up. Adele's seatbelt prevented her from flying forward, although she was slammed back as if an invisible force was holding her. She was able to reach and grab the plane's console with one hand and her seat with another. The blush drained from her face; it was now ashen with fear.

"Monsieur! Monsieur!" she screamed as she looked to him for help. He was gone.

Her eyes widened in terror when the plane took a nosedive. Outside, the clouds spun and parted fast allowing her to see the earth coming closer and closer at neck-breaking speed. She covered her eyes with her arms and screamed.

Adele sprung up in bed once again, gasping for air. Sweat was dripping down her face and neck. Her hands shook as they clutched the sheets. Realizing it was another nightmare she felt her heart slowly return to its normal beat. She let out a deep sigh of relief then reached around and grabbed her pillows. She propped them up against her headboard, leaned back, then covered her face in her hands and wept.

Later that morning, Adele watched the light snow fall all around as she sat in her car at the East Northport train station. Wearing her best coat and gloves, she sat stoically waiting for the train that would take her into Manhattan where she would deliver several new chapters of her manuscript and discuss, hopefully, the publishing of her beloved book.

She had thought about driving into the city herself, but with the weather being unpredictable, as it usually was when nearing the end of winter, she didn't want to risk getting stuck in traffic and be late for her appointment. She had come too far to jeopardize this opportunity.

Her thoughts stayed focus on how she would best present herself and the work. Although she felt the butterflies in her stomach at the prospect of her book being published, she knew this was business and had to keep her feelings in check. Still, her heart did race a bit faster when she heard the sound of her arriving train's whistle. "This is it," she thought to herself as she quickly collected her purse and satchel from the passenger seat, made sure she had her ticket in hand and got out of the car.

The ride on the Long Island Railroad was long and mundane. Adele was relieved once she arrived at Penn Station, though upon climbing the stairs from the train's platform, it saddened her to see again soldiers kissing and bidding farewell to their girlfriends and families, only this time their destination was Vietnam. "Hadn't we learned?" she wondered sadly. She knew that war, though sometimes necessary, only caused great destruction and loss. Those thoughts made her clutch tighter to her satchel, its contents containing the story of her own loss from a war so many years ago.

In the city, the snow swirled more aggressively, but didn't stick to the pavement, which Adele appreciated since she was wearing heels. If it had been spring, she would have happily walked the twenty-two blocks or so since she loved the sights and glamour of Manhattan, but on this day she was forced to take a cab, and forced to get out a block away from the publishing company since the street was congested with cars and the cab was barely moving. Again, she would walk the block instead of risking being late for such an important meeting.

A twinge of excitement shot through her when she looked up and saw the address for Knopf Publishers engraved on a stunning marble skyscraper just above a stately looking entrance. She paused for a moment to savor the moment then took a deep breath, released it and entered with stoic purpose and pride.

Adele went through the motions of going to the lobby's front desk and asking what floor her appointment was on, then riding the elevator up. She loosened the scarf around her neck and daintily shook off any flakes of snow that still clung to her coat. The smell of the elevator car made her smile slightly. Its scent was much like that of an old, treasured book mixed faintly with some male executive's musk cologne. It was how a publisher's elevator should smell, she thought.

Once she reached her floor, and the doors slid opened, she stepped out into a sparse yet intimidating reception area where a striking female receptionist sitting at a desk greeted her. Adele's arrival was announced to whomever the receptionist spoke on the phone then was asked to take a seat and wait, which wasn't long. About five minutes passed before a young executive stuck his head out from a door and asked her in a friendly manner to please step inside.

Moments later, Adele was sitting anxiously at a long table inside an even larger conference room with glass windows that looked out at other skyscrapers. Her chair was made of a masculine looking leather. Across the table from her sat a young publishing executive in his mid-thirties. He was the friendly, scholarly type in a tweed suit with a bowtie who exuded a slightly condescending air for business.

"We read what you've sent and were impressed by your," he paused, searching for the right word, "*documentation*," he said with a slight smile.

"I was there as his instructor," said Adele, subtly trying to stress the validity of her work. "But I was privy to his talent and his brilliance."

"Right," the executive said as he casually sat back, "Well, perhaps that's what's missing. Your book is interesting, don't get me wrong, but today readers want more."

"More?" Adele asked, unsure.

"Yes. Right now, your book as is…it's just a lot of facts," he answered as he sat forward. "Facts are necessary, of course, but it being 1965, readers are looking for something more to hold their interest. Can you recall anything that might make the book more…*provocative*? Anything that might have happened between, say, you and St. Ex.?"

Adele shot him an intrusive, angry look. "*If* anything happened, that would be private," she said, her jaws clenching.

"Yes, of course, but that's what sells books," he said, trying to be diplomatic, but also responding to her obvious discomfort, "*And* gets them published."

Adele knew what he was asking for, but what went on between her and Saint-Exupéry was not fodder for the masses. It was a true friendship, and something worth treasuring. She was not one now, or ever, to put to paper the special details, let alone her own personal feelings for the man. She sat still without saying a word. The executive waited then let out a sigh.

"Look, often retirees suddenly find that they have a lot of

time on their hands, so they decide to jot down their memories. We get it all the time."

"But this is not about *me*. It's about Monsieur de Saint-Exupéry," Adele exclaimed. "He was a very important man. Important to aviation, literature…humanity!"

"Yes. He was. I completely agree," said the executive. "And to be honest, you wouldn't be sitting here if not for him. The book is too simplistic. Surely, if you spent all that time with him, you must have more to share."

Adele, again, didn't like his insinuation. She sat forward and said in a tone usually reserved for her students, "Documenting his time in Northport was my only intention. I was there when he wrote *The Little Prince*."

The executive, tiring of this, said, "OK, but in this…" he lifted the manuscript then dropped it back on the table, "You come off as just a fly on the wall. And nothing happens. Sorry to be so blunt."

Knowing she was losing the argument, and her chance to get her book published, she stated simply, as her voice trembled, "I wanted him to be remembered."

"No doubt he will be, Miss Breaux," said the executive. Then he tapped her manuscript with his fingers and added, "But not from this. We appreciate your time."

He stood, lifted the manuscript and handed it to Adele. Adele, crushed, rose from her chair and took it from him slowly and bowed her head.

When she walked out into the reception area it was no longer intimidating, instead it felt callous and cold. So was the elevator ride down to the lobby. Stepping out onto the city street was just as unwelcoming, a hard slap in the face by a gush of icy wind. Adele walked several blocks, numb to her surroundings. It wasn't until her feet began to hurt that she hailed a cab back to Penn Station.

It was late afternoon by the time Adele caught a train home. It was before rush hour, but the train was still filled with tired passengers. Adele sat and stared sadly out the window. The sky was grey; the light snow had turned to rain. It matched her mood. She felt a failure. Worse, she felt old, very old. Yes, the train was taking her back home, but she felt she had nowhere to go. She saw no future for herself. The pain of this fact was overwhelming. She began to feel a tight feeling in her chest and a wave of sadness about to engulf her. To stop the pain, she thought of the past. There was a comfort there, especially when she was with *him*. That was where her thoughts took her. It was better than being on that slow moving, smoky train about to collapse in failure...

IT WAS 1942, AND though Adele didn't know it yet, it would be the best year of her life. She was in her bedroom wearily unbuttoning her blouse, ready to relax after a long day of teaching when the phone rang. She strolled lazily into the living room and answered it. On the line was Saint-Exupéry, speaking playfully in French.

"If you are without scruples, then you will come to the house today to teach!"

Adele brightened at the sound of his voice. "I will be happy to come...and without scruples!" she cheerily responded, then hung up the phone and began to quickly button up her blouse.

Less than thirty minutes later, Adele pulled into the driveway of the Bevin House and parked. She jumped out of her car and excitedly sprinted toward the house and onto the porch. After being let inside by the maid, she made her way down the hall to the parlor. Adele gaily untied the scarf around her neck as she got to the door. The maid opened it and Adele entered, smiling.

Adele's smile soon fell when she saw Saint-Exupéry staring out the window in deep thought, smoking deliberately on a cigarette.

"Monsieur?" she asked, wondering what it was that made him look so intense and sad. He turned slowly and looked at her with tired eyes.

"Mademoiselle, forgive me. I forgot I've asked you to come," he said with distracted regret.

Adele tried to hide her disappointment. "Is something the matter?"

Saint-Exupéry spoke in a somber tone. "A member of my old squadron, a friend, crashed his plane. I got the telegram shortly after my call to you. Again, my apologizes for having you come all the way out here."

"No. *I'm* sorry," said Adele as she walked over and stood next to him. They both stared out the window in silence. Adele hated the war and wondered how best to console her friend. Then Saint-Exupéry spoke.

"I am the last one," he said as he inhaled deeply from his cigarette making the glow bright red, then slowly released the smoke from his lungs. "In childhood there was never any concern for tomorrow. We knew it would come. Now, there is no promise of it."

Adele looked at him then back out the window, hating that truth. "This war seems endless," she said softly. "One can't help but feel…so powerless."

Again, they both stood there in silence, contemplating the destruction of war and the fragility of life. Saint-Exupéry glanced at her, appreciating her company at such a difficult moment. Suddenly, getting an idea, a spark came to his eyes. He turned and looked at Adele.

"Mademoiselle, one needn't feel so powerless. Perhaps you can use your abilities better for the cause. I can help you get a position with my friends in Washington."

Adele looked at him, stunned. "A p-position?" she stammered.

"Translator, possibly," he said with an excited nod of his head. "Your country needs...*encouragement*. Strength is found not just in weapons. "Here," he began, as he went over to the table and searched for a pen. When he found one, he grabbed a sheet of onionskin paper, sat and started to write. Adele watched, intrigued yet uncertain.

After he finished, he stood and carefully blew on the paper to dry the ink, then walked back over to Adele and handed it out to her.

"My recommendation for you. Use it to help get you started. You should be out in the world, a world that needs you. Please consider?"

Adele took the paper, read the recommendation, then looked back at Saint-Exupéry, deeply moved though somewhat anxious.

"Y-yes. I will. Thank you," she answered.

Saint-Exupéry smiled warmly then stared out the window again, his melancholy mood returning. A moment passed before he spoke without taking his eyes from the window. "I've finished my book."

Adele shot him an excited look. She searched to find the same excitement on his face about this grand accomplishment, but didn't find it. His mood remained somber, and she was confused by it.

"Winter is here," he said, "Our stay is ending. We'll be leaving very soon."

His words struck Adele hard, although she somehow managed to keep a neutral and brave face, but her thoughts of their association ending was flooding her brain, barely allowing her to hear much of anything after.

"Will you come Saturday for dinner?" he asked simply. "I'd like to see you again before I leave."

Adele looked at him despairingly. She heard his question, but didn't want to answer. It all seemed so final, and maybe if she didn't answer then she could suspend this moment forever. But the word fell from her lips, a soft, sad, "Yes."

"And you will bring your bill?" he asked.

"My bill?" she asked, confused. The last thing she was thinking about was payment for her time with him. She couldn't even fathom what he was talking about for a few seconds, then suddenly realized and answered, "Oh. Yes. Of course."

But as the words came out, they sounded so formal. Formality was suddenly a strange concept. Her heart was breaking. She felt split, bleeding even, and yet her constitution took over, and out of habit and will, not heart, she was able to conceal her true feelings.

Saint-Exupéry smashed his cigarette into an ashtray, and headed for the door. "Come – I will walk you to your car," he said almost in an uncaring manner.

What happened to the playful, spirited man that would have easily turned such a moment into a game? The one who loved to make Adele out to be the stoic stick in the mud, to which she didn't mind because it was he who was doing it? Saint-Exupéry was the only one who had ever broke through her rigid façade and made her life worth living, and the world a wonderland. Heartbroken, she moved slowly as she followed him out of the room.

Once on the porch of the grand mansion, Saint-Exupéry turned up his collar to the cold, walked Adele to her car and opened the door without a word, without a smile. Numb more to her feelings than the icy weather, she climbed in. As he was closing the door, he gave her a flat, "Au revoir," then the door was shut.

Adele was now locked into what felt like a small box and not a car. The silence was deafening. When Saint-Exupéry started back to the house, shoulders hunched and clutching his collar from the wind, he looked frail, older than his forty-two years. Adele watched him enter the house and close the door. There was no smile, no wave. She sadly started the engine as she fought back tears…

ON THE TRAIN, ADELE, recalling the memory, clasped the manuscript to her chest with the same profound sadness expressed on her face and fighting back tears, as she leaned her head against the train car window and stared out.

Chapter 24

No Regrets

It was early evening by the time Adele arrived home from the train station. She pulled into her driveway and sat in her car watching the rain for several minutes before gradually, as if in slow motion, unlocking her door, grabbing her satchel and purse and getting out. The rain had turned into a slight, cold drizzle, but she didn't bother to tighten her scarf or race to the door. She no longer cared. She put the key in the lock, opened it and entered.

Inside, she flicked on the light, tossed the keys on the table by the door, dropped the satchel on the floor and walked into her living room. She stood in the center of it contemplating what to do. It was too early for bed, and she hadn't the strength or appetite to fix something to eat. She removed her coat and threw it on the couch. Hanging it up would take too much effort. She pulled off the scarf from around her neck and threw that on the couch as well.

Adele was appreciative of the rainfall outside, slight as it was, because it created a sound and rhythm to what otherwise would have been silence. That was something she couldn't bear. She looked over at her dining room table. The typewriter along with all her notes and papers were where she left them. She walked into the dining room and looked down at her unfinished work. The book she now would never complete.

Adele opened the leather bound notebook that Beatrice had given to her and flipped aimlessly through the brittle, handwritten pages of notes. She was as brittle as they were, she thought, if not physically surely emotionally. As she did this, she found a small, handwritten receipt among the papers. She took it out and saw it was from a local Northport diner that was no longer in business. It had closed about ten years after the war, when newer businesses began to spring up on Main Street. Adele looked at the receipt wondering why she kept it.

"Hamburger with cheese, salad...liver with onions, two teas..." Adele read aloud, still wondering. Then it hit her.

"Ann had the burger and I had the liver," she said softly, recalling. "Oh, my," she murmured as she sat slowly in a chair remembering that meal at the diner back in 1942...

છ∘ત

IT WAS THE EVENING. Adele was sitting in a booth of a small Main Street diner, feeling anxious and depressed, as a corner jukebox played Vaughn Monroe's "My Devotion." A handful of locals were at other tables enjoying their meals. Adele barely touched hers. Across from her sat Ann finishing what was left of her cheeseburger.

"It may be the last time I'll see him," Adele said after a long silence where she had rearranged the liver and onions on her plate at least a half dozen times.

"You'll stay in touch with him," said Ann trying to cheer her.

Adele looked at her, despondent. "It won't be the same. This was our time. And now it's over." She looked down at her food, then added with false conviction, "Maybe it's time for me to leave as well."

Ann shot Adele a stunned, worried look. "What are you talking about?"

"Leave teaching and move on to something more important," Adele said almost matter of fact, though interested in seeing Ann's reaction.

"That's crazy," Ann responded as she wiped her mouth with her napkin.

"Why is it crazy?" asked Adele, a hint of anger in her voice.

"Because your life and your work are *here*," Ann answered annoyed that she needed to remind Adele of this.

"Here is where I'm trapped. I should be doing much more. Even he thinks so. He wrote me a letter of recommendation," said Adele in her own defense as she opened her purse, removed the letter and handed it to Ann.

Ann opened the letter, looked at it, then said in frustration, "It's in *French*."

Adele snatched the letter from Ann and read it aloud for her in English. "I heartily recommend Miss Breaux to any branch of the government having need of a collaborator knowing fluently the French language. It is of my opinion that Miss Breaux can fill any post with ease where finesse in the use of French is necessary."

"That's very impressive, Adele, but you can't leave. You have your career," said Ann trying her best to talk sense into her friend.

"And what else?" Adele asked impatiently as she folded the letter and put it back in her purse.

Ann didn't answer. She knew there was little else in both

their lives. She, too, had dreams and fantasies of exploring the world, enjoying the finer things in life, finding the right man, or any man, for that matter, who would sweep her off her feet and marry her, but she was sensible and accepted the reality of where her life was. She was smart, and that brought her a good career that she enjoyed. Ann knew she was lucky to have at least that and was grateful. She wished her friend would recognize this and do the same.

Just then, a waiter approached, dropped off their check with a friendly smile and walked away. Ann waited until he was out of earshot to ask Adele an important question.

"Be honest," she began, "are you doing this for yourself or for him?"

"Myself, of course," Adele answered, offended.

Ann shook her head, unconvinced. Adele noticed.

"He's opened a whole new world to me," Adele said, trying to add weight to her defense.

"He's opened your *heart*," said Ann, correcting her.

"I've encouraged him to fly again, and now he's encouraging *me*. It's what friends do for each other," Adele said, making a point.

"Then, as *your* friend, I ask that you not make any hasty decisions. Think this through," she responded.

Angry about the lack of support, Adele grabbed the check and her coat. "I'll be going to Oregon at the end of the school year. It'll give me time to think it all through. I'll make my decision then."

Adele slid out of the booth and walked to the cashier. Ann took one last sip from her teacup then slid out, too. Putting on her coat, she muttered, "Damn Frenchman."

Adele and Ann left the diner together, and walked the sidewalk in silence. The night was cool and clear with a mild, salty sea wind. Adele was in deep thought, as was Ann, as they passed the quaint shops that were already closed for the evening. Local couples from the town, including a spattering of servicemen, were either on their way to the movie theatre or to one of the nearby pubs.

Adele glanced at Ann and saw she was watching the pavement as she walked. She didn't like the silence between them and thought about what to say when she looked up ahead and saw Commander Bessette getting out of a car. She felt her heart skip a beat as she watched him step up on the sidewalk and head in their direction. As he approached, Adele stopped and called out his name.

Commander Bessette stepped toward Adele, not recognizing her at first. Ann made sure to hang back, not wanting to intrude, especially since she didn't understand French. That was the language Adele used when she introduced herself, and reminded him that they had met at the Bevin House.

Commander Bessette's eyes lit up and spoke happily in English, "Ah, yes! The teacher."

"You speak English?" Adele asked, surprised.

"Yes. Since a small boy," he nodded.

"Have you been visiting Saint-Exupéry," she asked, eager to learn any information.

Commander Bessette lowered his head and said with regret, "No. He refuses to speak to me."

Adele looked at him, confused. Commander Bessette noticed and hesitantly explained, "He...he wants to be a pilot again, but of course, he shouldn't. He can't."

Adele was stunned by this news. "But he is still capable, and belongs with his men," she argued in Saint-Exupéry's defense.

"No," assured Commander Bessette, "He is too old."

"Surely, that can't be the reason –" Adele said.

"Antoine is a brilliant aviator, but not a good pilot. He's

crashed many planes and has broken nearly every bone in his body over the years. He's not safe, and flying again could end his life."

Those words hit Adele hard. It was difficult for her to fathom such a thing. She looked at Commander Bessette, bewildered, and said softly, "But he's written all those books…"

"Beautiful as they are," Commander Bessette began, "the reality is he is no longer fit. Flying could do harm to him and perhaps others. I wish he would listen, but he has alienated those who know him best. I've heard he's reached out to General Eisenhower, but anyone that encourages him to fly is wrong."

Adele looked down at the pavement, pained that she'd been caught up in a fantasy of this romantic pilot, but still, how could any of this be true? He was so strong, intelligent, and capable. Commander Bessette took another step forward, as if to emphasize the importance of what he was about to ask.

"Perhaps you can say something to him?"

Adele quickly looked up, dumbfounded. "Me?"

"Yes. He listens to you. I could tell," Commander Bessette said with assurance, then smiled. "And maybe he will listen better to a woman. At least try?"

Adele was torn by this request. She glanced over at Ann who had overheard the conversation. Ann looked away, pained, knowing what an emotional dilemma this was for her friend.

Commander Bessette took a step back, returning to formality. "In any case, it was good seeing you again, Miss Breaux. Maybe we will run into each other again sometime. Good night."

"Yes, Commander. Good night."

She stood there as if paralyzed and watched Commander Bessette walk away. Ann slowly sidled up to Adele and stood next to her. She reached out and touched Adele's arm, sympathetically, but Adele pulled her arm away and began to walk. Ann followed.

Knowing her friend well, and needing to make sure she remained in reality, she said urgently, "Adele, you have to tell him."

This angered Adele. She stopped and turned to her. "I can't. You don't understand, it's all he has. He's a *pilot*!"

Ann responded bluntly, "That's the romance talking."

"*Romance*?" Adele asked, staring at Ann, confused.

"Oh, come on!" Ann said rolling her eyes. "It's obvious how you feel about him. It's *been* obvious."

Adele looked at her, shocked and embarrassed, then stoically stood straight and said with pride, "I have only the utmost respect and..." She stopped in mid-sentence seeing Ann giving her an incredulous expression. Whom was she kidding?

"And because you '*respect*' him you're going to give up your career and not tell him he could get killed if he flies again?" asked Ann. "This isn't one of his books, Adele. This is *real* life."

Adele looked at her with pleading agony, her voice trembling, "It's not my place. I can't."

"A friend *would*," Ann reminded her. "Maybe if you told him how you felt about him first, it'd be easier."

Just then, a cold wind began to blow. Ann clutched at her coat before adding, "You don't want to live with any regrets, Adele. I know I wouldn't," then walked away as Adele stood there, tormented, unable to move.

Later that night, Adele couldn't sleep. She was beyond restless. Even lying down was unbearable. She got up several times and paced her room. The words and request of Commander Bessette haunted her, but Ann's haunted her more.

Tell Saint-Exupéry how she felt about him? Impossible. She was just a lowly, sad, schoolteacher living in a little town with nothing to offer but how to change words from French into English.

And who was he, just a world famous author, and brave pilot, but more importantly a *married* man. It was unheard of, and improper, for a woman to confess such a thing. Also, once words like that are spoken, she would never be able to take them back. They would be out there, exposed, especially if they were not reciprocated. She would crumble if he responded with pity. Worse, she feared he would laugh hearing such words come from her lips. He more than likely had many women declare those sorts of sentiments to him, but those women were younger, more sophisticated and, of course, beautiful. She was none of those things, and couldn't bear the thought of rejection.

These thoughts raced brutally through her mind, along with her need to tell him not to fly. That pained her more since she had done nothing but encourage him to believe that he could again. She loved the look in his eyes, staring appreciatively at her, as she championed for him to do it. She believed in him. She understood he was lost being on the ground. That he felt half a man. His true happiness had been, and always would be, in the sky.

Who was she to discourage it? He counted on her. She convinced herself to be the only one that understood this about him. But what if he did fly and ended up doing harm to others? Or worse, she thought selfishly, to himself? How would she ever be able to live with herself if such a thing happened?

Adele began to worry about her own well-being. Was she really pacing the floor in the middle of the night over this? A pupil? She had seen many times a student develop feelings for a teacher, and how she and her colleagues, at first, would chuckle at the innocence of it, then discuss how to best discourage it. But in this situation, she was a teacher who had developed feelings for her student. She still believed it was something that needed to be discouraged, but was finding it nearly impossible telling that to her heart.

Chapter 25

Goodbye

That Saturday in 1942 came sooner than Adele had wanted it to. She drove to the Bevin House with great trepidation. Although the idea of stepping into the gorgeous mansion, this time as an invited dinner guest and not as the hired language instructor, was something she appreciated and even took great pride in, it was also her last opportunity to discourage Saint-Exupéry from flying and maybe tell him of her affections. Would there be any time to get him alone, she wondered, and if she did, would she be able to find the courage to do either?

The dinner was semi-formal with several other guests in attendance, mostly diplomats from Washington. The talk around the table was about the on-going war and how it might end, as well as the Saint-Exupéry's return to France as soon as it did. Saint-Exupéry himself was in fine spirits, and it was a delight for Adele to watch him entertaining the guests with his humor and intelligence. She said very little, feeling intimidated to be among such high ranking officials, and Consuelo, who made sure to ignore Adele throughout most of the evening. It was only the occasional wink from Saint-Exupéry that made her feel included, and she smiled every time he did.

It was after the guests had left and Consuelo retired upstairs that Saint-Exupéry led Adele into his study. She entered clutching her purse. He followed, closing the door behind him.

"Mademoiselle, I'm glad you came for dinner. However, you were very quiet. Why?" he asked as he made his way around his desk.

"I didn't know what to lend to the conversation," Adele said in a soft yet distracted voice.

Saint-Exupéry looked at her and smiled, understanding her shyness. He opened up the top drawer of his desk and removed a large checkbook ledger.

"So...what is it that I owe you?" he asked as he flipped open to a page of blank checks and grabbed a pen.

Adele opened her purse, took out a small piece of paper and held it out to him. "It's all calculated," she said, hating this formality, "The total comes to thirty six dollars."

Saint-Exupéry looked at her, surprised. "Thirty six dollars?" he laughed. "Surely, it must be more."

Adele didn't laugh. "No, I added it correctly," she said.

Saint-Exupéry took the piece of paper from her and looked at it. "Mademoiselle, this is not right. Did you add your time, petrol cost?"

"I did," answered Adele.

"But it should at least be a hundred," said Saint-Exupéry with a slight grin.

Adele didn't respond. Saint-Exupéry looked at her, wanting to give her more, but also knew she wouldn't accept it. Reluctantly, he wrote out the check, tore it from the ledger and handed it to her. She took it, again, hating this formal exchange, and put it in her purse.

She then carefully pulled out a copy of his book *Flight to Arras* that she had tucked inside her purse and asked, "Monsieur, if you don't mind, I have with me one of your books. Would you be so kind to sign it?"

Saint-Exupéry looked at her, surprised. "Mademoiselle, why didn't you ask? I would have given you a copy."

"I have all your books," Adele admitted, then blushed having revealed this truth.

Saint-Exupéry looked at her, flattered. He reached out, took the book from her and sat in his chair. With careful thought, he took his time inscribing it as Adele watched. When he was done he closed it, stood and handed it back to her.

"Thank you. I will miss you, Monsieur," Adele said stoically, doing her best to hide her sadness.

"As I you," Saint-Exupéry replied, but didn't hide his, as he looked at her with great fondness.

Adele stood there for a moment, struggling with her conscience. If there was ever a moment to tell him anything, it was now.

"Monsieur, I'd like to say something. It's about how I-I've..." she stopped, trying to find the words. "B-being with you..." she stammered, but stopped again.

Saint-Exupéry looked at her, interested to hear what she had to say. She looked at him and saw the eagerness in his eyes. This should be easy, she thought. This was her chance. She tried to speak again, but couldn't form the words. The struggle was too much. Losing all nerve and feeling defeated, a coward, she said softly, "Take good care, Monsieur de Saint-Exupéry."

He smiled, gave her a slight bow in reverence, and replied, "Mademoiselle Breaux."

Unable to bear another moment, Adele held the book tight to her chest, turned and quickly left the room. The maid helped her with her coat then did her best to keep up with her as Adele hurried down the hall. She rushed in front of Adele to the front door and opened it. She followed that with a polite bow.

"Good night, Mademoiselle," she said to Adele.

"Goodbye," said Adele without looking at her.

Adele made her way out of the house, down the steps and rushed into the dark night to her car. She got in, tossing the book and her purse on the passenger seat. Her hands shook as she put the key in the ignition. Before she started the car, she looked back at the house that had become her sanctuary from loneliness. The grief was too much to bear, so she lowered her head in profound sadness. She knew she was about to leave her only true happiness.

Chapter 26

Failing

Norman knocked on Adele's door several times before it slowly opened. Looking sad and tired, Adele managed a weak smile upon seeing him.

"Hello, Norman," she said, as she opened the door wider for him to enter. He did, looking at her with concern.

Adele closed the door and headed into the living room. Norman followed, asking, "Is everything OK? What happened with the publisher?"

"My book is not something they're looking for at this time," she said putting it diplomatically. She wasn't about to repeat what the publisher actually said, then added with a weary sigh, "I've decided to put it away for a while."

"You're still going to write it, though, aren't you? You're not going to stop just because of one publisher. There are others," said Norman, doing his best to encourage her.

"I don't know, Norman," Adele said, sounding worn out. "Perhaps it's a project too big and complex for someone like me."

Norman wasn't sure what she meant by "complex," but

didn't ask and said, "Well, I still think it's a great story, and should be written."

Adele smiled at him, appreciating his support. Norman wanted to say more, but didn't want to pry seeing she wasn't up for discussing it, so he changed the subject.

"Well, I stopped by to ask your advice. It's about my student again, Jack. I'm afraid I'm going to lose this battle."

"Has he returned to class?"

"No, but I saw him in the hallway today and asked him to. I doubt he will."

Adele looked at him, unsure what to suggest.

"It's just...I know he's a smart kid," Norman said in frustration.

"Where's your evidence of that?" Adele asked.

Norman, feeling foolish, admitted, "I have none. Just a hunch."

Adele said softly, "It is only with the heart that one can see..." She stopped, not wanting to finish the quote and looked away.

"Saint-Exupéry?" asked Norman.

Adele nodded yes. Norman chuckled. Adele gave him a quizzical look.

"Sorry. I can hope that one day someone will remember me as fondly as you do Saint-Exupéry," he said. "But whom am I kidding? I'm only a teacher, not a famous pilot."

Adele looked at him with sad wisdom in her eyes and said, "I've learned that it's not so much what we've done, but who we were to others that's truly worth remembering." She then returned to the subject of Jack. "I don't know what to tell you about your student, Norman. Sometimes the only thing you can do is nothing."

"Well, unfortunately, I may not have a choice," Norman said looking worried. "He's in trouble. At home. He has a black eye."

Adele gave Norman a look of grave concern. It was one thing for a student to not be doing well in class, but if there was a problem of possible abuse at home, and a teacher knew, there was a whole different set of rules to abide by.

"Have you told Morris or Dave Allardice?" she asked.

"Not yet," replied Norman.

Adele frowned at him for not following procedure.

"I will," said Norman, although with not much conviction. He then admitted, "I don't even know if that's how he got it. Another kid told me. I can't go on hearsay. Also, I know if, or when, I do bring in Morris or Dave, that will be the end of this kid. He'll drop out and I'll have lost my chance to…"

"Save him?" Adele quickly asked, feeling again her own pain from not speaking up to her most beloved student that might have changed his life.

"No," said Norman, "Keep him in school. If not he'll fall through the cracks and…" Norman looked at the floor. "I don't know. There has to be some way to get through." He then he let out a heavy sigh. "Failing as a student is hard, but it can be corrected. Failing as a teacher? You can never go back."

His words upset Adele. "No…you can't go back," she murmured softly as she began wringing her hands nervously. She then looked at Norman with tearful eyes and pleaded, "If there is anything you need to do or say to this student, Norman, do it now. You don't want any regrets. Don't wait. Please, please, don't wait."

Norman was taken aback by the desperate tone in her voice and look in her eyes. "Adele, are you all right?" he asked.

Adele anxiously pressed her hands down the lap of her dress several times to compose herself and answered calmly, "Yes. Yes, forgive me. You'll do the right thing, Norman…with your student. I know you will."

She then suddenly looked distracted. "Now, if you'll excuse me, I have some correspondences to get to," as she led him to the front door. When she opened it, Norman paused, worried and wanting to say something, but respected her privacy and left.

Adele closed the door and went back into her living room. She walked over to her record player and turned it on. Carefully lifting the needle, she placed it on the spinning album and soon an opera slowly began to float from the speakers.

Adele closed her eyes, taking in the rich voice of a tenor singing beautifully in Italian about love lost. She opened her eyes, walked over to a window and looked out. The sky was drab and grey. It reminded her of an afternoon in 1942, a month after her first lesson with Saint-Exupéry…

ঙ৹ঞ

IT WAS A COLD day in late October when Adele pulled into the driveway of the Bevin House. Once parked, she looked up at the sky. It was grey and overcast, giving off an empty, lonely feeling. When she stepped out of the car, she looked around. Everything seemed oddly still. Even being so close to the water's edge, there was very little movement. Not even the sand was being pushed by the wind across dunes. It was only the faint sound of seagulls heard in the distance that made her feel there was some sense of life on the planet.

Adele didn't like this weather and wanted to get as far away as possible from it. She strapped her satchel across her shoulder and was happy to be heading inside where it was warm and cozy, and where Saint-Exupéry was sure to lift her mood.

After entering the house, Adele walked into the parlor where she saw Saint-Exupéry at his table working on a watercolor. She watched him as she removed her coat and scarf, draping both over a chair. She appreciated and respected the laser-sharp focus he gave to his work and silently approached the table to get a better view of what he was doing. She was never one to ever disturb an artist at work, but she knew she would have to eventually since she was there to do a job. However, she would allow a few more moments before doing so.

She watched him stroke a small paintbrush across the onionskin paper several times then dip it carefully into the little plastic tray where several other colors sat in small holes. Adele eyed the plastic tray suspiciously and moved around the table to get a better look. It was just as she suspected.

"Monsieur, this paint set...it's for a child."

"Yes," he replied without taking his eyes off his watercolor.

"You've made all of your watercolors using this paint?" she asked, puzzled.

"Yes," he answered again, wondering why she was making an issue of it.

"But you should be using real paint. These pictures will be going into your book."

"This *is* real paint. I bought the kit in Manhattan at a Five & Ten Cent store. The children's toy department."

"But, Monsieur, don't you think your work deserves a more professional appearance? Think of what you can do with watercolors from a more proper set," said Adele.

Saint-Exupéry stopped for a moment and looked at her, worried. "Mademoiselle, do you not like my work?"

Adele looked at him; insulted he could ask such a thing. "You know I admire your work very much," she replied.

"So, there are none of these that are not pleasant to you?" he asked, pointing to several watercolors scattered across his table.

Adele looked at his other work and shook her head. "No, they are all lovely," she answered.

Saint-Exupéry smiled then returned to moving his paint-brush across the onionskin paper. Adele looked at him confused then realized it was rude of her to impose what she thought was better for his creativity. Feeling awkward and a little foolish, she took a seat at the end of the table and continued to watch him paint.

After a few minutes passed, a look of discouragement fell across her face. It occurred to her that Saint-Exupéry was very resistant to learning and that her time with him, although magical in its own way, was doing very little for either of them.

"Monsieur, I am worried," she softly as if not wanting to disrupt his creative flow.

Saint-Exupéry looked over at her and stopped. He grabbed a cloth and began to wipe the paintbrush.

"About?" he asked with a slight smile.

"Failing you as a teacher," she answered honestly.

Saint-Exupéry chuckled. "Mademoiselle, you are not a failure, nor at fault," he said, sincerely. "I have been resisting because I don't see the point in learning."

"But you *need* to. They expect you to speak and understand English in Washington," Adele said in frustration.

"Why should I learn? I need only to learn to hail a taxi to get me from one place to the next. Other than that, the rest would only spoil too many special opportunities," Saint-Exupéry said with a smile.

"Special opportunities? What special opportunities?" Adele asked.

Saint-Exupéry's eyes lit up, more than happy to explain, and put down his paintbrush.

"When I see a pretty woman in America, I describe what I need with gestures such as asking for a cup of coffee or a meal," he began, expertly pantomiming sipping from a cup, then holding a plate and eating from it. "This makes her smile," he grinned, then winked, adding, "Why learn English and lose that smile?"

Adele shook her head, disapproving. Saint-Exupéry saw this and decided to take his point further.

"A lot can be said between two people without language, Mademoiselle," he said as he walked over and took a seat next to her. He moved in closer and looked seductively into her eyes.

Adele blushed and looked away, trying not to smile.

"Ah! See?" Saint-Exupéry exclaimed. "I have just learned how you feel about me by what you just did." He leaned forward and asked sincerely, "Now, tell me with *language* how you feel about me?"

Adele looked at him, shocked. He stared at her, eager to hear her response. Caught off guard, she didn't know what to say. Her mind began to fill with so many things that were in her heart, such as how he brought color into her life, the same way he did with his art using that silly child's paint kit. And how he made the room burst with radiant sunshine while outside remained dark and depressing. But more than anything, she wanted to thank him a thousand times over for bringing the whole big beautiful world into her small one.

But when Adele opened her mouth to speak, but couldn't bring herself to say any of those things. Saint-Exupéry waited then eventually sat back with a soft, understanding smile on his face.

"Do not worry, Mademoiselle," he said with deep sincerity. "You are a good teacher..."

A SAD ARIA FROM the opera filled the room as Adele stared out of her window with tears in her eyes. The memory of Saint-

Exupéry telling her she was a good teacher sat heavily on her heart. Being a teacher was all she knew, it was her calling, and she believed she did it well...until now. Now she doubted everything in her life and wondered why her life turned out the way it had. Did she do everything wrong? Did she do anything right? One thing was for sure, and this weighed on her more than anything else; she had no one beside her at such a moment to discuss those deep and intimate issues with. And for that, she felt a failure.

Chapter 27

A Hat, A Snake

Norman was sitting at his dining room table that evening. Having just finished correcting the last of his student's papers, he rubbed his tired eyes, rose from his chair and turned off the light before leaving the room.

The house was dark and quiet. Josephine had gone to bed hours earlier. Now it was his turn. As he walked quietly toward his bedroom, he stopped first to check in on his sleeping infant son. The door was slightly ajar when he gently pushed it wider and entered. Once inside, with only the hallway light to guide him, he approached the crib, leaned in and gently stroked his son's soft cheek.

As he did this, he glanced over and saw on a table the copy of *The Little Prince* that Adele had given him. He picked it up, opened it and began to read. Instantly engrossed, he didn't take his eyes off the pages as he quietly walked out of the room. Soon after, he brought the book with him into the bathroom and leaned against the sink, still reading it as his toothbrush and pajamas sat waiting to be put to use. It would be another hour or so before they would be.

Norman lay awake next to his sleeping wife after finishing *The Little Prince*. He thought of the profound wisdom that filled its pages, as well as the poetic, even lyrical way the story, about the small boy on this alien planet, was told. It moved him immensely and he wondered if it might be something his students would enjoy. It certainly would be a great book to have a discussion about. His students for sure would get its meanings, he believed. Then he thought about one student in particular who might get it even more.

The next morning, Norman hurried down the hall of the high school with his briefcase in one hand and the copy of *The Little Prince* in the other. When he reached the administration office, he entered and approached a middle-aged secretary sitting at her desk.

"Hi. I'd like to use the copy machine," he said in eager excitement.

The Secretary looked at him, stunned by his request. The school had recently purchased an upgrade to a more modern way to make paper copies. A company with the funny name of Xerox had put out their latest model of copiers, the Xerox 914, just the year before, and by 1965 it became so popular it was selling in the hundreds of millions.

The Secretary replied, "I'm sorry, Mr. Orenstein, it's brand new and very expensive. It's reserved only for special projects."

"I have a special project," he insisted.

The Secretary looked at him, torn. She was given specific orders not to allow anyone near the copier, but she liked Norman. He was always so friendly and considerate to the administrative staff.

Norman appealed to her kindness. "Just one copy. I promise."

The Secretary glanced around. Seeing they were alone, she nodded and motioned for him to go ahead. Norman smiled as he went around her desk and into the small, private room located behind her. He placed his briefcase on a nearby table then stood and stared at the new clunky looking copy machine. Trying to recall the short demonstration on how to use it just months earlier, he opened *The Little Prince*, found the page he wanted to copy then lifted the copier's lid and laid the book flat on the glass. He closed the lid then searched for the right buttons to press.

Norman squinted as he read carefully the choices on the copier's keypad. There were many and it was very confusing. If he could only find the right one, he could hurry up and get out of there.

Without warning, Carmen entered the room, looking irate. "What do you think you're doing?" she barked.

Norman turned around, startled. Seeing it was Carmen, and fed up with her attitude, he went back to his search for the right button, and said with icy detachment, "I'm looking for your name on this machine, but obviously can't find it because it's *not* yours." He then turned and glared at her.

Carmen was stunned. Having no comeback, she let out an insulted huff and walked out. Norman smiled enjoying his small victory, then went back to his search. He eventually found the correct button and pressed it. The Xerox machine made a loud buzzing sound, much like that of a small car engine, and soon the paper copy came out, landing in a little tray. Norman looked at the near perfect quality of the picture with a smile. He removed the book from the copier then opened his briefcase and placed both the photocopy and the book inside. He snapped his briefcase shut and quickly left the room.

Norman eagerly anticipated the last period of the day. When it finally arrived, he stood at the door of his classroom and greeted each student that walked in with a friendly hello.

As he did this he kept his eye out for Jack among the sea of students that filled the hall, but he was nowhere in sight. When his class was nearly full and the last stragglers raced to get inside, Norman's hope of seeing Jack was fast slipping away. The bell rang and it was time for Norman to get inside and begin his lesson. He lingered just a few more moments, glancing up and down the now empty hall.

Discouraged, Norman turned to enter the classroom. As he did, he heard faint steps in the distance. He turned and saw it was Jack, who was lazily heading in his direction with his head down and his hands in his jean pockets. As Jack approached the door, he glanced up slowly and looked at Norman. Norman didn't say a word and watched as Jack brushed passed him and entered the room. Relieved and thankful, Norman entered, too, closing the door behind him.

After having a successful discussion with his students about the death of Romeo and Juliet and the impact their deaths had on their families, Norman asked his students to write a brief essay on how they would have rather seen the play end, or, if they agreed on its ending, to explain why. As the students wrote furiously on their one sheet of paper to be handed to Norman by end of class, Jack sat with his blank paper on his desk and stared out the window. Norman watched him then glanced up at the clock, impatient for his class to be over.

The last bell finally rang. Norman quickly rose from his desk. The students rose from theirs and, as they filed out, handed their papers to Norman. When Jack got up, he began to slink along the back of the room to make his exit without having to pass Norman. Norman saw this and called out to him. Jack stopped, hating this, and lingered alone in a corner. After the last student left the room, he shuffled slowly toward Norman.

"I told you I wasn't gonna write any paper," he grumbled defiantly before Norman could speak.

Norman nodded and said, "Yes, that was our agreement. I'm glad you showed up."

Jack shrugged. It didn't matter to him whether he did or not. Nothing seemed to matter to this kid. Norman straightened the papers that were in his hand and placed them on his desk. He then opened his briefcase.

"I have something I want you to look at," he said as he took out the Xerox copy he made earlier. He handed it to Jack. "Can you tell me what that is?"

Jack took the copy and stared at Saint-Exupéry's drawing of the boa constrictor from *The Little Prince* that most people mistake for a hat. He studied the drawing carefully then said, "It's a snake. It looks like he swallowed some kind of animal."

Norman broke into a grin. *There* was his "evidence." He reached into his briefcase, pulled out the copy of The Little Prince and handed it to Jack. "I'd like you to read this," he told him.

Jack looked at the book, insulted. "A children's book? You think I'm stupid," he snapped, his voice filled with anger.

Norman quickly shook his head. "No, no, I don't. And, yes, the book is a children's book, but for adults as well."

"A children's book for adults?" Jack asked snidely, wondering what sort of game this teacher was playing.

"Yes. Please, just read it?" Norman asked with sincerity.

Jack looked at him, unsure, then slapped the book against his other hand in frustration and lazily walked out of the classroom. Norman watched knowing this was a long shot, and possibly his last, with Jack.

Chapter 28

Sad Affair

Adele was at her dining room table, putting her typewriter back in its case. She had become resigned to the fact that the book she wanted to write was not something anyone wanted, or needed, which was much like how she felt about herself. The sting of rejection felt more like a slap, and it made her numb. She snapped the typewriter case shut and placed it on the floor in a corner then went back to the table, letting out a heavy sigh seeing all the papers and note pages scattered about.

She ran her fingers through her hair, exasperated by the mess. Since it was early evening, she thought about dealing with it in the morning, but didn't want to wake up to it, so she decided to get it out of the way right then and there.

At first she tried to sort everything in order, then realized there was no point, so she began to grab stacks of papers and place them on top of others, not caring. Having no place to put everything, she saw the box that Sara had dropped off almost a year ago and decided to use that.

Adele removed the lid and grabbed the manuscript that was rejected by the publisher, as well as the file folder that held all the other letters of rejection and went to place it inside when something caught her eye. Putting the manuscript and file folder aside, she reached in and took out the old yellowing sheet music that Beatrice gave her. She stared at the picture of Bing Crosby with the Andrew Sisters and the title of the song, "I Can Dream Can't I?" then read again what Beatrice had inscribed in the upper corner.

Adele, Don't let your heart be a 'sad affair' – Love, Beatrice.

Adele sadly shook her head, opened it and began reading the musical notes. After catching on to the melody, she softly hummed the tune to herself. Interested, she walked over to her piano in the corner of her living room, sat on the bench and placed the sheet music in front of her. She studied the notes again for a moment then began to play the song.

Her playing was slow, careful…beautiful. The melody was smooth and melancholy. Adele played the first page then stopped and perused the song's lyrics.

Straightening the eyeglasses on her face, she began to play again, and gently sang along. Her voice was sad, but lovely. It matched perfectly the words that were about being in love with someone you could never have. Adele sang without realizing the depths of the word's meaning until she turned the page and sang the words, "My heart is…"

She paused momentarily, then sang slowly, "A sad affair…"

Adele stopped and stared at the sheet music, now knowing why Beatrice gave it to her. It was her way of letting Adele know she understood her. Beatrice always had – with the sheet music, the leather notebook she gave her, even all the prying comments she made when it came to Saint-Exupéry. Beatrice *knew*.

Adele hung her head in sorrow thinking about her friend and the unbearable loss. She looked back at the sheet music and turned to the next page, determined to finish the song if only to honor her deceased friend. She put her hands on the keys. When she looked up, she saw an old and faded piece of paper stuck tight to the second page.

Adele gently peeled it off and looked at it. Her hands began to shake as she carefully unfolded what she soon realized was the old, brittle newspaper clipping from the newspaper that Sara read to her at breakfast that morning in Oregon. The headline read:

PLANE OF FRENCH PILOT
AND WRITER MISSING IN MEDITERRANEAN

Adele stared at it, paralyzed. Seeing it again hit her harder than it did back in 1944. She began letting out short gasps of air from her lungs, as if short of breath. She stood and held onto the piano for support, as she gently beat her chest with one hand and held the newspaper clipping clutched tight in the other.

She was able to stop gasping and looked down at the crumpled newspaper clipping in her hand. Unable to bear this repeat of horrible news, she quickly shoved the clipping back between the pages of the sheet music and staggered over to the dining room table where she shoved the sheet music back in the box along with the manuscript, rejection letters and all the other piles of paper and notes she could gather.

She closed the lid shut, keeping her trembling hands on top of it, as if to prevent it from ever opening again, although more for support since she felt her legs becoming unstable and fought back tears that already began to fall.

Not wanting to give in to this cruel and unbearable pain, she pushed the box angrily away and walked to her bedroom, having to stop twice to grip a chair for stability when it felt as if her legs were about to give out. When she finally made it inside her bedroom, she slammed the door shut behind her. The world, and everything beyond that door, could go on without her. She was finished with all of it, just as it obviously was finished with her.

⊱♥⊰

ADELE SAT IN THE co-pilot seat of Saint-Exupéry's small plane. Outside there was mild turbulence, which made her anxious, unlike Saint-Exupéry who, as usual, was next to her, flying the plane immune to any danger. He hummed and whistled a happy tune, until Adele finally looked over at him, annoyed.

"What is that silly song?" she asked, hoping he'd stop.

Saint-Exupéry smiled and began singing the lyrics of the silly love song to her in French.

"If one day I come back...I'll know your heart will be waiting...I will not forget the days we were together...Never give up searching, I beg...For I will be searching, too...And we will love each other again..."

Adele was touched deeply by this. She turned, faced him and, mustering up all the courage she had, spoke with brave sincerity.

"Monsieur, it's time I tell you what I've waited too long to say..."

Saint-Exupéry looked at her. His seductive eyes stared deeply into hers. They made Adele nearly swoon...until she saw them slowly transform from deep brown to steel grey. She sat back, alarmed and confused, as she watched them form into solid stone, then crumble, turning to sand, and pour out of the sockets down the front of his face, leaving two empty, hollow holes.

Adele panicked and reached for his face, as if touching it would reverse this nightmare, then stopped abruptly and let out a terrified shriek. Her hands were now aged and wrinkled with noticeable blue *veins protruding from thin, transparent skin. She fearfully pulled them back and stared at them. They trembled as she touched her face and felt the lines and sags that were now there. Adele turned and caught her reflection in the plane's window. She saw the old woman that she now was staring back.*

Her throat was filled with panic as she began to stammer, "N-no...no.

M-monsieur. Monsieur!"

She turned to Saint-Exupéry, but he was gone. Alone in the plane, Adele lost control of herself and began hyperventilating, barely stuttering out the words, "No...no...no. . !"

Just then, the plane started to shake violently. Adele held on to the console as the plane started to make a steep, terrifying decent. Fear swelled deep inside her and rushed up into her lungs, then throat, causing her to let out a loud, desperate and final scream, "No!!"

Adele sprang up in bed, wheezing for air. Her eyes were filled with fright as she tried to focus on something, anything, familiar in her dark bedroom. She reached frantically for her glasses on the nightstand, haphazardly put them on, then bolted out of bed. She fumbled and nearly fell as she hurried out of the room.

Making her way down the hall, Adele was too crazed with fear to turn on a light, so she pressed her hands along the walls for guidance. She was still choking for air when she stopped at a closet and pulled it opened. She reached inside, yanked her coat off its hanger then quickly put it on and headed for the front door. As she passed a hall mirror, she caught a glimpse of herself in the darkened shadows. She froze when she saw the elderly woman that was staring back. Reality raced fast forward and finally caught up with her.

Overpowered by panic and despair, she shouted, "No...no...this isn't happening..." then searched and found her car keys on a table, slipped into a pair of shoes that were near the door, grabbed at the handle, turned and opened it. A gust of winter wind whipped her hair back as she ran out into the cold, dark night.

Adele fought the wind that was pushing her back and hurried to her car. As she struggled to insert the key to get inside, a vivid memory flashed through her now terror-filled mind...

IT WAS OF THAT last evening at the Bevin House in 1942 after Adele gave Saint-Exupéry her bill of thirty-six dollars and said goodbye. She sat in her car in the driveway, unable to bring herself to start it and drive away from the only place she felt connected, exceptional, a part of something. She lowered her head in profound sadness when suddenly, she heard a muffled voice come from outside. When she looked she saw Saint-Exupéry clutching his jacket with the collar up walking fast toward her car.

"Mademoiselle!" he shouted as he stepped up to her window.

Confused, Adele quickly rolled it down.

"Mademoiselle...it is not the end. You and I. You must come to New York!"

Adele looked at him, unsure what he meant. Saint-Exupéry saw the confusion in her face and added, "For dinner. Next week!"

Realizing he, too, didn't want it to be over, she began laughing happy tears that quickly replaced the sad ones.

"Yes. Of course. I'd love to," she said as she delicately wiped the tears away with her fingers.

Seeing this, Saint-Exupéry broke into a warm smile. "No tears, Mademoiselle," then added in his best broken-English, "It is not – tidy."

Adele laughed out loud, still unable to resist his charm. He grinned and said with optimistic delight, "So, next week? You will phone?"

"Yes. Yes! I will," she answered nodding her head enthusiastically and with a giggle.

He gave her a small wave then rushed back toward the house. Adele watched him, smiling with relief and excitement…

ଓ⚮ல

THE MEMORY CAUSED ADELE'S foot to step on the gas pedal, which made her Renault bolt out of her driveway and speed fast down the street. The car swayed and swerved along the darkened streets of Northport until it reached Eaton's Neck, where it swerved again as it made its way down the long strip of road to Asharoken. The headlights bounced and flashed on the dark beaches, shining on the desolate dunes and sand swept paths. Thankfully, it was after midnight. There were no other cars on the road.

Adele drove as if trying to get to a destination she was late for, but more to outrun the memories that were coming on stronger and more vivid, filling her with fear and regret…

ଓ⚮ல

IT WAS EARLY EVENING when a taxi pulled up in front of an historic looking brownstone in New York City. Adele stepped out wearing a new coat and scarf. Her hairstyle and make-up were perfect. Feeling and looking like a high society woman, she dashed up the steps in her heels to the front door, anxious to see Saint-Exupéry again. This was something she'd always dreamed of, how she'd always imagined it should be.

She rang the bell. A buzzer let her in. Moments later, Adele was led into the living room of a handsome apartment by a maid. Standing near the fireplace was Saint-Exupéry. Though dressed handsomely in a dark suit and tie, he looked seriously bothered by something.

Adele was oblivious to his mood, just happy to see him again and approached him, smiling, as she began unraveling her scarf. A cheerful greeting of "Monsieur...!" sprung from her lips.

Saint-Exupéry turned around, angry, and snapped, "I will not work on it!"

Adele was quickly taken aback, confused, then realized he wasn't speaking to her. She turned and saw Consuelo sitting on a couch across the room with a drink in her hand. She was wearing a festive dress, but her mood was dark. Adele's happy eagerness faded upon seeing Consuelo causing her to become timid, even borderline obedient.

"Bonsoir, Madame," she said lowering her head in respect.

Consuelo got up and walked past Adele, ignoring her. She stood next to a large table that was near her husband. Saint-Exupéry took a step away from her and said with determination, "I will have them come for it in the morning."

"It's the one *I* chose! I like *this* one," Consuelo shouted in defiance.

Saint-Exupéry shouted back, "But I am the one who will be working on it!"

Consuelo gave him an angry scowl. Saint-Exupéry was not about to lose this fight. He looked at Adele and asked as he pointed to a table, "Mademoiselle, do *you* like this table?"

Adele froze not wanting to be put in the middle of a domestic dispute. She looked at the table then began cautiously, "It's nice..."

"But it's too *big*!" exclaimed Saint-Exupéry, not caring that he interrupted her, then added, "I prefer the one I had at the Bevin House. You remember?"

"Yes. Of course," answered Adele. She remembered every last detail of that house, let alone every minute she spent with him.

"Then how can I work on this monstrosity? Tell me!" he demanded.

Adele looked at Consuelo as if seeking permission to speak.

Consuelo glared at her and said, "Yes, go ahead. Tell him."

Hesitant, Adele cleared her throat and spoke diplomatically. "If the purpose is for your work, Monsieur, then you should get a table that will inspire your creativity."

Saint-Exupéry gave her a heartfelt smile. He then looked at Consuelo and gave her a winning grin. "Ha! There it is! I will order a new table in the morning."

He grabbed his drink from the table and finished it as Consuelo shot Adele a threatening look. Adele looked away, intimidated. Saint-Exupéry slammed his glass down in victory and shouted, "Let's eat!"

"I'm not hungry," Consuelo said in a passive-aggressive manner, still irate.

Saint-Exupéry looked at her and said, "We have a reservation," then took a step toward his wife and coddled, "Don't be a sore loser."

Consuelo turned away from him. "I won't eat. It will be a waste of money."

Saint-Exupéry, used to dealing with this, coddled her more, as he fetched her coat that was on the couch. "We'll go where *you* want to go," he said affectionately.

Consuelo looked at Adele as if plotting. She then put down her wine glass and allowed Saint-Exupéry to help her with her coat...

୫୬୰ୡ

ADELE'S CAR FOUND THE familiar address in the darkness and pulled into the driveway of the Bevin House. The car's headlight illuminated its now dark and haunting exterior. She sat staring at the ominous looking fortress before her. The howling wind outside only added to the distress that was mounting on her fragile psychological state. She shook her head left and right as if trying desperately to stop the painful memory…

୫୬୰ୡ

ADELE, SAINT-EXUPÉRY AND CONSUELO sat at a small, cramped table in a half empty café in Manhattan. It was a mediocre establishment, not the elegant restaurant that was obviously planned, or that Adele had hoped and dressed for. What was worse, she watched helplessly embarrassed as Consuelo treated the waiter as her own personal slave, and could barely stand to see the humiliation from it on Saint-Exupéry's face.

"And bring us rolls," Consuelo demanded to the waiter, "Warm. And *fresh*. None that have been out, or there will be no tip!"

The waiter nodded respectfully as he took her menu and left. Consuelo looked at her husband. He had turned in his chair, facing away from her, and withdrew into himself. She looked at Adele, and in a snide manner asked, "Is *this* table good for you?"

Adele feigned a smile and nodded. She looked at Saint-Exupéry for help, but he couldn't even make eye contact. He let out a defeated sigh and leaned his chin on his fist, tired. And that's how the rest of the dinner went. Small talk, dominated by Consuelo, mixed with a lot of misery.

Later, in front of the café, Saint-Exupéry led Adele to the edge of the sidewalk as Consuelo stood several yards away, looking cold and cranky. Saint-Exupéry placed his hand on Adele's back and smiled playfully.

"Watch this!" he whispered with excitement.

Adele was taken by his ability to put that treacherous dinner behind him so quickly and become the playful scamp she adored. She watched with interest as he stepped from the curb and waved at the passing cabs, calling out, "Taxi! Taxi" to each one.

Within moments, one of them slowed down and pulled up in front of him. He peered inside the passenger window that was half open and said to the cab driver in perfect English, "Take her to the train, please," then turned and grinned victoriously at Adele.

Adele let out a happy giggle, proud of her student. She loved it more when he winked at her. She melted, and it gave her the nerve to step forward, ready to tell him finally what was in her heart.

"Monsieur, there is something I…"

But Saint-Exupéry was too distracted by the taxi. He eagerly opened the cab door for her. She hesitated, then acquiesced and started to get in…

১০৫৫

ADELE GOT OUT OF her Renault that was still running, and stepped onto the gravel driveway of the Bevin House. The headlights still shone on the silent and uninviting estate. Alone in the cold darkness, she began to walk toward it. As the freezing wind whipped her face, she clutched the collar of her coat and tried to bring it to her ears as the memory of being on that New York sidewalk in 1942, still raced through her mind…

SAINT-EXUPÉRY HELD THE door as Adele, clutching the collar of her coat, got into the cab and got comfortable in the back seat. As he was about to close the door, Adele quickly sat forward.

"Monsieur..." she called out.

Saint-Exupéry opened the door wider, leaned in and looked at her with encouraging eyes.

"Monsieur, I have been wanting to tell you how I feel about..." she said with courageous excitement, when suddenly, she caught the ominous reflection of Consuelo in the glass of the cab's window. She was standing in the distance staring at the taxi with impatience and contempt. This caused Adele to silently panic and stop speaking.

Saint-Exupéry leaned further into the cab, wanting to hear what Adele had to say, but her lips barely moved. She was unable to get out any words. Saint-Exupéry looked at her, intrigued, wanting to know her secret.

"Tell me. Please," he said ready to hear...

STANDING NOW IN FRONT of the Bevin House, Adele paused. The reality of her beautiful past now gone, and faced only with the harsh, lonely present, brought tears to her eyes. She breathed in sharply, trying to control her overwhelming emotions, but it was no use. The floodgates opened and she began to sob uncontrollably. She was nothing more than a sad, broken woman with only painful memories of a long forgotten past now.

She held her face in her hands, weeping hysterically. Suddenly, from the distant sky, a small, plane's engine was heard. Adele lifted her head, turned and looked up hopeful, as if it were Saint-Exupéry himself coming to her rescue.

As it approached she let out a pant of relief. The plane was silver and flew directly above her. It was in clear sight against the black sky. Adele closed her eyes in expectation as the memory from that night in 1942 came to its conclusion...

ço∘∂

ADELE WAS IN THE cab, sitting forward on the edge of the seat. She looked into Saint-Exupéry's eyes as if desperate for him to understand without her saying what was so difficult for her to express. She tried to speak, her lips moved slightly, but, again, no words came out. She felt her body tremble, her heart pounding...now was the moment. She had to tell him. She knew it would be her only chance.

But she couldn't, and with her heart breaking and her soul defeated, she said in barely a whisper, "Au revoir...Monsieur."

Saint-Exupéry smiled tenderly and said, "Au revoir, Mademoiselle."

He then stepped back on the sidewalk and closed the taxi door. With sad, tearful eyes, Adele looked at him longingly through the cab's window. As it started to pull away, Adele slowly disappeared into the darkness of the back seat...

ço∘∂

ADELE STILL HAD HER eyes closed and her face up to the sky as the silver plane flew directly overhead. When she opened her eyes and saw the plane fly away, her expression went from desperation, to sadness, to deep regret.

In a soft, trembling whisper, she finally spoke the words Saint-Exupéry would never hear, "I love you," then watched the plane's tail lights fade away into the night sky.

Chapter 29

Acceptance

The next morning, Norman was in his classroom closing his briefcase, ready to take his first break. Much to his surprise, Jack shuffled in, without his head down, and approached Norman. Although his appearance was the same, Norman noticed something different in his demeanor. Jack was less suspicious and distant. Now there seemed a kind of connectedness in his attitude.

He glanced awkwardly at Norman, in a shy way instead of defiantly, and tossed the copy of *The Little Prince* on his desk.

"I read it," Jack said in a lowered voice.

Norman was greatly taken aback, but didn't show it. He asked, "What'd you think?" hoping for a positive response.

Jack reached in his pocket and pulled out a folded, crumpled piece of paper. "I figured you'd probably ask me to write a paper about it, so here."

He handed it to Norman. Curious, Norman unfolded the paper and looked at it. His eyes widened with surprise, then softened, visibly moved by what Jack had written.

"See you in class?" Jack asked as he glanced again at Norman, with a look of a possible future in his eyes.

Stunned by his question, Norman went speechless and simply nodded yes. Jack hesitated for a moment, as if he wanted to say something, but didn't. He turned and quietly shuffled out of the room. Norman looked back at Jack's paper as she sat in his chair. He then let out a relieved, "Wow."

Later, Norman walked down the school hallway and stopped in the doorway of Morris' office. Morris was at his desk, reviewing some papers.

"Do you have a minute?" Norman asked softly.

Morris looked up and motioned for Norman to come in. Norman entered, saying, "Jack Doleman turned in a paper today."

"He did?" asked Morris, his eyes wide with surprise.

"I had him read *The Little Prince*," Norman replied, confident.

Morris looked at Norman, unsure, and watched as he took Jack's paper from his jacket pocket.

"Let me read to you what he wrote," Norman said, as he cleared his throat and read aloud, "The Businessman in The Little Prince is like my father because like the stars, he thinks he owns me. Unlike the Little Prince with the rose, he doesn't know how to take care of me."

Norman handed Morris the paper. Morris looked it as he rubbed his chin then back at Norman, concerned.

"*The Little Prince* is not in our curriculum, Norman," he said in a tone of disappointed authority.

Norman froze. He did it again, he thought, straying from procedure, as he did in New Jersey at Cranford. It wasn't something he meant to intentionally do, but he did it nonetheless, for the sake of a student. Fear and worry welled up in Norman. He knew he was in trouble and was sure to be written up, or worse, as in Cranford, be forced to find new employment. He felt his heart sink.

"I-I know," Norman stammered. "I should have consulted with you first. I – I'm sorry."

Morris stood up shaking his head with regret, then looked Norman square in the eye, broke into a grin and said, "Ah, hell, at least you got him to read a book! That's one battle won!"

Norman looked at Morris, surprised and relieved.

"Nice job, Norman. Keep up the good work," Morris added as he handed him back Jack's paper and stepped around his desk. He grabbed his jacket and put it on as they both walked out of his office.

Once in the hallway, a group of female students walked by. As they passed Morris and Norman, they all called out, "Hi, Mr. O!"

Norman said hello in return and watched as they passed.

Morris, seeing this, patted Norman on the back, impressed, and said with a grin, "You've arrived." He then casually walked away.

Norman stood there, smiling, knowing he finally belonged.

Chapter 30

What Was Learned

That afternoon, Adele sat at her dining room table, depressed. The night before confirmed the fact that the past was gone. Her career was gone. Saint-Exupéry was gone, and all that was left was an unknown future. She fought off her fears as long as she could, but now they caught up to her and so she sat, nearly paralyzed, contemplating her very existence.

Suddenly, the doorbell rang. Her first instinct was to ignore it. She wasn't expecting anyone and was in no mood to talk, not even to the postman whom she thought it might be. The doorbell rang a second time. Giving in, she rose slowly from her chair, went to the door and opened it. Standing there was Morris with a wry grin on his face.

"I don't get it," he began, sounding playfully sarcastic, "Used to be you were like a bad penny turning up everywhere, and now I gotta come and *find* you?"

"I don't know why you bother," Adele said in defeat as she sadly turned and went back into her living room.

"Uh-oh," Morris muttered as he stepped inside, closed the door, and followed her.

Adele took a seat by the window and stared out.

"What's wrong?" asked Morris.

"I'm old, that's what's wrong," said Adele followed with a sigh.

Morris smiled. Adele looked at him, not amused.

"You're smiling because you agree," she said, looking away, hurt.

"No," Morris said, sincerely, "because you're brave."

He walked over, sat next to her and said with encouragement, "So, you tried to write a book. At least you took a chance."

"And *lost*," Adele said, sounding bitter.

"What have you lost?" Morris asked, confused.

"Everything. I feel forgotten. Left behind."

"By whom?" Morris asked, still perplexed.

"By...life," answered Adele, discouraged.

"Because no one wants your book?" Morris asked trying to understand.

Adele let out another sigh. "I wanted the world to know that he was *here*," she said in desperate exhaustion.

"No. I think you wanted the world to know that you were here. That book is about *your* life, Adele, when he was in it. Not you in his. He was in *your* life. A life that isn't finished yet."

Adele stared out the window again, sad. A moment passed then she said softly, "I encouraged him to fly, Morris."

"He *needed* encouragement?" asked Morris with a chuckle.

"It *killed* him," Adele snapped, not thinking any of this was funny.

"And you feel guilty for that?"

Adele nodded her head slowly. Morris looked at her, knowing that was absurd, but also that this was her wound. He thought for a moment then asked, "Hey, do you think

Harriet likes it when I fly? She knows the risks, but she also knows how much I love it. It's part of who I am."

"But *why* take the risk?" asked Adele thinking he was as stupid and reckless at Saint-Exupéry.

Morris thought for a moment then said, "Probably because the way I feel about flying is the same way you feel about Saint-Exupéry. I can't help myself."

She shot him a guilty look.

"It's really no secret, Adele. Come to terms with that and you'll be all right," he said with an accepting smile, then stood and added as only an educator would, "There's a life out there, you know. Don't let it get away from you."

Adele turned her head and stared out the window again.

Morris waited a moment for her to respond, but she didn't. He knew she needed to be alone, but hoped she heard him and that his words made some sort of impact. Before he left, he gently reached out and gave her arm a loving squeeze.

ৎ৯৵

SEVERAL DAYS PASSED BEFORE Adele finally left her home. She decided to go to Oscar's Bookstore, a large, inviting place that was a favorite among the locals in the town of Huntington, a thriving community approximately six miles from Northport by car. Oscar's was one of Adele's favorite places to find books and bargains. She could, and would, spend hours in there. On this day, it was overflowing with customers. Adele enjoyed browsing the shelves. Being among books was always a comfort. It was a place where she could easily lose herself.

As she was perusing a section of new arrivals, she noticed a small group of people, most of them college students, listening to a book panel discussion. Intrigued, she wandered over, stood nearby, and listened intently to what was being said.

Two male college students, one bearded, the other with shaggy hair and glasses, sat pompously in front of the group on a small dais and spoke arrogantly about literature.

"Well, the other books mentioned obviously carry more social substance. I think *The Little Prince* is more a novella *masquerading* as a children's book," the bearded college student said in a pseudo-intellectual tone. "Unlike Hesse and Tolkein, who were actual scholars, Saint-Exupéry was, at best, an over indulgent, has-been aviator who wrote the book while vacationing on a beach."

Adele felt her blood boil with rage from what she just heard. Infuriated, and unable to control her anger, she muttered loudly, "Over-indulgent, has-been aviator? I never heard such blatant disrespect!"

The students in the group turned and looked at her as she spoke louder and more clearly, "Saint-Exupéry wasn't at all what that...that...*imbecile* called him!"

The shaggy haired speaker with the glasses looked at his associate and said with a laugh, "Someone apparently disagrees with you."

Adele stepped forward, ready for a fight. "That's right! How dare you speak about Monsieur de Saint-Exupéry that way?"

The bearded student sat forward and addressed Adele. "Hey, it's only an opinion."

"A wrong one!" Adele snapped back in fierce anger. "Monsieur de Saint-Exupéry was not over-indulgent and not on vacation when he wrote *The Little Prince*. He was working for our government during the war."

The bearded student chuckled and said glibly, "Ah. The war. I stand corrected."

The small group laughed. Adele grew angrier. "And you stand to look like a complete ass who knows *nothing* about literature, let alone *history*."

The group let out a collective "oooh" as the two students on the dais looked at each other. Was this old lady really challenging them?

"Whoa, grandma! Cool it. We're just having a friendly discussion here," said the bearded student to Adele.

"Your discussion is neither friendly *nor* accurate," shouted Adele, not about to back down.

"OK," said the shaggy haired student, "So you're a fan of *The Little Prince*. We all have our favorite books and get attached, but it doesn't make us experts."

"But I *am* an expert!" Adele shouted.

The students on the dais, as well as several people in the group, started to chuckle. This caused Adele to finally defend what she felt was rightfully hers.

"I knew him while he was writing that book. I was *there* when he wrote it. He was someone extremely important. Someone I deeply respected and admired. Someone…"

She hesitated and began to tremble, then finally said with bold honesty and truth, "*I loved!*"

Having finally said it out loud, Adele put her hand to her fast beating heart. The two students on the dais, as well as the entire group, looked at her, dumbstruck. Seeing she was now the center of attention, Adele quickly turned and walked away.

Feeling the rush of embarrassment on her now blushing face, Adele made her way toward the front of the bookstore, wanting to get out as fast as she could, when a young woman followed and caught up to her.

"Excuse me…" she said eagerly.

Adele stopped and turned around. She looked at the young woman hard, expecting to hear more youthful arrogance, and put up her guard.

"I heard what you said back there," the young woman began.

"You were pretty passionate. Did you really know Saint-Exupéry?"

"Yes. Very well," Adele answered, as if defying the young woman to question her any further.

"Have you ever thought of writing about your experiences with him?" the young woman asked, enthusiastically.

Adele's defenses were still up. She gritted her teeth and said, "I already have, but like those young men, all the publishers I've approached have little interest in the past."

The young woman smiled. "Well, I'm very interested in the past, and in *your* story," she said as she opened her purse, took out a card and handed it to Adele. "Here is my card. I'm with the Fairleigh Dickinson University Press. We're relatively small, but we love history and I'd love to read whatever you have."

Adele looked at the card then back at the young woman, stunned. The young woman smiled warmly. "Please contact me next week?"

"Y-yes. I will," said Adele, her mood shifting to excitement. "My name is Adele Breaux."

"Lois Carmichael," said the young woman, shaking Adele's hand. "I look forward to hearing from you," she smiled, then walked out of the bookstore.

Adele stood there in disbelief. She looked back at the card then held it to her chest, barely able to contain her happiness.

ॐॐॐ

SEVERAL DAYS LATER, ADELE left her house and walked cheerfully to her car carrying her purse and a book. As she did this, she looked across the street and saw Norman pulling into his driveway. She stopped and waited until he got out of his car then called out, "Yoo-hoo! Norman!"

Norman saw Adele and was surprised by her upbeat demeanor. Last time he saw her she was distracted and depressed. Interested in what caused such a drastic change, he crossed the street to say hello. As he approached her, he said with a touch of suspicion, "Hi, Adele...you seem happy."

"I am!" she exclaimed in a sunny, sing-songy voice. "I have a publisher!"

Norman shot her a surprised and happy look. "Really? That's fantastic! Way to go!"

Adele beamed with delight as she placed her purse and the book on the hood of her car then, uncharacteristically, reached out to Norman with open arms and gave him a huge embrace. Norman was taken aback at first then smiled appreciatively.

As she held him tight, she whispered, "Thank you, Norman. Thank you," then pulled away.

"For what?" Norman asked as Adele stepped over to her car and collected her purse and book off the hood.

"For being a good friend," she answered sincerely, then she opened her car and got in.

Norman stood there and smiled before he headed back home. Inside her car, Adele neatly placed her purse and the book on the passenger seat. As she put the key in the ignition, she stopped and looked at the book. It was the copy of Saint-Exupéry's, *Flight to Arras* that she asked him to sign all those many years ago.

She reached over and opened it. Seeing Saint-Exupéry's small, scratchy handwriting again warmed her heart as she read the inscription he wrote in French:

For Miss Adele Breaux who has guided me into the mysteries of the English Language. With a very friendly recollection.
   Antoine de Saint-Exupéry

Adele smiled then stared straight ahead for a moment before slowly closing her eyes, allowing herself to be taken back to one of the last memories she had of her long, lost friend in Asharoken...

ی۔۔۔ی

ADELE ARRIVED AT THE Bevin House on time for another afternoon lesson with Saint-Exupéry. The maid greeted her at the door and told her that Saint-Exupéry had not yet come back from the beach, which was not far from the house.

The beach? Adele wondered as she followed the maid down the hall toward the parlor where she was expected to wait. Bothered that he wasn't taking his lessons, or her time, seriously, Adele stopped midway and told the maid she didn't want to wait for him in the parlor. Instead, she wished to go outside and see Saint-Exupéry there. The maid nodded obediently and led Adele to the other end of the house, opened a door and pointed toward the water.

There was a fierce chill in the air as Adele carefully made her way toward the beach, walking clumsily over rocks and sand. It was a difficult trek, one that made it look as if she was trying to perform a balancing act, but she was determined to get to where she was going.

Not far ahead she saw Saint-Exupéry standing in the ocean with his pants rolled up to his knees. He was holding a wooden toy boat in one hand while vigorously swiping his other in the water. As Adele headed toward him, annoyed and frustrated, she called out, "Monsieur!"

Saint-Exupéry was too engrossed with his toy boat to hear her. When Adele got closer, she stopped near the water's edge, placed one hand on her hip and asked angrily, "Monsieur! Did you forget we have a lesson today?"

Saint-Exupéry quickly turned around, startled. Happy to see her, he grinned and shouted, "Mademoiselle! Hello!"

His cheerful demeanor only annoyed Adele more. She said sternly, "Monsieur...our lesson? *Your* lesson?"

Saint-Exupéry, seemingly oblivious to the cold weather, pulled his hand from the water and, being barefoot, walked carefully onto the beach. He wiped his wet hand on his pants and looked at Adele with childlike excitement.

"I was testing the motion of the waves. I believe their velocity at the surface, and the ones below might power a submarine!"

He looked like a little boy to Adele, standing there, holding his toy boat and smiling enthusiastically. She let out a futile sigh and said, "This isn't working."

"What isn't?" asked Saint-Exupéry, perplexed.

"Teaching you anything. It's been nearly two months and you've hardly learned a thing from me," she said with more regret than disappointment.

Saint-Exupéry looked at her surprised she would think such a thing and said quickly, "Oh, that is not true. You have taught me a great deal."

"Like what?" she asked knowing there was nothing he could say to convince her.

Saint-Exupéry took as step forward and looked up at the sky, thinking. Adele stared at him, waiting. His gaze lingered on the clouds. Adele watched him, growing impatient. Suddenly, with a slight smile, he looked back at her and said with reflective sincerity, "You have taught me –*profound loneliness.*"

Adele took a step back, stunned and embarrassed. She clutched at her coat feeling exposed and hurt.

Then Saint-Exupéry added, "And that is what I know I will feel once we are parted."

Adele looked at him with sad surprise as he took another step forward and stood directly in front of her. He looked

deep into her eyes and said, "But when my loneliness is comforted, I will be content to have known you. As I hope that
you will be just as content to have known me."

He then looked down and flipped the toy boat in his
hands, as if suddenly shy, or once again, preoccupied in
thought. Adele stared at him, moved beyond measure...

BACK IN HER CAR, Adele opened her eyes and smiled. She
looked at his inscription one last time, then closed the book
and started her car.

Chapter 31

No One Dies

A small Piper Cherokee airplane made its way down a narrow airstrip preparing for take off. Within minutes, it gained speed and quickly lifted up and headed for the sky. Inside the cockpit was Morris, doing what he loved the most...flying. Sitting next to him was Adele. Once they were at full altitude, the engine began to quiet down and slowly leveled off. They were flying in calm, clear skies when Morris looked over at Adele, eyeing her with concern.

"How ya doing?" he asked.

Adele smiled, fascinated by the flight. "It's beautiful up here. Exhilarating."

Morris was relieved. "Hey, I wanted to tell you something. The state legislature overturned teacher mandatory retirement at age seventy. That means you're welcomed to come back to teaching if you want to."

Adele looked at him, surprised, then stared straight ahead, thinking. Slowly, a smile crept across her face as she realized she didn't need teaching anymore. She felt free of the occupation that started out as only a means to survive the Great

Depression. And although she was good at it and grew to love it dearly, it was also the thing that kept her feeling trapped, grounded. The future was now in front of her and it was time for her to finally fly.

"No, Morris," she said turning to him, "Teaching was once my whole life, my identity, but it's not anymore. There is a whole world down there," she said pointing to earth, "that I need to be a part of. It's time." Then she added, "Plus, I have a book to finish, which I expect you to help me with."

"Me? I thought Norman was doing that," he said, surprised.

"You both are," she replied.

Morris smiled. Just then, the plane jerked and started to sputter. Morris became slightly panicked as the plane jerked hard a second time. He checked the controls, worried, and said, "I think I better land this thing. We don't want to die."

He looked at Adele, expecting to see her out of her mind with fear, but instead, was surprised to see that she was uncharacteristically calm.

Adele looked at him, smiled and asked, "Who says we die?"

The End

Epilogue

Adele Breaux stayed in Northport another seven years after publishing her book, *Saint-Exupéry In America, 1942 – 1943 A Memoir,* in 1971. She dedicated it to Morris. She moved back to her home state of Oregon in 1978.

Morris Saxe remained Assistant Principal at Northport High School until 1975. He and his wife, Harriet retired to Northern California.

Norman Orenstein remained a teacher of English at Northport High School until he retired in 1990 and moved to Florida.

Consuelo de Saint-Exupéry wrote a memoir of her marriage to Saint-Exupéry entitled, *The Tale of the Rose* then sealed it away in a trunk in her home. In 1979, the manuscript was discovered and published in France in 2000. It became a national bestseller.

On the evening of July 31, 1944, **Antoine de Saint-Exupéry**, on an assignment to collect intelligence on German troop movements, left from an airbase on Corsica and was never seen again.

The Little Prince was written in the summer and fall of 1942 and published in 1943. It has been translated into more than 250 languages and sold more than 140 million copies making it one of the best-selling books ever published.

Afterword

The novel, *Lonely Heart Of The Little Prince*, was inspired by the true story of Adele Breaux, the woman who was hired to teach English to renowned French aviator, Antoine de Saint-Exupéry, during the months he was writing his classic story, *The Little Prince*, one of the most beloved books of all time.

The story of Adele and Saint-Exupéry is unique in that there is little information available about the period of time Saint-Exupéry wrote *The Little Prince*. He worked in a remote mansion, in a small hamlet, in my hometown of Northport, Long Island. Adele, being one of Saint-Exupéry's few, yet frequent, visitors, saw first-hand his masterpiece in progress, as well as came to know the man.

When I first learned of this story (told to me by my former high school English teacher, Norman Orenstein, who was Adele's neighbor and friend in Northport for close to fifteen years), I was impressed just by the fact that *The Little Prince* was written in the town in which I grew up. However, that was until Norman shared the captivating story of Adele, who fell in love with Saint-Exupéry, while tutoring him, and remained haunted by her unrequited feelings for him, for the rest of her life.

As a writer, this piqued my interest and I wanted to learn more. I began researching every book, article, interview, etc., I could find about Adele and had many lengthy phone calls and email exchanges with Norman about his memories of her. Throughout these talks, Norman said often, "The person who knew Adele best was a man named Morris Saxe. He was her colleague at the high school years before I got there, and her confidant."

With Norman's help, I found Morris and his wife, Harriet, and interviewed them. Morris and Harriet had both known Adele since 1950, and told me from the day they met her, she spoke frequently about Saint-Exupéry and was "very much in love with him, even more so after his tragic disappearance in 1944."

They shared their stories of Adele, the person, and described in detail the many conversations she had with them about Saint-Exupéry. This story is unique in that Morris, Harriet, and Norman were Adele's closest friends and the only ones privy to these conversations. They have all generously given me permission to their memories and recollections of Adele, and about her personal association with Saint-Exupéry, for the purpose of my book.

My intention was to turn this story into a screenplay. Being a screenwriter, I was first struck by its cinematic value, however, upon completing the script, I decided it would best to turn the story into a novel. A screenwriter is limited to roughly 120 pages, and I found myself having to cut out many important details that were needed to tell the whole story. I thought of writing it as a biography, but felt it would become bogged down with facts. Choosing to write it as fiction, allowed me to create a richer and more compelling story, which remained closer to the heart of Norman, Morris and Harriet's memories.

It was a labor of love, if you will, to bring to life the story of the woman, the "lonely heart," who lived behind the creation of one of the world's most treasured pieces of literature, and its strong, romantic, heroic and wonderfully playful author. There are so many who have been fortunate enough to be witness to the world's most gifted artists, such as Saint-Exupéry, but sadly they fade into obscurity. It was my honor to bring Adele's story to light and share it with those who love *The Little Prince* and the works of its beloved author.

About the Author

LeeAnna Neumeyer grew up in Northport, Long Island, where Antoine de Saint-Exupéry wrote and completed his classic book, *The Little Prince.* She is a graduate of the State University of New York at New Paltz, and has a degree in English. She is currently working on her next novel.

6881808R00166

Made in the USA
San Bernardino, CA
19 December 2013